THE ANUNNAKI MYSTERY

By Ken Warner

MW00667039

© 2022 by Kenneth H Warner, II

All rights reserved.

Contents

THE ANUNNAKI MYSTERY

Chapter One

Jaden Kwan ran up the steps. Reaching the second-floor landing, he opened the door cautiously, only far enough to fit his hand through the gap. He turned his palm one way, then the other. The nanobots embedded under his skin relayed their scans to his neural implants. There was nobody out there. He opened the door wider and stepped into the corridor.

Creeping over to the main hallway, he stopped at the corner, once again checking with one hand to make sure the coast was clear. But this area was empty, too. Jaden moved into the corridor, laser pistol at the ready in his right hand, using his left to scan the rooms as he passed.

He felt skeptical that Isis and her hybrids would make an appearance here. There had been no confirmed contact with them in almost three years. After her failed attempt to exterminate humanity, Isis had gone entirely off the grid. They'd tried to track her down, but every lead turned into a dead end.

On the other hand, this summit represented a turning point in world affairs. It had taken the Collective months to arrange. Representatives from every country in the world would be attending. Jaden knew this meeting was mostly a formality; the treaty's language had been negotiated ahead of time. But he also knew that symbolism was important. And the significance of Earth's peoples coming together to recognize the legitimacy of a coalition made up primarily of alien species could not be understated. From now on, the Collective would be a nation unto itself. If Isis were going to choose any moment to return to the world stage, this would be it.

But beyond the symbolism, Jaden had no doubt she'd have pragmatic reasons for sabotaging this event, too. Part of the treaty outlined the technology the Collective would be sharing with the rest of the world. Surely, Isis would not want to see that come to fruition.

Jaden reached the end of the corridor without finding any evidence of intruders. Since their last encounter with Isis, they'd developed the technology to detect holographic emitters. It turned out that the devices leaked a small amount of high-energy radiation previously unknown to Martian or Othali science. The Othali warship had detected its signature here, in this building, less than twenty-four hours before the summit was scheduled to begin. The delegates had already started arriving, but they'd evacuated the building, monitoring the exits for any sign of the telltale radiation.

From orbit, it was impossible to pinpoint the source of the emissions. The Collective had to deploy its security forces to search at close range. One of the conditions upon which the world's major powers had insisted was that emitter tech be forbidden from the premises for the duration of the summit. The Collective had agreed. So, either one of them had screwed up and activated their emitter by mistake, or Isis had an agent or agents here. Nobody else on the planet possessed the technology.

"This is Jaden," he announced through his implants. "Level two is clear."

"Understood," Salvatore's voice replied. "Proceed to level five."

Jaden knew they'd sent other agents to the third and fourth floors. He entered the south stairwell and ran up to the fifth floor. Emerging into the corridor, he proceeded cautiously, scanning his surroundings as he passed.

But suddenly, he caught a blip at the far end of the hallway. It vanished again as abruptly as it had appeared, but there had to be someone down there. Only an emitter could produce radiation in that frequency.

"That had better not be you, Griffin," Jaden called out. Griffin was one of the other security agents. He was one of the hybrids they'd captured from the compound in South America but confirmed to be a member of the resistance. Only a few years older than Jaden, he was also Malia's boyfriend. But there was no reply. Jaden didn't think this was Griffin. He was something of a practical joker, but not even he would screw around in a situation so serious.

Jaden proceeded along the corridor, pistol at the ready, scanning the area as he moved, but the signal did not repeat. He reached the short hall leading to the second stairwell without finding anyone. "This is Jaden. I caught a blip on the fifth floor, but there's nobody here."

"Understood," Salvatore's voice replied. "Proceed to level eight.

Use extreme caution—that frequency is not naturally occurring. Someone is up there using an emitter."

"Roger." Jaden entered the stairwell, scanning above and below before hurrying up the steps. But as he reached the eighth floor, his implants registered another ping. Jaden halted, scanning the area around him, ready to fire his pistol. But there were no more blips. Isis must have discovered the stray radiation and found a way to reduce it. The Collective had done so with their devices as well.

Jaden was about to open the door to the corridor when something slammed into his chest, knocking him down the steps. Regaining his feet, he fired his weapon toward the landing above. But the shot hit the door. Reaching out with his mind, he tried to find the intruder using his telepathy but couldn't locate him. Suddenly the eighth-floor door flew open; Jaden fired again, but the blast hit the far wall.

Using his telekinesis, Jaden flew up to the landing and through the door, scanning the corridor, ready to fire again. But there was no sign of the intruder. Isis had definitely found a way to reduce the stray radiation.

"This is Jaden. I've made contact on the eighth floor."

"I'm sending reinforcements," Salvatore replied.

At that moment, a laser blast hit the wall right next to Jaden. He dropped to his stomach, pointing his weapon up the hallway and firing again. No luck. Reaching out telepathically, he tried to locate his adversary again but came up empty. Jaden didn't understand this. Had they found a way to shield themselves from telepathy? It was certainly possible. Isis possessed the same abilities, and they'd had three years to develop new tech. They could have used her powers to test new equipment.

There was another laser blast, this one hitting the floor directly in front of Jaden. And this time, he'd spotted its source. Reaching out with his mind, he found the intruder. Jaden penetrated his thoughts, forcing him to become visible. It was a male, roughly six feet tall, with short, blond hair. But an instant later, the hybrid pushed Jaden out of his mind, vanishing from sight.

But Jaden had him. Isis wasn't the only one who had had time to develop new tools. Jaden had discovered that he could use his telepathy to control artificial neural processors, like those that powered the emitters. He penetrated the hybrid's unit and sent a command that overloaded its circuits, rendering it inoperative. The intruder became visible, and Jaden fired, hitting him in the leg. The hybrid hit the floor with a yelp.

Jaden got to his feet, running toward his quarry and using his telekinesis to lift him off the floor. But he managed to fire his weapon, hitting Jaden in the shoulder. A jolt of pain exploded down his arm, and he dropped his pistol. Reaching out with his mind, Jaden disarmed his opponent, slamming him into the wall. He fell to the floor with a grunt as Jaden reached him. Using his telekinesis, he lifted him up again, pinning him against the wall. "What are you doing here?" he demanded out loud. "Why did Isis send you here?"

"Why do you think?" the man replied with a sneer. "We're not going to stand by and let you give the human scum our technology."

"*Your* technology?" Jaden repeated. "How do you know anything about what we're doing here?" The man said nothing, returning Jaden's stare in silence. Jaden penetrated his mind telepathically, trying to discover how Isis had learned about their activities, but the hybrid pushed him out again. "How are you doing that?" Only the Martians had ever been able to eject him from their mind like this. Tapping into the magnetic field to augment his power, Jaden tried again. He managed to surface some thoughts this time before the hybrid kicked him out again.

"Jaden!" a voice yelled from the opposite end of the hall. It was Griffin. He hurried toward Jaden, picking up his pistol on the way and handing it back to him.

But at that moment, the hybrid kicked Jaden in the chest with both feet, vanishing again as Jaden smashed into the opposite wall, dropping his weapon again.

"Dammit!" Jaden yelled, trying to regain control of the intruder, but he was gone. How had he managed to reactivate his emitter? That should not have been possible.

"Where'd he go?" Griffin shouted, frantically scanning the area with one hand.

Something slammed into Griffin, sending him crashing to the floor. An instant later, an unseen fist collided with Jaden's head. He saw stars but stayed conscious. Reaching out with both hands, he managed to grab the hybrid. He took another swing, but Jaden could feel it coming and shielded his head with one arm. At the same time, he used a hip throw to take the man down.

When they hit the floor, Jaden put him in the mount position.

He and Malia had spent most of the last three years training in martial arts with Bastet, and he'd found he possessed an affinity for grappling. As the hybrid struggled to free himself, Jaden reached out with his mind and overloaded his emitter again. The hybrid became visible.

Griffin had regained his feet and come running over. But at that moment, someone shot him with a laser blast. Griffin fell unconscious. Trying to glance over his shoulder to see who had fired, Jaden lost his focus for a moment, and the hybrid managed to squirm free, toppling Jaden onto his back.

Jaden jumped to his feet. The intruder was running down the corridor, but Jaden couldn't see the new arrival. He had to be using an emitter to stay invisible. Grabbing his pistol, he fired at the visible hybrid. The shot hit him in the back, and he dropped.

A moment later, something smashed the window at the far end of the hallway. It had to be the second hybrid. Using his telekinesis, Jaden flew up the corridor and out the window. "Intruder down on the eighth floor. Griffin's down too. Requesting assistance. A second hybrid just flew out the window. I'm pursuing."

"Negative," Salvatore's voice responded. "Stand down and remain on level eight."

Jaden ignored him. Summoning his saucer, he flew into the airlock and hurried up to the cockpit. His implants were limited, but using his ship's scanners, he flooded the area with scanning beams and detected an enemy saucer just before it took off to the north.

The resort they'd selected for the summit was nestled in the

Bavarian Alps. Jaden launched a small projectile at the enemy saucer moments before it disappeared between two peaks. But the missile had found its target, attaching a tracking beacon to the hull.

"Gotcha," Jaden yelled. He set the navigation system to pursue and engaged the engines at full power. Isis would track his engine output this way, but it didn't matter. They'd realize he was in pursuit regardless.

The hybrid flew a wild course through the mountains, but the two ships' capabilities were identical, and he couldn't escape. Jaden set his weapons to fire automatically if they could get a lock on the target, but he was flying so erratically that this wasn't possible. He fired a few times manually, but his every shot flew wide.

"Jaden, return to the resort. That's an order," Salvatore said through his implants.

"No can do," Jaden replied. "This is the first contact we've had in years. I'm not throwing away this opportunity." He switched off his transponder and cut communications. Salvatore would still be able to track his engine output, but it didn't matter. His lead was too great for them to catch him.

The enemy saucer changed course, flew high over the mountains, and fired on Jaden. It was a direct hit; his shields fell to seventy percent. Jaden returned fire, trying to take out his engines. The blasters found their target but weren't enough to penetrate his shields. Jaden fired the plasma cannon. This brought the hybrid's shields down to thirty percent. One more hit, and he should be able to disable his engines.

But suddenly, something slammed into Jaden's saucer. Shields were down, and engines were reduced to half capacity. Losing velocity, Jaden watched on sensors as the enemy saucer shot out of range. As he tried to bring the shields back up, Jaden searched the area to see who had fired on him. The saucer didn't possess the firepower to cripple him like this.

But before he could find the second ship, another shot rocked his saucer, opening a gaping hole in the hull. Engines failed, and external sensors went down. Suddenly, staring out the cockpit windows, he spotted a massive vessel materializing dead ahead. It was Isis's chariot.

"Oh, shit," Jaden muttered, dropping through the floor. He flew past the main deck and into the airlock. Flying out of his saucer, he turned in time to see the chariot fire again and vaporize it.

Chapter Two

Jaden had made himself invisible on the way out of his saucer, but it didn't matter. The chariot was able to track him using active scanning beams. He flew as fast as he could, alternately climbing and diving, banking one way and then the other, but it was no use. Even tapping into the magnetic field, he could not outrun this ship.

The chariot kept firing its blasters, barely missing him each time. In the past, Isis had wanted to capture Malia and him. But now that she had their clones in her possession, her people were shooting to kill.

Jaden thought of trying to access the thoughts of someone on the chariot telepathically or the ship's control systems, but it was all he could do to avoid being incinerated. "This is Jaden. I require assistance! The chariot destroyed my ship, and I'm taking heavy fire!" His neural implants showed that he was connected to a Collective network, but he had no idea if anyone could hear him.

Just then, the edge of a blaster shot singed his right calf. The pain exploded in his mind, and he knew he'd lost a chunk of flesh. Losing his concentration, he tumbled out of the sky, dropping like a stone. His leg would heal, but if he couldn't focus past the pain, he'd splatter on the rocks below.

Concentrating with all his might, he regained control of his descent and flew away from the nearest mountain and into the valley below. Soaring past the tree line, he had an idea. He flew lower, weaving through the trees. The going was slower this way, but the trunks should provide some cover from the weapons fire.

An instant later, a blaster shot hit a nearby tree, shattering its trunk and engulfing it in flames. The heat of the blast blew Jaden off course, and he nearly flew into a tree. Maybe this wasn't such a good idea.

Jaden soared high above the trees. Quickly reversing course, he headed back toward the nearest mountain. The chariot fired again, narrowly missing him. He flew between two peaks and rounded one, trying to put the mountain between him and the chariot. Flying in closer, he flattened himself against a sheer cliff face, scanning the sky for Isis's ship. But it was nowhere to be seen.

Descending cautiously, he reached a saddle point between the two peaks and landed on the rocky ridge. His leg was throbbing but seemed mostly healed already. Struggling to catch his breath in the thin air, he searched the sky, ready to fly again if the chariot showed up. He found he was shivering and realized how cold it was here. There was a stiff breeze blowing up from the valley.

"You're stronger than I remember," a voice called out from behind him. Turning, Jaden spotted a woman moving toward him, her long, dark hair blowing wildly in the wind. She was wearing a skintight leather jumpsuit. An angry red scar ran down one side of her face.

"Isis," Jaden muttered, his heart hammering in his chest. He tried flying away, but Isis overpowered him, using her telekinesis to keep him grounded.

"Your people are fools," she told him. "If you share your tech with the humans, they'll only use it against you. Maybe not right away. But it's only a matter of time before they turn. They're animals. You know it as well as I do."

Jaden glared at her. Reaching out with his mind, he tried to penetrate her thoughts. But she was ready for him. She ejected him from her mind, then used her powers to lift him off the ground.

"You and your sister are still welcome to join me. There is much I could teach you."

"And help you exterminate our people? No thanks, I'll pass."

"The humans are *not* your people. But we have a new goal. We're getting off this rock, and you could help us. Take your place by my side, and together we will rule a whole new world."

"What new world?" Jaden said skeptically.

But at that moment, Isis turned, gasping in surprise. Jaden followed her gaze and spotted the chariot becoming visible in the sky behind her. Another vessel was firing on it—the Othali warship.

Isis dropped him and vanished. The chariot returned fire on the warship but then moments later disappeared again.

"Jaden, this is Commander Anhur. Are you all right?"

"I'm fine," he replied with a grin. "But man, am I glad to see you!"

Jaden boarded the ship through the hangar bay. Landing on the docking platform, he found Nadia waiting for him.

"Salvatore's pissed," she told him. "We're taking you back to the resort, but watch out. He's gunning for you."

"Yeah, I bet he is. But thanks for the warning."

Only minutes later, they reached their destination.

"Come on, I'll take you down there in a shuttle," said Nadia.

"Nah, I'm good." Jaden bade her farewell, then flew out of the hangar bay. He landed in front of the resort to find Salvatore striding toward him.

"That was reckless. And you defied my orders. If you were anyone else—"

"It's a good thing I went. I met Isis. They're planning to leave Earth."

"And go where? Not back to Mars, surely."

"I don't know, but she said I could help her."

Salvatore considered this for a moment, giving him a puzzled look. But then he shook his head and said, "We'll discuss this later. Right now, we have another problem. One of their agents planted a fusion grenade in the basement. We need to get everyone out of here."

"Couldn't you disarm it?'

"Negative. No access."

Using his implants, Jaden scanned the area for Martian devices. Sure enough, he found the grenade in the hotel basement. But Salvatore was right: he couldn't gain access. He could probably crack the security, but that would take time. Reaching out telepathically instead, he probed it with his mind and identified its control processor. It took a few seconds, but he managed to override its security protocols. "It's on a timer," he told Salvatore. "Set to detonate tomorrow morning."

"Right in the middle of the summit," Salvatore noted. "Can you disarm it?"

Jaden focused for a moment. He was able to issue a command to disable its triggering mechanism, rendering it inert. "Done."

Salvatore breathed a sigh of relief. "I'll never understand how you do what you do."

"Me neither," Jaden replied with a grin.

"Jaden, can you tell if it's one of mine?" a voice said through his implants.

"Hey, Venus," Jaden replied. "Spying on us?"

"Monitoring communications, not spying, you brat."

Jaden returned his attention to the grenade. He scanned its systems but couldn't tell for sure who had manufactured it. "It looks like one of ours, but I don't know its circuits well enough to say for sure."

"See if you can bring it back to the nest," said Venus. "Our inventory doesn't show any missing units. Which means either Isis figured out a way to infiltrate the compound without our knowledge, or—"

"Or she managed to copy your design and make her own," Jaden finished for her. "I'm on it." He took a step toward the building, but Salvatore grabbed him by the arm.

"This is dangerous. Isis could still detonate it remotely."

"No, she couldn't. I disabled the trigger. It's a dud now."

"You can't know that for sure. She may be able to override your command."

"We need to ascertain her capabilities," Venus said. "Use your saucer to initiate a dampening field around the building. That will prevent any signal she sends from reaching the device."

Salvatore frowned for a moment but then nodded. "Very well. Give me a minute, Jaden." His eyes went unfocused for a moment, and Jaden knew he was accessing his ship's control systems. "It's ready. But act quickly. Isis may still find a way around this."

"You got it," Jaden replied, trotting off toward the building. He ran into Griffin halfway there. "Hey, come with me. I could use your help."

"But there's a nuke in there! I thought we were evacuating?"

Jaden ignored him, continuing on his way. He reached the entrance with Griffin right behind him. They hurried through the lobby and into the service corridor. Running down the steps, they moved through the basement and found the grenade attached to a steel support beam.

"Is that one of ours?" Griffin asked with a tone of surprise.

"Sure looks like it," Jaden replied. He scanned it again, this time with an active beam to get a more thorough look at its inner workings. If it wasn't one of theirs, it was indistinguishable. He grabbed ahold of it and tried to remove it from the beam. "Magnetically locked, just like I figured."

"Now what?"

Jaden ran one hand over the top of his head, considering the dilemma. He'd gotten rid of his braids in favor of a buzz cut only recently and still wasn't used to it. "We've gotta cut it off," he said finally.

"This pillar is load-bearing," Griffin pointed out. "You remove a section, and the whole building could come down on top of us."

The beam was H-shaped, with the puck-shaped grenade affixed to the center section.

"I'll make the cut right around the base of the device. The beam should be plenty strong with the two crosspieces intact. But you monitor the stress. If it goes critical, we'll get out of here."

"You're going to fire a laser that close to a nuclear bomb?" Griffin asked, his expression a mix of concern and disbelief.

Jaden shrugged. "It'll be fine."

"I hope your hand is steady," Griffin muttered. He held out one hand, and Jaden knew he was initiating his measurements. "I'm ready."

Jaden set his pistol to the exact frequency required to cut through the steel. Holding the weapon with both hands, he initiated the beam. Slowly, he began making his cut.

"We're at fifty percent of tolerance and holding steady," Griffin told him, his voice shaky.

Jaden continued his work. Griffin updated him every few seconds, but the change was negligible. Finally, Jaden finished the cut and removed the grenade, taking the circular steel slab with it. "See?" he asked with a grin. "Piece of cake."

"Yeah? Then why are you sweating so much?"

They headed back up to the main level. Jaden accessed the device's control chip again to make sure it was still inert. But suddenly, the grenade armed itself. "Shit—move!"

Running through the lobby, Jaden bolted out the doors, right past a startled Salvatore. "It's gonna blow!" he shouted, taking to the air. Jaden flew as high and as fast as he could, hurling the nuke toward the sky and using his powers to accelerate it. Moments later, there was a blinding flash as the grenade exploded. Shielding his eyes, Jaden tried to return to the ground before the shockwave hit him. But it was no use. The wave slammed into him and knocked him through the air. Jaden hit the ground hard and tumbled down a grassy hillside. Finally coming to rest, he realized he'd broken his left leg; the femur was poking through his jeans.

Jaden knew the injury would heal itself, but the bone needed to be set before that happened. He shuddered to imagine what would happen if it healed like this. Grasping his thigh just above the knee, he tried setting it himself. But the pain was too intense; he nearly passed out.

"*Salvatore, I need you,*" he called out in his mind.

"*On my way.*"

Jaden lay flat on his back, clenching his jaw against the pain. After what felt like an eternity, Salvatore strode into view, Griffin right behind him. The Martian kneeled by his side, examining the injury. "I'm going to set this. It's going to hurt."

Jaden nodded. "Do it."

Salvatore gripped his lower thigh with both hands. "One... two... three."

Everything went black, and Jaden knew no more.

Jaden opened his eyes. He was lying on the floor of the resort lobby. Griffin was sitting in a nearby chair. Seeing that Jaden was awake, he rushed to his side. "Man, you are a lunatic," he said with a grin.

Sitting up, Jaden ran one hand along his left leg. It had already healed. The area was sore, as if from a workout, but he could tell that Salvatore had managed to get the bone in place before the injury healed. "Where's Salvatore?"

"He's outside. I'm supposed to let him know when you wake up."

Jaden got to his feet, but Salvatore was already striding into the lobby to check up on him. "All better?"

"Good as new," Jaden confirmed. "Are you still pissed at me?"

"It's not me you have to worry about," Salvatore replied. "Let's go."

Jaden and Griffin followed him outside. They boarded his saucer and moved up to the cockpit. The moment Salvatore engaged the engines, Jaden heard his mother contacting him through his implants.

"*What the hell were you thinking*?" she screamed.

Jaden tried to explain what had happened, but Melissa wasn't interested in hearing it. He figured the lecture would last the entire trip back to the compound, but thankfully, Venus interrupted.

"Send me all the data you collected on that device through your implants," she said. "Can't examine the thing myself now that you've managed to blow it up, but hopefully, I can glean something useful from your scans."

"*I* didn't blow it up!" Jaden protested. "That was Isis!" He sent her the data. "How the hell did Isis get a signal to that thing through our dampening field?" he asked out loud.

"That's not clear yet," Salvatore replied. "We've got some ideas, but nothing we can confirm yet," he added cryptically.

Minutes later, they reached the compound and docked in the hangar bay. Disembarking, they found Melissa and Malia waiting for them. Malia had recently grown her hair out in locs, and Jaden still wasn't used to it. She ran over to Griffin and hugged him, tears streaming down her cheeks. But Melissa approached Jaden, resuming her tirade at the exact word where she'd left off.

"Mom, all right, I get it," Jaden said, throwing up his hands in surrender. "I'm sorry. Next time I'll obey orders, I promise!"

Melissa glared at him for a moment longer, then burst into tears and hugged him so tight he thought his ribs might break. Jaden managed to break free after a minute, and they followed the others out to the central corridor. Melissa started berating Jaden again, but as they reached the access tunnel, Venus stepped through the wall.

"I've got good news and bad news," she reported. "What do you want first?"

"How about the good news?" said Salvatore.

"Isis didn't get that grenade from our stores."

"Which means she figured out how to make her own?" asked Jaden.

Venus fixed him with an ominous stare. "That's exactly what that means."

Chapter Three

Malia frowned for a moment. "How were you able to determine this?"

"Come with me, and I'll show you," Venus replied. The five of them followed her into the access tunnel and down to her lab.

Once inside, Jaden spotted a holographic image of a Martian neural processor along with some circuitry. "What is this?"

"This is the control unit for Isis's fusion grenade," Venus explained.

"*You're* the one who can talk to computers, and you didn't know that?" Malia asked sarcastically.

"Shut up, Whoopi."

"Oh, there you go again—"

"Would you two please *stop*?" Melissa pleaded. "I can't stand this constant bickering lately!"

Jaden opened his mouth to reply but then thought better of it. "This image is from my scans. How can you tell it's not one of yours?"

"I thought it was, at first," Venus replied. "The design is almost identical. But there are some small differences. Look." She called up a second hologram next to the first. The two looked the same to Jaden. But then Venus enlarged them both, focusing on the chips' interfaces with the rest of the circuitry. "The one from the resort has a sixteen-gigabit memory bus. That's twice the bandwidth of ours. You can see here that the physical connection is different."

Looking closely, Jaden could indeed discern that the two components were not an exact match. The one from the resort was thicker.

"The differences are minute," Salvatore pointed out. "So much so that we must conclude that Isis somehow gained access to our schematics. How could she have done that?"

"We planted enough of these things in her compounds," Venus replied with a shrug. "She could have had a rogue process running on one of the control systems that we missed and used that to take scans. Or she could have had some sort of remote device on-site that we didn't notice."

"Like a drone or something?" Jaden asked.

Venus nodded. "I've done a full security sweep here, and I'm confident she didn't acquire her scans from this facility. But the missions to the other compounds were somewhat chaotic. There could be a dozen different ways she obtained her scans. And once she had them, reverse engineering the device wouldn't have been that hard. Her people were already familiar with the tech involved."

"Well, it was only a matter of time before Isis developed a weapon like this," Salvatore said with a sigh. "At least now we know about it."

"What are we going to do about the summit?" Malia asked.

"I'm not sure yet," Salvatore replied. "We'll be holding a meeting at fourteen hundred hours to discuss this."

Jaden headed out of the lab with Malia and Griffin. They were going to the cafeteria, and he was starving. But Melissa held him back in the corridor.

"What is it, Mom?" Jaden said impatiently.

"I'm not done with you yet," she said, poking him in the sternum with her index finger. "Not only did you put yourself in mortal peril unnecessarily, but you disobeyed a direct order from your superior officer. If you pull another stunt like this, I'm going to recommend that you be removed from the security forces. Do you understand?"

"*Mom*, you're overreacting. It all worked out in the end. And now we've got some good intel on Isis. And besides, I'm practically an adult now. You can't ground me like I'm still fourteen—"

"You are *not* an adult yet."

"Only because *you* vetoed the measure to make seventeen the age of majority!"

"None of us have veto power. I simply convinced them to see things my way. And I did that because of *you*, and with good reason, based on your behavior today. You cannot act on every wild impulse. There is a command hierarchy in place, and if you can't adhere to that, then you don't deserve to keep the role I've allowed you to take."

Jaden took a deep breath. "I'm sorry. You're right. I was out of line. It won't happen again, I swear."

Melissa held his gaze a moment longer, her expression intense, but finally sighed and hugged him. "I'm glad you're all right."

"Thanks, Mom. Me too."

Jaden hurried up to the cafeteria to catch up with Malia and Griffin. He sat down with them once he'd grabbed some food.

"I honestly thought Mom was going to kill you this time," Malia told him.

"Yeah, well, I'm sorry to disappoint you," Jaden replied sardonically, taking a bite of his sandwich. "We could've used you out there today. I broke my leg after that nuke went off. Salvatore did a good job setting it, but I would have felt more confident if you were doing it."

Malia had shown an affinity for medicine. It turned out she could use her telepathy to affect a person's internal organs in much the same way Jaden used it to communicate with neural processors. They'd both been able to access other people's minds and control their bodily processes to some extent for years now, but for Malia, it had gone beyond this. It seemed as if she could somehow extend her healing abilities into another, something that had not been possible for either of them until the last year or so. Neither of their newfound powers made sense to them or anyone else in the compound. It didn't seem like they should be able to do these things based on their established understanding of their powers. On the other hand, that established understanding was flimsy at best.

Bastet had taken over their academic instruction, in addition to their martial arts training, right after their last battle with Isis. Jaden and Malia had completed the equivalent of a high school education in only two years. Since then, Malia had gone to work with her mother to learn medicine. Jaden, meanwhile, had taken on an apprenticeship with Venus and Salvatore to learn Martian systems technology. His newfound powers had lent themselves perfectly to this pursuit.

Bastet was going to continue training them in martial arts until she abruptly announced her resignation from the Collective only a few months earlier. She told them that she needed to return to her temple without further explanation.

"So… did you see any of uh… my people when you were fighting the chariot?" Griffin asked.

"Nah. It must have had a full crew, but those two inside the resort were the only cat-eyed ditto heads I saw."

"*Jaden*!" Malia said, her eyes wide.

"Sorry, present company excluded, of course," Jaden added with a nod to Griffin. "I know you're not a ditto head—I've been inside your skull before. Of course, that was before you were banging my sister. I don't think I'd want to visit again."

"At least I'm getting some," Malia chided.

"Ouch," Griffin said with a grimace. "Savannah's still holding out, huh?"

Jaden rolled his eyes. "She had a strong religious upbringing, all right?"

"Are you gonna propose just so you can get laid?" Malia asked with a sly grin.

"Go to hell. I'm not in any rush. There's a lot more to *our* relationship than just sex."

"You're right," Malia said with a shrug. "It's purely physical for us." She leaned over and made out with Griffin. Jaden chuckled, shaking his head. He knew that wasn't true but couldn't help feeling jealous. Although there was no way he was ready for marriage, he did wish Savanah's attitude were a little less restrictive.

"Hey, what happened to that hybrid I left behind when I went after the other one?" Jaden asked.

"Fake tooth," Griffin told him, clamping his jaws exaggeratedly.

"Damn. I wish I could've questioned him."

"Yeah, well, that's what you get for disobeying orders," Griffin replied.

After lunch, they bade farewell to Griffin and headed to the conference room. Melissa, Venus, Sydney, and Vincent were already here. Commander Anhur was present via hologram. But neither Salvatore nor Brian had arrived yet.

They had established the Collective almost two years ago, with the intention of declaring nationhood. After negotiations with the governments of Algeria and Fiji, they had purchased the land around their compound here, as well as the Fijian island they'd been using for recreation. But achieving worldwide recognition as an independent power had taken much more work. Brian and Salvatore had spearheaded the effort, and the upcoming summit represented the culmination of nearly two years of work.

Officially, their citizenry included the three remaining Martians, the hybrids who had renounced Isis, Melissa, Malia, and Jaden, and the handful of humans who had taken up residence in the compound, including Sydney, Miguel, and Babcock and his granddaughters. Carl had chosen to live on the Othali warship but had the freedom to come and go as he pleased, as did the Othali.

For now, the Othali intended to remain in their solar system. Their ship orbited the planet, but many of their people spent time in the compound and at their resort in Fiji. But they had not yet decided to stay here permanently. Jaden suspected that's where things were headed, and if they did eventually make that choice, their citizenship in the Collective was a foregone conclusion.

After much deliberation, the people of the Collective had decided to elect a governing council to lead them. That body included Venus, Salvatore, Melissa, Sydney, and Vincent, one of the hybrids. Only Vincent had chosen to run for the position. The others had been nominated against their will but agreed to serve when they won the most votes.

Jaden's uncle, Brian Kwan, had received more votes than Melissa but refused to serve. Jaden wasn't too surprised by this; Brian had always expressed distrust of other world governments, so it made sense that he didn't wish to become part of one. But he did agree to function as an ambassador.

Malia, Jaden, Brian, and Commander Anhur were not officially part of the governing council. But they always invited Anhur to the meetings as the Othali liaison. And Jaden, Malia, and Brian's central roles in defeating Isis had earned them standing invitations.

Jaden couldn't bring himself to trust Vincent. He and Malia had probed the thoughts of every hybrid when they first took the compound to verify their resistance to Isis's goal of exterminating humanity. Malia had confirmed Vincent's loyalty, but Jaden couldn't help but wonder if she'd missed something. And like everyone else, the hybrids had to take an oath of allegiance to become citizens. Jaden had taken the same oath.

Many other hybrids had joined the Collective since the early days. Sydney had found a team of experts specializing in helping people rejoin society after leaving a cult. That group had helped dozens of hybrids and brought them to the point where they could become citizens.

But Jaden harbored doubts. These people had spent most of their lives actively supporting genocide on a scale never seen before in human history. How could they move past that in only a year or two?

Salvatore walked in then, interrupting Jaden's thoughts. "I'm sorry for the delay," he said, taking his seat at the table.

"Where's Brian?" asked Melissa.

"On his way to Moscow. The Russians pulled out of the summit after the attack on the resort."

"What? Why?" asked Sydney. "It took ages to put this together—why would they back out now?"

"Their government has expressed doubts about our ability to protect their delegates from further attacks," Salvatore explained. "Don't worry. Brian will sort it out."

All of the Martian and hybrid members of the Collective had long had neural implants that allowed them to interact with the Martian control systems, including those on the flying saucers. The implants were nanobots that interfaced with the brain stem and cerebral cortex. Malia and Jaden had had them injected into their bodies years ago. They'd added the gravitational nanoparticles to their systems more recently, although Jaden still preferred using his telekinesis to fly. The rest of the human members of the Collective, and Melissa, had opted to add the nanotech to their bodies since then. And Jaden knew that Brian had recently learned how to fly the saucers and was probably taking one to Moscow.

"Very well," said Venus. "In that case, let's get started. We will relocate the summit to the backup location one week from today. The delegations are aware of the new date, but as before, we will not divulge the location until two days before the event."

"That precaution didn't prevent Isis from learning about the Bavarian resort," Sydney pointed out. "Why do we think it'll stop her this time?"

"It probably won't. But we're beefing up our security. I think perhaps we let our guard down a little too much after having no contact from her for so long."

Jaden remembered very well the debates they'd had in this very room about the security for the first location. The others felt that posting too heavy a guard would be intimidating for many of the delegates. Sydney herself had said that it made them seem more like a military junta than a legitimate nation. Only Salvatore and Venus had supported deploying a more potent force.

"We've been able to analyze the emitter the intruder was using," said Venus. "Isis must have discovered the same radiation leak that we did because she's modified the device to minimize it. But she couldn't eliminate it, and we've been able to adjust our sensors to improve our ability to detect it. I don't think her people will be able to get past ours this time."

"I overloaded the circuits on that thing, but that hybrid managed to get it working again," Jaden told her. "I don't understand how he did that."

"*He* was nothing special," Venus said. "The emitter's got redundant circuitry. So once you'd knocked it out, he went to the backup system. Almost seems like Isis anticipated this kind of attack."

"That explains it," Jaden said with a nod. "But that hybrid was different, too. I penetrated his mind, but he was able to kick me out. They couldn't do that before. I managed to surface a few things when I went in the second time. He's part of an elite team Isis has trained herself to fight us. She calls them the Omega Group. They drill against telepathy and telekinesis."

"But how did she find out the location in the first place?" Melissa asked.

"There are 193 countries sending delegates to the summit, plus their support staffs," Salvatore pointed out. "That provides hundreds of avenues through which Isis could have acquired the information. It's impossible to know."

"Unless it was one of *our* people," Jaden said, staring pointedly at Vincent. He returned his gaze with a smirk but said nothing.

"You are out of line, Jaden," Salvatore told him. "And my patience is wearing thin. Vincent swore an oath to uphold and defend our charter, as have you. And he has done nothing to deserve your distrust."

"A leopard can't change its spots. That's all I'm saying."

"Jaden!" said Melissa, her tone outraged.

"Unlike any of the delegations, we monitor all communications from our compound with the outside world," Salvatore pointed out. "If Vincent or anyone else were providing Isis with information, we would know it.

"The simple fact is that there is no way we can control the spread of information once we release the new location to the delegates. The best we can do is fortify our defenses, as I advocated doing before the initial event. But unlike then, now we know for sure that Isis represents a specific threat, and we can respond accordingly.

"So, unless you have something constructive to contribute, please refrain from further comment."

Jaden gave Vincent one last frown, then nodded with a sigh. "All right."

"Do we know why Isis sabotaged the summit?" asked Sydney. "If she's looking for a new way to exterminate us, I'm not sure I see how blowing up the resort would have helped her."

"She told me they don't want us sharing technology with the humans," Jaden said. "She said they'd only find a way to use it against us one day. But she also said they have a new goal. Something about moving to a new planet."

"A new planet?" asked Melissa. "Where?"

"Well, I'm paraphrasing. Her actual words were, 'we're getting off this rock.' But she wants me to join her. She said that I could help her, and that I could rule a new world with her. So, I mean, that sure sounds like they're moving to a new planet."

"Isis doesn't possess the technology to make it to a new star system any more than we do," said Venus. "I don't know what she's blabbering about."

"We possess the tech," Anhur pointed out. "The Othali, that is. Isis could be planning an attempt to take the warship. Or at least to acquire schematics of our engines to build her own. And that could be the kind of help she's hoping to get from Jaden—he has access to our systems."

Jaden knew that the Martians and Othali had made very different technological advances over the millennia. While the Martians had managed to harness the fundamental force of gravity, and the Othali had not, the Othali had developed the ability to move through dimensions of spacetime not usually accessible from the normal universe. And they were jealously guarding that knowledge. The Collective had agreed to share the science behind the Martian gravitational engines and devices with the people of Earth. Still, they would not be sharing weapons technology and did not themselves possess any knowledge regarding the mechanics of delta shifting.

"The Othali aren't the only ones who possess transdimensional engine technology," Vincent pointed out. "The Malor developed this as well."

"True, but the Malor don't currently possess the ability to delta shift radio transmissions, much less matter," said Salvatore.

"Last we knew, that was correct. But we don't currently have any information regarding their whereabouts," Vincent pointed out.

"If I recall correctly, Majestic was dismantling the crashed Malor mother ship at one point," said Sydney. "Is it possible they took their engines?"

"According to the data we retrieved from their systems, that ship's engines were destroyed in the fire," said Salvatore. "They were able to retrieve some of their weapons, which they reverse-engineered and used to enhance their capabilities. But they were unable to gather any data regarding their transdimensional drive. Regardless, Jaden has no special knowledge about the Malor, so I doubt Isis was referring to them.

"But a transdimensional engine isn't necessarily required to reach another star system. The Othali were planning to make that journey using only their hydrogen engines. Isis and her people could get there faster than that with their gravitational drive."

"She wouldn't need Jaden's help to do that," said Venus. "And don't forget the signal we detected at the resort."

"I'm sorry, what signal?" asked Malia.

"My mistake," said Salvatore. "I should have brought this up earlier. We put a dampening field in place at the resort. So there should not have been any way for Isis to get a signal to her fusion grenade to re-arm it. But the Othali detected a delta-shifted transmission only moments before the detonation."

"That would mean her signal didn't have to penetrate your

dampening field," said Anhur. "It moved transdimensionally from her location to the grenade."

"Precisely," Salvatore agreed.

"Well, that seems to prove Isis is already working on transdimensional tech," said Melissa.

"It took our people thousands of years to make the jump from delta shifting radio transmissions to doing the same with matter," Anhur told them. "Having one does not lead directly to the other. You'll have to trust me on this."

"There's another possibility," said Malia. "What if the transmission was made biologically, not technologically?"

"I'm sorry, *biologically*?" Salvatore asked. "How is that possible?"

All eyes turned to Malia expectantly as she gathered her thoughts. "Before the Othali arrived here, Nadia saw visions in her dreams. When we first met her, she performed a brain scan on me and determined that the magnetic field was delta-shifting my brainwaves. The visions she was having were *my thoughts*.

"What if Isis has developed the same ability to delta-shift her brainwaves, as well as Jaden's power to access neural processors with her thoughts?"

"That would mean that she could have armed that nuke from any distance with a thought," said Salvatore.

"Maybe we're thinking about this the wrong way," said Sydney. "Given everything Isis can do now, it might be better to *give* her the warship, just to get her off this planet!"

The others chuckled, but Jaden thought she was on to something.

Hell, they could offer to transport Isis and her people to a new planet, thereby eliminating her as a threat.

"Irrespective of Isis's intentions regarding a new world for her people, it is clear that she will try again to sabotage our summit," said Venus. "I move that we put into place the security plan Salvatore and I outlined before the first event. All those in favor?"

This time, the council voted unanimously to implement the tighter measures. The meeting adjourned, and Jaden hurried out of the conference room.

Chapter Four

Jaden hadn't taken more than three steps up the corridor when his mother emerged, calling him back.

"You were *completely* out of line in there! I cannot believe you would be so *rude* to Vincent. What's gotten into you lately?"

"Mom, I'm sorry, but I don't trust him. *Someone* leaked the location of the summit. And only the ruling council knew about the resort. Who else could it have been?"

"You heard Salvatore. Any member of the delegations could have been the culprit. Vincent is a duly elected member of the council. You cannot talk to him that way. Am I making myself clear?"

"Sure, Mom. Whatever." Jaden turned his back on her and walked away.

"Jaden!" she called out, but he kept going.

He had to confess that he wasn't sure why he suspected Vincent. There wasn't any evidence that he was a traitor. But Jaden had a gut feeling about him that he simply couldn't shake. Maybe it was that smirk of his. It reminded Jaden of Lucifer. Could it be nothing more than that? Only time would tell.

Jaden ate only a light dinner, saving his appetite. Later that evening, he boarded his saucer and took off toward Savvy's place in

Texas. Accessing his iPhone with his implants, he shot her a text to let her know he was on his way.

Brian had figured out a way to provide them all with iPhones that could interface with both cellular networks and their satellite network. This enabled them to communicate "normally" with people outside the Collective.

But Salvatore had been the one to find a solution for connecting the devices to their neural implants. He'd made a simple change that allowed the Martian system to communicate over Bluetooth. Jaden could use his telepathy to access the neural processors the Othali and Martians used, but that didn't work as robustly on human computer chips; they weren't sophisticated enough. Salvatore and Brian had taught him how to hack into human systems using his implants, but Salvatore's modification made the process much more straightforward and provided access to all of their people, not only Jaden.

He reached Savannah's cottage and set the saucer to hover over the front yard. Jaden had to give Savvy a lot of credit. Her grandfather—"Pappy," as she called him—had passed away from a heart attack only a few weeks after Jaden first met them. Her aunts and uncles refused to take her in, so Savvy was on her own.

It turned out that her grandfather had squirreled away a small fortune and left it all to Savannah. But his surviving children had contested the will and held up the estate in probate for more than a year. He'd taken out a loan for the campground, but Savvy had no way to make the payments, and the bank foreclosed. She'd moved to Texas and rented a mobile home, earning a meager income waitressing at a local diner.

But finally, the court upheld her grandfather's will and awarded Savannah her inheritance. She paid off the estate's remaining debts, purchased this cottage on the other side of the lake from the mobile home, and was now putting herself through college.

But Savannah also loved to cook. Jaden caught the delicious aromas of whatever she was preparing for dinner as he climbed the front steps. He walked into the house and embraced Savannah.

"I've missed you," he said, kissing her neck.

"Aw, you're sweet," she replied, kissing him back. "I hope you're hungry!"

She'd cooked some sort of Indian dish. Jaden enjoyed it, but it was so spicy that he had to take a break between bites and eat plenty of rice to cool off his mouth. He told her about the incident at the resort while they ate. Jaden trusted her but always left out details that could compromise their security. Despite the lack of contact with Isis, Jaden had always worried that she'd be back. And they couldn't get information out of Savannah that she didn't have.

But he and Savannah also made sure to keep their relationship under wraps. They never posted anything on social media about each other or their relationship. And Jaden only ever used his saucer to visit her, and Isis had no way to track his movements. At least, none that the Collective knew about.

After dinner, Jaden heard a commotion outside as they were

clearing the table. Looking out the window, he spotted a dozen cars and vans parked out front.

"What the hell is this?" he muttered, heading toward the door.

"Oh, it's just the news people," Savanah told him, peering out the window. "They showed up earlier, too, but I told them to get lost."

"News people?" Jaden repeated. "What the hell do they want?"

"They were asking about *you*," she told him.

"Me? How the hell do they know we're together?"

"No idea. Someone must have seen you coming and going, I guess."

So much for their secrecy, Jaden thought. "Well, I'm gonna get rid of them," he said, heading out the door. The moment he stepped onto the porch, they accosted him, pointing their lights and cameras at him. "Listen, this is private property. You all need to get out of here, or I'm calling the police."

"Mr. Kwan, is it true that your Collective is being recognized as its own country?" one of them shouted at him.

"We're hearing reports that the original site of the summit was attacked. Can you confirm this?" another yelled.

"I'm sorry, I have no comment. Now, please, leave! All of you!"

Jaden had to walk toward their vehicles to get them to leave the property—they followed him like a pack of hungry wolves. But finally, he convinced them to depart, and they started packing up their gear and driving away. As he headed back toward the cottage, he spotted one more of them lingering by the back corner of the house. Jaden approached him. "Hey, man, come on. Get out of here. I told you, if you don't leave, I'm calling the cops."

"I'm not a reporter, Jaden," the man said, stepping out of the shadows. "But I would like a word with you."

Jaden got a closer look at him. He looked vaguely familiar, but he couldn't place it. The man wore jeans and a black turtleneck shirt. There was something on his neck. Getting a closer look, Jaden realized it was a tattoo—it looked like a dragon. Not the winged type commonly found in western fantasy stories, but more of a serpentine one. "And who the hell are you, exactly?"

But at that moment, the man pointed something at him. Jaden thought it was a weapon, but there was a blinding flash before he could react, and he had to cover his eyes. He could see nothing for a moment, and by the time his vision recovered, the man was gone.

"Hey! Who the hell are you?" he demanded, circling the house in search of the stranger. But he couldn't find him anywhere. Holding out one hand, he tried scanning the area for infrared signatures but realized that the inputs were washed out. He couldn't see *anything* this way. Whatever that man's device was, it had rendered his implants useless.

Jaden circled the property once more, moving out toward the road to search for a vehicle, but there was no trace of the intruder. Giving it up as futile, he went back inside.

"What was that flash?" Savannah asked, her voice full of concern. Jaden told her what had happened. "And he was just *gone*?"

"Yeah, I couldn't find him anywhere," he said with a shrug.

"Probably just another reporter."

"Yeah, maybe."

But Jaden wasn't so sure. What was that device he had? And how was he able to disable Jaden's implants like that? They started working again after a half hour or so. But still, Isis could use something like that as a weapon against them if she were to acquire it. Jaden would have to mention this to Salvatore and see what he thought.

There were security cameras set up around the property. Jaden accessed the system through his implants and checked the footage. It showed the mysterious man interacting with Jaden, but that device he'd used had blinded the cameras, too. They had returned to normal by the time Jaden checked the footage but didn't show where the man had gone.

Jaden locked the door and armed the security system. Brian had installed it soon after Savanah moved in. The deadbolt locks came from some company in Sweden and used rotating discs instead of the usual pin-and-tumbler mechanism, which meant they couldn't be picked. Steel beams reinforced the door frames, making it impossible to kick them in. The windows all contained quarter-inch polycarbonate, which was bulletproof. And there were sensors protecting every door and window. With the system armed, Jaden felt confident that the strange intruder wouldn't be able to break into the home. But just in case, he also put his saucer in sentry mode. It would alert him through his implants if it detected anyone near the property.

Savannah and Jaden sat up late watching a movie, then went to bed. They lay in each other's arms, kissing and cuddling for a while. Jaden desperately wanted to make love to her, but Savannah wouldn't consider it. Jaden was in love with her but in no hurry to get married. They were only seventeen and nineteen, after all.

Jaden enjoyed the time he spent here with her. It made his life feel normal, if only for a little while. Ever since the police had shown up at their house and killed their dad, what seemed an eternity ago, he'd longed for a return to the ordinary. Granted, he still had Martian implants in his body and a flying saucer hovering above the property, but this was the closest to normalcy he was ever likely to get.

Finally, they fell asleep. But Jaden's implants woke him a few hours later. He jumped out of bed, worried that the mysterious stranger had returned. But it was only a message from the compound. They were holding a meeting in the morning and wanted Jaden to be there for that. He had plenty of time still but couldn't get back to sleep. He tried to get dressed without waking Savanah, but she heard him stirring.

"What's going on?" she asked, her voice groggy. "Did that guy come back?"

"No, there's been no sign of him. I just have to get going. They're having a meeting, and I need to be there for it."

"Aw, I was hoping you'd stay for a couple of days."

"I know," he said, crawling back into the bed and kissing her. "I'm sorry. I'll be back as soon as I can."

Jaden left the house and locked the door. Accessing his iPhone, he armed the security system again, then boarded his saucer and took off. Back at the compound, he caught up with Malia and Griffin at breakfast.

"You'd better watch your tongue at the meeting this morning," Malia told him by way of greeting. "Mom's *so* pissed at you for the way you treated Vincent yesterday. She was planning on having them disinvite you from the council, but I managed to talk her out of it."

"Well, thanks for that," Jaden said with a sigh. "But I just don't trust these hybrids. No offense, Griff."

"None taken," he replied.

"Your attitude is so hypocritical," Malia said with a scowl. "You and I are hybrids, too."

"Semantics," Jaden replied, rolling his eyes. "The fact of their being hybrids isn't the reason I distrust them. It's because they spent their lives trying to exterminate humanity."

"For what it's worth, I don't trust Vincent, either," said Griffin. "We were both stationed in the South American compound when you all took over. And he was in the commander's inner circle. I'd only just started working as an adult, so I wasn't what you'd call 'in the know.' But I don't see how someone in a leadership position like that could lack loyalty to Isis."

"You're not helping," Malia told him with a frown.

"That's what I'm saying!" said Jaden. "He was pretty eager to join the council, don't you think?"

"The hybrids represent a huge majority of the Collective," Malia pointed out. "They deserve representation in our government."

"Not saying they don't," Jaden agreed. "But he shouldn't be the one."

Once they'd finished eating, they headed down to the conference room. The others were already here; Jaden avoided making eye contact with Vincent. Commander Anhur joined them by hologram moments later. Jaden told the group what had happened with the strange intruder at Savannah's house the night before.

"That's concerning," Brian said with a frown. "Could you tell if he was a hybrid?"

"I don't think so," Jaden replied. "His pupils were round, and I didn't detect an emitter before he blinded me."

"And your implants work now?" Salvatore asked.

Jaden nodded. "The effect lasted only a half hour or so."

"We should bring Savannah here," Melissa suggested. "She's not safe out there."

She had suggested this before. It surprised Jaden in a way; though she didn't say anything, he suspected she didn't entirely approve of his cohabitating with Savannah. But her reasoning had always been that Isis might use the girl to get to Jaden. Bringing her to the compound would eliminate that weakness.

"Nah, Mom. She's got a life of her own. Going to school and whatnot. It would be too much of an interruption. And with Brian's security system, she'll be fine. Dude was just a man. And besides, he was interested in me, not Savannah."

Jaden believed what he'd said, but there was more to it than that, for him, at least. Bringing Savannah here would eliminate the one escape he had from the fantastic world of living in a Martian compound.

"She's still vulnerable coming and going from her car," Salvatore pointed out. "Your mother's right. She'd be safer here."

"Savannah can take care of herself," Jaden insisted, shaking his head. "She grew up with guns—she carries a Glock in her purse, and she's got a shotgun in the cottage. Trust me, she'll be all right. This guy was interested in me, anyway, not her."

They let the matter go. Salvatore updated everyone on the preparations for the summit. The Russians had agreed to return, but only if it took place in their country. As a result, it was being held in an elegant riverside hotel in Moscow. The Kremlin would be providing security. In addition, they'd not only agreed to Salvatore and Venus's measures but insisted upon them. So, Jaden would be taking part in a thorough sweep of the venue ahead of time. The Collective security forces would be working side-by-side with their Russian counterparts, and they'd have multiple saucers flying a constant air patrol of the area.

"We'll be moving the warship into the airspace in the hours leading up to the event, as well," Anhur told them. "If Isis shows up with the chariot, we'll take care of her."

"I'll be heading to the venue the day before the summit with our security forces," Salvatore concluded. "Venus will remain here, and we'll double up on our air patrol."

"Good thinking," said Sydney. "It would be just like Isis to attack the compound while our attention is focused elsewhere."

"Yes, exactly," Salvatore agreed. "Very well. That concludes our business for this morning."

Chapter Five

Malia spent the day working with Melissa in the medical bay. Afterward, she went back to her quarters and changed into her workout clothes. Melissa had surprised Malia and Jaden each with their own apartment for their seventeenth birthday. Malia's quarters were next to Jaden's and on the same level as Melissa's, so it wasn't that much of a separation. Not like she would have had if she'd gone off to college like *ordinary* people her age. But she still appreciated the privacy.

She headed down to the compound's gym. Despite Bastet's departure, they still had an area dedicated to martial arts training. In addition to teaching Malia and Jaden privately, Bastet had trained the entire security force in hand-to-hand combat.

Malia ran through her tai chi form. She loved the combat arts, but there was something special about practicing tai chi. It provided a level of focus and serenity she found in little else. And although she wasn't sure if she believed in "chi" per se, as Bastet had explained it, she *did* feel a kind of energy flowing through her body as she moved through the form.

Bastet alone had been unsurprised when Malia first used her powers to heal someone else. The woman believed that Malia was transferring her chi into her patients' meridians. Malia didn't buy it, but nobody else could offer a better explanation.

Malia had long suspected that Bastet possessed hidden talents of her own. When Malia had first met her at her temple in China, one of her pupils had jumped into a pit, landing safely even though she didn't possess nanoparticles or telekinesis. And on many occasions, when sparring with Bastet, it almost seemed like she knew what Malia would do next before she did it.

Although Malia had asked Bastet about these abilities, she'd avoided providing a direct answer, instead hinting that Malia would know more one day. But unfortunately, Bastet's sudden departure had precluded that possibility—for now, at least. Nevertheless, Malia felt sure that if she and Jaden could have learned her secrets, it would have enhanced their already formidable array of talents, which would be invaluable in their conflict with Isis and her hybrids.

They'd had minimal contact with their enemies in recent years. But Malia had always believed that Isis would be back, and current events had proven her correct. After derailing Isis's plans to exterminate humanity, members of the Collective had spent months helping the world's governments eradicate her forces from their institutions. The Americans, Russians, and Chinese had been particularly aggressive in rooting out the hybrids. Venus's discovery of the telltale emitter radiation had helped tremendously. They'd shared the information with many countries' law enforcement agencies.

The hybrids adapted, relying more on contact lenses than emitters to mask their cat-like pupils. Unlike the Martians, they didn't have scales, making them harder to spot. But the major governments had still managed to find them.

But tracking down the hybrids in the world at large had proven much more difficult. The ones who had infiltrated the world's governments and financial institutions didn't live in compounds or bases. Instead, it turned out that they had embedded themselves in the community, indistinguishable from the humans. As a result, the Collective had had only limited success in finding them. But about six months after Isis's defeat, the hybrids had seemed to disappear altogether.

Many had defected from Isis's organization, turning up at the compound to join the Collective. And some of those had stayed in the field to help round up the others. But then their contacts all went missing.

Malia finished her tai chi practice as Jaden and Griffin arrived. They were sharing a laugh about something but wouldn't share when Malia asked what was so funny. She didn't mind; she knew she'd get it out of Griffin later.

Griffin asked them what was going on with the summit while the boys warmed up. Malia told him about the problem with the Russians and that they'd moved the event to Moscow. She was sure Griffin would probably end up on the security detail with Jaden.

Jaden had learned tai chi from Bastet, too, but hadn't kept it up after she'd left. He said it was boring. But Malia and Jaden both continued working on their sparring and grappling skills, and Griffin had started working out with them, too. Malia had developed a slight edge against the boys when it came to sparring. She was able to beat both of them more often than not. But Jaden had far exceeded them both in grappling. His skill was uncanny.

They decided to focus on grappling today. Jaden and Griffin went first, and Jaden managed to get him in a chokehold after only a minute or so. Malia fought Jaden next. She lasted a little longer and almost thought she had him when she got him in her guard. But Jaden escaped and put her in an armbar. Malia had no choice but to tap out.

Malia and Griffin went next, and this match lasted longer than the first two combined. This time, Malia eked out a win with a chokehold, but she and Griffin were an even match.

They spent more than an hour working out, and by the end, Jaden hadn't lost a single match. Malia was glad he wasn't cocky about it. Had this been a few years ago, she was sure his gloating would have been unbearable.

After their workout, Malia and Jaden headed back to their quarters. They were meeting Melissa for dinner and a movie, and they both wanted to shower first. Malia had noticed that Jaden and their mom were at odds more than ever lately, and she'd suggested this weekly get-together as a way to help bridge that divide. They'd always been close with Melissa growing up, and Malia still was, but she spent long hours with her in the infirmary every day. Jaden didn't, and now that they were living separately, the council meetings accounted for the bulk of their contact with each other. Malia didn't think that was conducive to maintaining a healthy relationship, given how contentious those meetings often became.

Malia kissed Griffin goodbye when they reached their quarters. He stayed with her most nights these days but gave her some space when they had these movie nights with Melissa. Jaden had befriended him soon after he'd arrived at the compound three years earlier. There weren't too many people their age, and only Griffin seemed to feel comfortable around them. The others kept to themselves. Malia supposed this was to be expected; they'd been enemies before, despite these particular hybrids' resistance to Isis's organization.

Malia had found Griffin a little annoying in the beginning. He reminded her of Jaden's old friend, Seth—they were both kind of goofy and nerdy. Griffin was learning computers and control systems along with Jaden and shared his affinity for the work, lacking only Jaden's telepathic control of neural processors.

She'd been mortified when Jaden first told her that Griffin was interested in her; the feeling had *not* been mutual. But Griffin had started hanging out with them more, and he'd grown on her. Although the first time he'd suggested doing something together without Jaden, she'd flatly refused. Griffin was persistent, though. Eventually, they'd started dating. And now that Malia had her own quarters... well, their relationship had blossomed in ways she would never have predicted.

Once she'd showered and gotten dressed, Malia walked next door to get Jaden, and they went to meet Melissa. But the moment they'd sat down in the cafeteria, the klaxon sounded.

"What on Earth?" Melissa said. "Tonight, of all nights?"

Jaden furrowed his brow for a moment, then said, "I'm sorry, I've gotta go. I'll try to come back, though."

"What's going on?" Malia asked as he got to his feet.

"Transdimensional radio signal coming from the hangar bay," he said before hurrying off.

Malia watched him leave, desperately wanting to know what was going on. She didn't want to leave their mom hanging like this, but the whole point of the evening had been for *Jaden* to spend time with her. But when she turned to face Melissa, she found her smiling at her.

"Go ahead," she said with a sigh.

"No, Mom, it's our special night—"

"It's all right. Find out what's up, and then you can let me know."

Malia shot her a grin. "We'll be back—both of us. I promise."

Malia ran off after Jaden. She got to the hangar bay at the same time as Griffin, and they both went inside. Jaden was standing by one of the saucers with Salvatore and Jasper, one of the other security agents.

"I'll take care of it," Salvatore said to Jaden. "Do not interfere."

"Yeah, but I *told* you—"

"You have your orders," Salvatore said calmly before striding away with Jasper close behind.

"What was that all about?" Malia asked.

"They traced the signal to *this* saucer," said Jaden. "It's Vincent's," he added in reply to Malia's blank stare.

"But our saucers don't have delta shifting radios," Malia said.

"No, but the signal was only incoming, not outgoing," Jaden replied. "And our radios can *receive* that kind of transmission, just like that fusion grenade at the resort."

"Any idea who sent it?" asked Malia.

"There's no proof—the data was wiped from the saucer, but who do you think it was?"

"Isis?" Malia asked. Jaden only gave her an ominous look in reply. "But that means she's communicating with someone here!"

"And it's got to be Vincent," said Jaden. "We have proof, now."

"Except that you don't because someone erased the data," Malia pointed out.

"Yeah, that's what Salvatore said, too," Jaden said with a sigh. "But it's *obviously* Vincent. I have to give him credit, though. Using the saucer's system was smart."

"Why?" asked Malia.

"It's independent of the compound," Jaden told her. "Meaning it's not monitored."

Malia shook her head. "He's on the council—he's got a security clearance. And that means he can initiate unmonitored communications from the compound."

"Yeah, but there would be a record of him doing that, which would raise suspicions given everything that's happened with Isis and the summit," said Jaden.

"Sure, but so would using a saucer's radio from inside the hangar bay," Malia pointed out.

"That's just it, though," Jaden said with a grin. "He would have gotten away with it if we hadn't started monitoring for delta-shifted transmissions."

"Yeah, when *did* we start doing that?" asked Griffin.

"Well, *we* didn't. Salvatore set it up without telling anyone else right after the attack on the resort."

"I thought he didn't think we had a traitor?" asked Malia.

"No, he just doesn't think it's Vincent. Even now, which is maddening." Jaden shook his head. "And no doubt, Vincent will deny any knowledge of this, and Salvatore will believe him."

"But internal sensors will show if he was in the hangar bay," Malia said.

"Not if he wiped the sensor logs, too," said Jaden.

"Which he can do with his security clearance," Malia acknowledged with a nod.

"And anyway, I'm sure he probably *wasn't* in the hangar bay. But he didn't need to be. He can access his saucer's systems through his implants."

"Good point," Griffin said with a nod.

"Well, I'm gonna start a process on the control system to monitor his activities," said Jaden. "Which *I* can do because security forces have clearances, too."

"Jaden, no!" said Malia. "If Salvatore or Mom find out that you did that, then they're sure to suspend you!"

"I'll do it," Griffin offered. "I've got the same clearance that you do, but I'm not on Salvatore's shit list. Worst I'll get is a reprimand. *If* they catch me."

“You’re no help,” Malia told him with a frown.

“Yeah, maybe you should be the one to do it,” Jaden agreed. “I appreciate it, man.” He bumped fists with Griffin, and the two of them headed out of the hangar.

Malia followed them out, shaking her head.

Chapter Six

Jaden and Malia went back to the cafeteria and updated Melissa, leaving out only the part about Griffin spying on Vincent. Malia had promised Jaden she'd keep that to herself. They enjoyed a meal together and then went back to Melissa's to watch a movie. But Jaden couldn't stop thinking about that transdimensional signal. If it was incoming only, then how was Vincent responding to Isis? The Collective didn't possess the ability to *transmit* transdimensionally.

Well, he realized, it would be easy enough to take his saucer out for a little excursion and contact her with a conventional signal while he was out. The compound wouldn't detect it, and he could erase the logs when he was done.

Jaden checked in with Salvatore later that night, but sure enough, he told Jaden there was no evidence connecting Vincent to the transmission. Sure, Jaden thought, except the fact that it was directed to *his* saucer. But Vincent insisted he didn't know anything about it until Salvatore told him. Jaden found this extremely difficult to believe; his saucer would have alerted him to an incoming message, transdimensional or not.

But Griffin kept an eye on Vincent for the next few days, and he didn't do anything suspicious—nor did he leave the compound.

The day before the summit, Jaden headed to the hangar bay with Salvatore. The rest of the security detail was waiting for them there, including Griffin. They boarded their saucers and took off for Moscow.

They reached the city, and Salvatore pointed out the venue. It was an enormous steel-framed, concrete edifice located in a bend of the Moskva River. Most of the hotel was nine or ten stories tall, with a central tower rising thirty-four floors. This building was much larger than the first location; Jaden thought it was a good thing they'd more than tripled the security complement for this mission.

The dozen or so saucers they'd assigned to air patrol began their watch. Jaden descended through the airlock and joined the rest of the group assembling in the courtyard in front of the tower. He spotted Salvatore moving toward the building entrance and then saw a group of Russian security officers approaching him. Jaden positioned himself so he could listen in on their exchange.

The Russian leader introduced himself to Salvatore, and they discussed their progress. Jaden's implants provided a translation of the man's words. They'd evacuated the building and were ready to begin their security sweep.

Salvatore addressed their group. Each member of the Collective's force would be paired with a Russian officer. Once he was done explaining the plan, he sent them their assignments. Jaden met a young-looking officer named Kira. She introduced herself, and he replied with the help of his implants. The nanobots took over control of his speech to provide his response in perfect Russian; Jaden didn't know if he'd ever get used to the sensation of his mouth forming words he didn't know how to speak.

Jaden followed Kira into the building. They'd been assigned the first floor of the tower. Jaden pulled up a map of the building with his implants, but Kira seemed to know the building well. They moved through the central corridor, Jaden scanning the area with his implants. Kira guided him into the banquet room they'd be using for the summit the next day. Jaden found nothing anomalous—no unidentified devices and no sign of any hybrids. Once they'd completed their sweep of the first floor, Jaden reported to Salvatore.

It took a couple of hours to complete the work, but the Russians let the guests return once they'd cleared the entire complex. Jaden spent the rest of the day monitoring the first floor with Kira. Griffin was at the front entry with Salvatore, scanning everyone who entered the building. Salvatore would be joining Brian inside the next day to represent the Collective, and Griffin would take over the lead role at the main entrance.

Delegations arrived from around the world throughout the rest of the day, but there was no sign of Isis. By the time Jaden's shift had ended that night, he was exhausted from remaining so alert for so long. He bade farewell to Kira, met up with Griffin, and went to find some food. They dined in one of the hotel's restaurants, then made their way up to the room Salvatore had assigned them for the night.

They had a smaller crew patrolling the building overnight. With barely anyone coming or going, they needed to monitor only the entrances. The air patrol guarded the exterior.

Jaden climbed into his bed and started dozing off almost immediately. He'd be up before dawn, so he was eager to get as much sleep as he could.

"You're lucky, you know," Griffin's voice said from the next bed.

"Huh?" Jaden replied, starting awake.

"Malia," he replied. "You're lucky to have your sister still. I wish mine were still here."

In a way, all the hybrids were half-siblings with half of the others. Every one of them had been created with genetic material from either Isis or Lucifer combined with human DNA. Jaden knew Griffin and his "sister," Judith, didn't share the same biological father but had both inherited their Martian genes from Isis. Griffin and Judith had grown up together in their compound and remained close their whole lives. Perhaps they weren't siblings in the usual sense of the word, but their relationship had been very similar to Jaden's with Malia.

Judith had been patrolling the airspace around their Fijian island six months ago when she'd detected an anomaly suggesting the presence of an enemy saucer in the area. She'd pursued, and the ship had fired on her.

They found her saucer's wreckage on a nearby island, but there was no sign of Judith. Despite an exhaustive search of the entire area, they'd never found her or any evidence of her whereabouts. And other than her reports during the encounter, there was no other sign of the enemy vessel. None of the other ships in the area had detected it, and someone had wiped the memory on her saucer.

"I know. I'm sorry, man," Jaden replied. He wondered what had prompted Griffin to bring this up out of the blue like this, but he said nothing more. Jaden heard him snoring minutes later.

Jaden slept fitfully. He woke up from disturbing dreams a couple of times, borne of memories from his time in captivity in Lucifer's compound. But he jumped out of bed when his implants woke him, ready for the day.

Once they'd each showered, Jaden and Griffin headed downstairs for breakfast. After they'd eaten, they parted ways, Griffin taking up his post at the main entry and Jaden by the doors to the banquet room with Kira. They unlocked the doors and stood guard, ready for the delegates' arrival.

Within the hour, the first staffers began arriving. Jaden scanned every person to make sure nobody was wearing an emitter. Salvatore and Brian showed up a little while later. Salvatore checked in with him, but there was nothing to report. He told Jaden that there had been no suspicious activity overnight, either.

A few minutes later, Melissa and Malia arrived. Melissa was deep in conversation with one of the other delegates and didn't seem to notice Jaden standing there.

"*She's not still angry with me, is she*?" he asked Malia telepathically as she went by.

"*She'll get over it. As long as you stop acting like a jackass.*"

"*Great, thanks,*" he replied sarcastically.

Malia rolled her eyes at him before disappearing inside. Not long after that, the last of the delegates arrived, Jaden and Kira closed the doors, and the ceremonies began inside.

Jaden listened as the first few speakers took the podium to address the summit. They each offered praise for the new treaty, outlining the benefits it would provide to humanity as well as the Collective.

It was Jaden's understanding that they would be providing only the Martians' gravitational propulsion and manipulation technology, the nanotech they'd used to create the antiviral response to Isis's plague, as well as certain other medical applications for the nanotech. But they would not be supplying equipment, only the theoretical underpinnings of each technology. Early in the negotiations, this had been a sticking point, as the world's largest powers demanded that only they receive such advanced equipment. But rising nations balked at this, pointing out that this would give the already-dominant countries an even more unfair advantage than they already had.

Salvatore had proposed giving every country the science behind their inventions but none of the equipment. This, he suggested, would provide a level playing field for all the nations involved. Jaden didn't think this was accurate, as the superpowers would still have a much better chance of building the devices, but in the end, everyone agreed to this plan.

Suddenly, something caught Jaden's eye. Someone was loitering at the far end of the corridor. "I'll be right back," he said to Kira. "I want to go see who this is." She nodded, and Jaden jogged up the hall.

Using his implants, he could get a closer look at them, but whoever it was had their back turned. But as Jaden approached, they turned to see who was coming. It was Vincent from the Collective governing council.

"What are you doing here?" Jaden called out. Vincent was supposed to be at the compound as far as he knew. But the man only shot him a smirk, then left the building through the adjacent exit.

Jaden reached the end of the corridor and hurried out the door but didn't see Vincent anywhere. One of their agents was stationed out here with her Russian counterpart. "Did you see where Vincent went?"

"Vincent?" she asked with a puzzled look. "He's back at the compound, isn't he? We haven't seen anyone out here."

Jaden scanned the area anyway but found no evidence of anyone else nearby. This didn't make any sense. He was sure the man he saw was Vincent. And he'd scanned for an emitter's telltale radiation, but there was none. There had been something odd about his appearance, though. Jaden couldn't put his finger on it. It was almost like he was a little fuzzy around the edges. He'd have to take a closer look at the data later on; right now, he had to get back to his post. Kira gave him a questioning look when he returned, but he shook his head.

Jaden listened to the next couple of speakers. Then one of the doors opened, and Melissa strode out of the banquet room, looking distressed, clutching her purse in one hand.

"Mom? What's wrong?"

"What? Oh, nothing," she replied as if noticing him there for the first time. But she seemed distracted as if her mind were elsewhere.

"I just have to use the ladies room." She looked back and forth up the hallway, searching for one. Jaden directed her back toward the lobby, and she hurried off.

"*Malia, can you hear me*?" he called out telepathically.

"*Yeah, what's up*?" she asked.

"*What's going on with Mom*?" He explained what had just happened.

"*She seemed fine before she got up to leave. I'm sure she's probably just nervous about her presentation—you know she hates talking in front of a lot of people. But she'd better hurry back. I think she's next.*"

Sure enough, the moderator announced her presentation a few minutes later. But Melissa had not returned.

"*Jaden, go see if you can find her*!" Malia said in his mind.

The moderator told the group that they'd be skipping to the next presenter instead and rescheduling Melissa for after lunch. Jaden hurried over to the lobby. But before he reached the restrooms, he received an alert from Salvatore.

"The Othali warship just reported an anomalous sensor reading headed toward the hotel at high speed. We haven't been able to confirm this, but only Isis's ships could move at that speed. So we're going to play it safe and evacuate the building. I've just informed the moderator. All agents, stick to your posts and help facilitate a swift and orderly exit."

"Shit," Jaden muttered out loud, turning around and hurrying back to the banquet room. He reported his odd encounter with Vincent to Salvatore.

"Jaden, that's impossible. Vincent is back at the compound—I spoke with him only minutes ago. I don't know whom you saw, but it had to be someone else."

"But it could have been a hybrid," Jaden replied.

"Perhaps. But you showed no emitter radiation, and the agents at the entrance didn't detect anyone in the area. So stay alert, and notify me immediately if you see him again. But I don't think this is related to Isis."

Moments later, the doors opened, and the delegates began streaming out of the banquet room. Malia checked in with him on her way by, but he let her know that he hadn't had time to look for Melissa. Malia nodded and hurried off.

Jaden tried to follow her progress and see if she could locate her. He also tried contacting his mother through his implants, but there was no reply. But suddenly, Jaden spotted a familiar face coming from the direction of the restrooms. It took him a second to place it, but this was the man who'd shown up at Savannah's place the other night. He was wearing the same jeans and black turtleneck. Getting a closer look with his implants, Jaden could see the dragon tattoo on his neck.

"Where are you going?" Kira demanded as Jaden tried to push his way through the crowd and intercept the man. But it was no use. The last he'd seen him, he was heading toward the main exit, and there was no way Jaden could get through the press of bodies in time. Frustrated, he took to the air, flying over the heads of the delegates to the lobby. People gasped in surprise as he passed overhead and landed in front of them, but he ignored him. He ran out through the doors. But he didn't see the tattooed man anywhere.

"Hey, Griffin, have you seen a man come through here wearing a black turtleneck with a dragon tattoo on his neck?" His friend gave him a puzzled look and shook his head. "Damn," Jaden muttered, hurrying out the door.

"Salvatore, this is Jaden. I just saw that guy from—"

"Jaden, get out of that building—NOW!"

Before Jaden could reply, he spotted the chariot swooping in from across the river. The warship materialized right behind it, firing weapons. They hit the giant saucer, but not before it launched two missiles at the hotel. Jaden flew high into the air as the weapons hit the tower and exploded in a massive fireball. The chariot disappeared again as the tower collapsed onto the lower sections of the building. A giant dust cloud emanated from the site as flames engulfed much of the remaining structure.

Jaden covered his mouth with his sleeve to avoid breathing too much dust as he summoned his saucer. Once he was on board, he flew up to the cockpit, surveying the destruction below.

There were still dozens of life signs inside. Many of those people were probably trapped by fallen debris or fire. Jaden focused his saucer's sonic emitters on the flames and fired. Several other ships did the same within moments. The soundwaves put out the fire.

Jaden left his saucer again, hit the ground running, and headed toward the main entrance. He ran into Griffin on the way; he was unharmed.

"Salvatore, are you all right?" Jaden asked through his implants.

It took several seconds, but he finally replied. "I'm here. Heading back inside to start rescue efforts. We've got a lot of people still in there."

"Understood," Jaden replied.

He and Griffin tried to get inside, but the doors were jammed shut. They were about to move to a side entrance, but suddenly, something blasted out the adjacent section of the wall. Malia emerged through the wreckage, covered in dust but otherwise uninjured.

"Jaden," she said, tears streaking down her cheeks. "I couldn't find Mom—she wasn't in the bathroom. She must still be in there somewhere!"

Chapter Seven

Jaden held Malia's gaze for a moment longer before turning his attention to the destruction of the building. "Mom!" he called out through his implants. "Mom, can you hear me?" There was no reply. He reached out telepathically, too, but still couldn't make contact. Scanning the rubble again, Jaden checked all the life signs, but none were Othali.

"Jaden and Malia, we need you over here by the east entrance," Salvatore said through their implants.

Jaden and Malia took off, flying around the corner of the structure, and found Salvatore standing in the adjacent street.

"What's going on?" Jaden asked.

"We've found an air pocket with at least six people trapped inside, but we can't get to it. Come with me."

Malia and Jaden followed him through a hole in the wall. They moved about fifty feet through the rubble, unable to see much through the dust. Jaden heard the surrounding debris piles creaking and groaning ominously.

They reached a staircase, and Salvatore led them down to the basement. At the bottom, the corridor was mostly intact, with only a handful of holes in the ceiling. But they rounded a corner and found an area where the ceiling had collapsed completely.

Climbing over some rubble, they reached a dead end. There was a massive chunk of concrete obstructing their way.

"We're detecting life signs in a cavity on the other side of this slab. I'm reluctant to use the saucers' gravitational beams to clear it because it's weight-bearing," Salvatore explained.

"So if we move it, the ceiling on the other side might collapse on the people in there?" Malia asked.

"Exactly," Salvatore said with a nod.

"I'll brace the ceiling; you get this concrete out of the way," Jaden suggested to Malia. She nodded, furrowing her brow as she gathered her strength. Jaden tapped into the magnetic field, then scanned the cavity with his implants. Taking a deep breath, he reached out with his mind, holding up the ceiling inside. "I'm ready. Do it."

Malia concentrated with all her might. The concrete slab began shaking, then slowly rose, a few inches at a time, until there was enough room for someone to crawl underneath.

"That's as high as I can get it without bringing down a bunch of rubble from above," Malia told them.

Salvatore nodded, then crawled through the opening. Jaden monitored his progress with his implants. Salvatore reached the cavity, then started the return trip moments later. Three other people were coming with him. As they cleared the concrete slab, Jaden realized that one of them was unconscious, and Salvatore was hauling her out.

"The other three are unconscious, and one is stuck under some debris," Salvatore reported. "Can you keep your hold on the ceiling and join me inside at the same time?"

"Yeah," Jaden replied, taking a deep breath. Then, focusing his attention on holding up the ceiling telekinetically, he dropped to his stomach and crawled through the opening, Salvatore right behind him. Inside, he found a man and a woman lying side by side in the rubble. There was a second woman, only her head and torso sticking out from a pile of debris. "This is gonna be tough. Let's get these two out of here first, and then I'll come back for her."

Each of them grabbed one of the victims by the arms, then slowly dragged them out of the cavity. There was no easy way to do this. Jaden lay on his back, holding onto the woman's hands and using his arms and legs to wriggle back to Malia. But finally, they made it to the corridor.

Jaden hurried back to the cavity. He tried pulling the last woman free, but she wouldn't budge. "*Malia, can you hold up that slab and the ceiling in here at the same time? I'm gonna need my powers to pull her free.*"

"*I'll try—don't let it go yet.*" Jaden could feel Malia's power adding to his own. "*All right, I've got it. But you need to hurry. I won't be able to hold this much weight for very long.*"

Slowly, Jaden released his control of the ceiling above. The weight shifted slightly, and a stream of dust fell on his head. Brushing it off, Jaden turned his focus to the trapped woman. Reaching out with his mind, he managed to lift enough of the rubble to free her. She was in bad shape. Blood was dripping from at least three different wounds, and he spotted a bone protruding from her thigh.

"*Jaden, hurry!*"

Moving as quickly as he could, Jaden wriggled his way back through the gap, pulling the woman along by the arms. Finally, he emerged with her into the corridor. He added his power to Malia's, and slowly, they lowered the concrete slab again. There was a rumbling sound from beyond it. Scanning the area with his implants, Jaden could see that the ceiling inside had collapsed.

"Not a moment too soon," he muttered. "Malia, these people are hurt pretty bad. They're going to need your help if they're going to get through this. So let's get them outside, then you work on them, and I'll come back for more survivors."

"I should come back and help, too," Malia insisted. "You and I are the only ones with telekinesis."

"Jaden's right, I'm afraid," Salvatore told her. "Some of these people will die without your help."

"I'll call you if we need two of us again," Jaden assured her.

Malia agreed with a sigh.

Salvatore called for more help as they began transporting people up to the surface. Once they got them all outside, Jaden scanned the debris pile again. There were more life signs on the other side of the structure. So he flew over there with Salvatore, and they began searching for an access point. But they couldn't find a way in from here. The rest of the basement had collapsed, and there was no clear path to the cavity where the people were located.

Salvatore called in one of the saucers. Jaden focused on holding up the rubble above the people as the saucer went to work using its gravity beam to haul away large chunks of concrete from the top of the pile. It was slow going, but finally, they removed enough material for Jaden to dig a path to the cavity with his telekinesis. It took a few trips, but he finally freed five more survivors from the rubble.

Jaden raced back into the cavity to retrieve the last person, an older man who'd been knocked unconscious by falling rubble. But as Jaden reached him, the tunnel he'd used to get there collapsed. The rubble overhead began rumbling, and Jaden knew collapse was imminent. So, reaching out with his mind, he suspended the debris directly above as the rest of the area crashed down around them.

"Salvatore, we've got a little problem in here," he said through his implants.

"We see it, too," Salvatore replied. "Hold tight. The saucer will remove everything above your position."

Only moments later, Jaden could hear the rubble overhead shifting as the saucer went to work. It took a couple more minutes, but finally, a shaft of sunlight reached them. Jaden blew the opening wider with his telekinesis, then lifted the man through the gap and brought him to Malia.

For the next couple of hours, Jaden rescued the remaining people trapped in the debris, with help from the saucers as needed. And Malia did everything she could to ensure they lived. But then, there were no more life signs. And they still hadn't found Melissa. Jaden tried scanning the debris field for Othali remains but came up empty.

He contacted the warship and asked them to see if they could find anything. Their sensors were far more powerful than his implants. Sure enough, they found traces of Othali DNA buried deep under the rubble. Jaden contacted Salvatore, sent him the scan results, and requested permission to go down there and find his mother.

"I'm sorry, Jaden," came his reply. "There's no air pocket down there—Melissa could not have survived this."

Jaden felt his eyes burning, and his body convulsed with a sob.

"Maybe Malia can save her," he insisted. "Let me at least try."

Salvatore didn't reply for a moment. Then, finally, he said, "Malia's done everything she can here. I'm sending her over to you. Let her help you from above while you go down there. We don't need the whole pile collapsing on you."

"Understood."

Malia reached him moments later. She fixed him with a gaze, tears in her eyes. There was no need to say anything; they both understood the gravity of the situation.

Jaden flew straight into the air, scanning the debris field below with his implants to find the most direct route to the remains. He settled on a starting point to the northeast of the rubble pile. Landing on the street, Malia by his side, he reached out with his mind and started removing debris. Malia assisted him until they'd cleared an area down to ground level.

Spotting an opening where the basement used to be, Jaden flew into the hole. Malia stood at its edge, ready to help. Jaden went to work, using his telekinesis to burrow a hole into the ground. Once he'd gotten within a foot or so of the remains, he dropped into the pit as Malia used her powers to keep the tunnel from collapsing on him.

Jaden reached the bottom. He scanned the area again to get his bearings, then started digging with his hands. Finally, he uncovered a patch of black leather. Digging it out, he realized it was his mother's purse. He checked the area around it, but there was nothing else here. Then, opening the purse, he found a hairbrush. And scanning that, he found traces of Melissa's DNA.

Heaving a sigh, Jaden wiped the tears from his face on the sleeve of his shirt. This was all there was? Where was her *body*? Jaden checked the area more thoroughly through his implants, but there were no other remains here. He was detecting something strange, however. There was a slab of concrete nearby, and it was emitting low levels of an odd sort of radiation that Jaden had never seen before. Scanning it more closely, he made sure to save the data, then made his way back to the surface.

Returning to ground level, he handed Malia the purse and hairbrush. She looked at the items in dismay for a moment, then dropped them on the ground and grabbed Jaden in a hug. Malia sobbed uncontrollably for a minute; Jaden held her, crying freely. He'd expected to find their mother's body down there. But somehow, even that had been taken from them.

Back at the compound, Jaden received a text message from Savannah. She'd seen the news coverage of the attack. He assured her he was all right, but she was in the middle of her class and couldn't chat for long.

A few hours later, Salvatore called a council meeting. Malia and Jaden entered the room together, and the others offered them their condolences. Only Commander Anhur was missing.

"Brian and I met with the other delegates at a secure government building in Moscow and held a brief signing ceremony," Salvatore announced once he'd taken his seat. "Despite the rest of the day's events, we have a treaty. The Collective is now its own nation, recognized in the eyes of the entire world."

"Do we have any idea what happened to Melissa's body?" Sydney asked, her eyes red and puffy.

Before Salvatore could answer, Commander Anhur's hologram appeared. "I'm sorry I'm late. But I've got some important news. As you know, the warship was monitoring the area before the chariot's arrival. And only minutes before that, we detected a blast of transdimensional radiation."

"Meaning what?" asked Vincent. "Isis didn't need to detonate a bomb this time. Instead, they destroyed the building with the chariot's weapons."

"No, you misunderstand me," said Anhur. "It wasn't a transmission this time. Someone transported matter out of that hotel by delta-shifting it."

"What?" asked Jaden. "Could someone have taken Mom?"

"That's what we suspect," Anhur confirmed. "But unfortunately, we're not able to pinpoint the location of the transfer. It happened somewhere inside that building, but that type of radiation is difficult to localize from a distance."

"You mean... our mom's *alive*?" Malia asked incredulously. Jaden felt his heart soaring at these words.

"There's no way to confirm that," Anhur replied. "But we

have run thorough scans of the building, and there are no more traces of Othali DNA down there. Melissa's body is gone. Based on the evidence, all we can say is that something, or someone, was transported out of that building immediately before Isis's attack."

"Hey, when I found her purse, I detected some strange radiation coming from a concrete slab nearby," Jaden told the others. "Could that have anything to do with this?"

Anhur frowned. "Send me the data, and I'll have my team take a look." Jaden used his implants to send his scans to the warship. A minute later, Anhur said, "What you detected is a transdimensional signature. Delta shifting matter leaves a residual trace of radiation. So whatever was removed had to have been located near that section of concrete."

"And that's where Mom's purse was," Malia said, excitement in her voice. "They must have taken her! She's got to be out there somewhere!"

"But who would take her?" said Brian. "And why?"

"Could it have been Isis?" asked Sydney. "We know she used a delta-shifted transmission last time..."

Anhur shook his head. "That's unlikely. A radio signal is one thing. Transporting matter this way is radically more sophisticated. I find it difficult to believe Isis could have accomplished it."

"We're left with the same conundrum we faced before," said Vincent. "Only someone who possesses transdimensional technology could have done this. And that means the Malor."

"When they escaped from Guantanamo, they were nothing

more than a disorderly mob, reduced to traveling on foot," said Brian. "I can't believe they have anything to do with this."

"Do we have any idea where they are now?" asked Sydney. "It couldn't hurt to check in on them, just to be sure."

"We have detected random activities at various points around the globe that could be attributed to them," said Anhur. Jaden listened intently. "But we'll have to investigate and see if we can track them down. They must have established a base of operations somewhere."

"The Othali possess transdimensional technology as well," Venus pointed out. "Is it possible we have a traitor aboard the warship? Could they have transported Melissa from there? Or could someone have taken a device from your ship to do it?"

Anhur shook his head. "The only transdimensional tech we possess are the transmitters, a telescope, and our primary engines. The telescope and transmitters are incapable of delta-shifting matter. And our engines don't work that way. We can delta-shift our ship to a different location, but there is no way to redirect the engine output to transport anything outside this vessel."

"You have been refining fuel, though, to replenish your supplies," said Brian. "Is it possible someone found a way to adapt your engines for this purpose?"

"If they did, they'd have to possess much more knowledge about our engines than anyone we have on board," said Anhur. "My chief engineer has assured me she has no idea how it could be done. And on top of that, we've confirmed that the engines have not been reactivated since we used up our last supply of fuel."

"There's something else," said Jaden. He told them about the man with the dragon tattoo showing up again at the summit. "He overloaded my implants the first time, blinding me for about thirty minutes. And then I saw what must have been a hologram of Vincent at the summit minutes before spotting the man in the same area where Mom went. I'm almost certain he's human. Could he have something to do with Mom's disappearance?"

"Send me the data from your encounter with Vincent's hologram, please," said Salvatore.

Jaden sent it. "He didn't have an emitter. I'm sure of that—there was no telltale radiation."

Salvatore examined the data for a moment, then a holographic image of the hotel corridor appeared above the conference table. He zoomed in on the figure standing at the end of the hallway. "This is a holographic projection. But it's not one of ours. Notice how the edges are blurry. This is a primitive attempt to duplicate our technology. But our projections are solid, and this is nothing but light waves."

"But that projection opened the door," said Jaden.

Salvatore advanced the footage. Sure enough, it looked as if the hologram had opened the door. But Salvatore froze the image and zoomed in closer. Finally, it became apparent that the movement was only a projection. Beyond the hologram, the actual, closed door was faintly visible.

"I don't know who that man might be or what he was doing at the summit," said Salvatore, "but based on this poor attempt to mimic our emitters, I cannot believe that he possesses the ability to delta-shift matter."

They sat in silence for a minute, no one able to come up with any other possibilities.

"We'll double-check our data here," Anhur said finally, "and confirm that our engines haven't been used. And we'll assemble the information we've collected about possible Malor activity and see if we can tease out a possible location for them."

They adjourned the meeting, and everyone got up to leave. Jaden made his way to the hangar bay. Once he was alone, he contacted Anhur and requested access to the information they had on the Malor.

"Give my people a little while to analyze it, and we'll send the council a detailed report," the commander replied.

"Sir, if you don't mind, I'd like to see the raw data myself."

There was no reply for a moment.

"Very well. Stand by."

Chapter Eight

Sitting in his saucer's cockpit, Jaden called up the data from the warship. The first thing that caught his eye were radar contacts—lots of them, all around the world. Vessels traveling faster than anything the humans possessed. But none of these contacts could be correlated with Collective activity. The contacts' locations seemed to be random in nature. But the majority of them did seem to be centered in South America, somewhere in the Amazon River basin.

Jaden sent the signal to open the hangar bay doors and flew his saucer out of the compound. Once he'd cleared the threshold, he set a course for South America and engaged his engines.

"Jaden, this is Salvatore," his voice said over Jaden's implants. "Where are you going?"

Jaden hadn't filed a flight plan or cleared this excursion with anyone. "Out. I need to get away for a little while."

There was no reply for a moment. "Please tell me you're not hunting Isis."

"I'm not. I swear."

Another pause. "Very well."

Jaden knew they'd be monitoring his saucer's transponder, so they'd be able to track him down if need be. But he *wasn't* looking for Isis. Based on everything he'd heard, he didn't believe for a second that she possessed the ability to delta-shift a person.

Once he'd reached the Amazon, he began scanning the terrain below for any sign of Malor technology. The Othali had long ago identified their unique energy signature; nothing else on Earth matched it. Jaden checked all the areas with the highest incidences of unidentified radar contacts but couldn't find anything that didn't belong.

"Now what?" he muttered with a sigh. It did seem a little surprising that the Malor possessed anything that could fly at the speeds indicated by the radar contacts. As far as Jaden knew, they'd been locked up without any of their technology. But upon escaping from Guantanamo, they'd somehow obtained vessels capable of speeds in excess of Mach ten. How? Had they built new saucers somehow? The first radar contacts in the Othali data were dated only months after the Malor's escape from Guantanamo. Could they have acquired the tools and materials necessary to build such craft so quickly?

Jaden remembered the Malor camp they'd encountered out in the Arizona desert. They'd had a few saucers there. But the American military destroyed those. Did the army manage to capture other Malor vessels somewhere? Maybe the Malor found those and retook them once they'd escaped. Jaden decided it was time to visit Guantanamo. He laid in the course and accelerated away.

Only minutes later, Jaden reached the island of Cuba. His saucer flew in low toward the bay near the southeastern tip of the landmass. It stopped above a building his implants identified as the base headquarters. Dropping down to the lower level, Jaden focused for a moment, creating a cocoon of stillness around himself. He'd learned this technique while training with Bastet. As long as he maintained it, his telekinesis would stop any object coming close to him. He took a deep breath, descended through the airlock, and flew down to the ground. Three soldiers rushed toward him, pointing their weapons at him.

"Stop right there and put your hands on your head," one of them ordered.

With a thought, Jaden plucked the guns from their hands and threw them toward the sea. The men turned to flee, but using his powers, he lifted them a few feet into the air, turning them to face him. He realized that his actions could be construed as an act of war and spark an international incident between the Collective and the United States. But he was hellbent on getting some answers. And besides, Brian could probably smooth things over. "Who's in charge here?" he asked.

"Rear Admiral Miller," one of them said. "He's the base commander. In that building right behind us."

"Thank you," Jaden muttered, returning the men to the ground. They dashed off.

As Jaden approached the building, he heard gunfire. A dozen bullets penetrated his telekinetic bubble and froze. Identifying snipers on the roofs of three nearby buildings, Jaden used his powers to seize their weapons and cast them aside. Several more soldiers emerged from the headquarters building. The ones closest to him had their guns drawn and pointed at Jaden. Once again, he grabbed the weapons out of their hands and threw them away. The men made to rush him, but a voice from behind them called out, "At ease, soldiers." Jaden got a view of the man. He was older, his hair balding. Holding a cigar in one hand, he flashed Jaden a smile. "Son, you are trespassing on a high-security United States naval base. Care to tell me what it is you think you're doing here?"

"Are you Miller?"

"That I am. And you're one of the kids who defeated that alien mother ship *and* stopped that Martian bitch from killing off the entire population of the world. So. Now that the introductions are out of the way, what the hell do you want?"

"I need to talk to you about the Malor that were being held here."

"Son, that's classified. As much as I appreciate what you and your sister have done for this planet, I am, unfortunately, not at liberty to discuss that topic."

Jaden and the officer stared at each other for a moment longer. Then, with a sigh, Jaden took to the air, using his telekinesis to take the base commander with him. He flew them into his ship's airlock and up to the cockpit. "Have a seat, sir," he said, sitting down himself and issuing a command to take them into low-Earth orbit. Miller took a puff of his cigar, staring out the windows as the ship rose through the atmosphere. Then he sat across from Jaden, crossing his legs.

"Son, I hope you aren't trying to intimidate me. Because I'm afraid that isn't going to happen."

"Not at all," Jaden replied. "Just removing any distractions. You had the Malor in your detention camps. But then they escaped. Do you know where they went?"

"I am not going to discuss classified intelligence with you. Now why don't you take us back the base, and I'll be on my way."

"Did you have any Malor ships on your base? Or just the aliens?" Miller took a drag from his cigar, saying nothing. "Do you know if your military has any of their ships somewhere else, at some other base?" Miller ignored him.

Jaden took a deep breath. Then, reaching out with his mind, he penetrated Miller's thoughts.

"Hey, now, what the hell do you think you're doing?" the man demanded, showing the first signs of distress since Jaden had met him. He sprang to his feet, lunging at Jaden, but Jaden arrested his motion telekinetically, forcing him back into his seat.

Jaden searched the man's mind for memories of the Malor. Images surfaced of a military transport plane landing at the base's airfield. Roughly a hundred of the aliens disembarked, shackled and chained. They marched them onto barges waiting at the shore and transported them to the windward side of the base and into the detention camp.

More memories came to the captain's mind. Several more transport planes arrived over the course of the next several months, each carrying dozens of Malor. Jaden could feel the captain's distrust of the aliens. Their presence on his base made him nervous—more so than the island's natives constantly patrolling their border. More so than any other detainees they'd ever held here.

"Listen, son, I'll tell you what. Get out of my head, and I'll tell you whatever you want to know. How's that?"

"Why the sudden change of heart?" Jaden asked, searching now for memories of Malor spacecraft.

"They told me you could read people's minds, and truth be told, I didn't believe them. But it would seem that I was wrong. And now, the trouble is that I'm privy to way more secrets than just those aliens of yours. So I'm willing to cut my losses at this point."

Only a handful of images had surfaced featuring Malor ships. Like most of the world, the captain had watched the Malor mother ship on television. And during the invasion, a couple of their scout ships had shown up above the base but moved on after a quick scan. It didn't look like they'd stored any captured vessels at the installation.

"All right," Jaden agreed, leaving the captain's mind. "You didn't have any Malor ships here."

"That's correct," Miller confirmed, taking a puff of his cigar.

"Did the military capture any?"

"They did. Most of them were wrecks. Seems those boys lost power once the mother ship went down. Some of them regained flight after that, but our planes managed to shoot most of those down. But they captured a handful more or less intact."

"And where did they take them?"

The admiral took a deep breath, letting it out in a long sigh. "Wright-Patterson Air Force Base in Ohio."

"And they're still there?"

"As far as I know. They have a team trying to crack the alien tech that flies the things, but last I heard, they weren't having any luck."

Jaden nodded. If he were the Malor, that's the first place he would have gone upon escaping from Guantanamo. "How did the Malor escape?"

"Son, that virus the Martian lady released decimated Gitmo. Only about a dozen people survived on the entire base. Didn't take much for those aliens to overpower them."

"Where did they go?"

"Damned if I know. The boys who remained had the presence of mind to sabotage the aircraft. So the aliens took whatever boats they could find and left by sea."

Jaden considered this for a moment. "And you don't know anything about where they might have gone after that?"

"Haven't heard a thing. They assigned me to Gitmo after you folks squashed the virus. Took months to rebuild the place. But we're back, and I can tell you, if they were to retake those aliens, they'd send 'em right back to us. And that hasn't happened. So I'm willing to bet money they're still out there somewhere, roaming free, doing whatever it is they do."

Jaden took them back down to Guantanamo. He scanned the entire base using his ship's sensors, but the only life signs were human. Miller was telling the truth. Jaden escorted him back down to the airlock, bade him farewell, and lowered him to the ground with the ship's gravitational beam. Then he set a course for Ohio. Only minutes later, he arrived at Wright-Patterson Air Force Base.

But as he set his ship to hover above the facility, a couple of fighter jets swooped out of the sky above, opening fire on his saucer. Their bullets bounced harmlessly off the ship's shields.

Jaden's implants alerted him to an incoming radio transmission. "Unidentified craft, you have entered restricted airspace. Leave immediately, or we will be forced to shoot you down."

"Yeah, you already tried," Jaden muttered. "How'd that go for you?" He exited the saucer and descended to the ground. The base was ready for him—Miller must have alerted them. As Jaden walked toward the headquarters building, dozens of soldiers closed in on him, all bearing weapons.

"Hold it right there!" one of them shouted. "Get down on your knees, or we will open fire!"

Jaden reinforced his bubble of stillness and continued forward. Then, reaching out with his mind, he pushed the soldiers obstructing his path out of the way.

"Open fire!" their leader yelled.

They showered him with gunfire. Jaden couldn't help but flinch, but the bullets hit his bubble and froze. Then, with a sweep of his hand, they fell to the pavement. Reaching out with his mind, he sent the soldiers flying across the base, close enough to the ground to prevent serious injury. But when he reached the entrance to the headquarters, several more soldiers emerged, pointing their guns at him. Jaden disarmed them telekinetically. "Who's in charge here?"

"Colonel White is the base commander, but she's not here," one of them replied.

"Who's second in command?"

"I am," the soldier replied. "Colonel Sharp's the name."

"Great. I'm—"

"I know who you are. But you're trespassing—"

"Yeah, yeah, I know. But I need some info, Colonel. So, we can do this the easy way or the hard way. Your choice." The colonel only stared at him, his eyes narrowing. "All right, it's the hard way then."

"Wait—tell me what you want, and maybe we can work something out!"

"I've been told that you've got some Malor saucers here. I'd like to see them."

The colonel hesitated for a moment, then said, "I don't know what you're talking about. We don't have any alien ships."

"You're lying." Jaden reached out telepathically and penetrated the man's thoughts. Immediately, he saw images of Malor vessels in a hangar somewhere. "Take me to that hangar."

"Not on your life, kid," Sharp replied, his body tensing.

Jaden accessed his ship's sensors through his implants. He scanned the base for any trace of Malor technology but came up empty. "According to my scans, those saucers you deny knowing about aren't here anymore. So where did they go?" The puzzled look on the colonel's face told Jaden that this revelation had surprised him. Jaden was tiring of this game. Reaching out with his mind, he lifted the colonel off his feet.

"Whoa, now! Hangar eighteen. That's where they are. Now, put me down!"

Jaden returned him to the ground. "Take me there."

Reluctantly, the colonel agreed. He led Jaden across the base. They reached an enormous aircraft hangar with guards posted at every entry. The colonel ordered the soldier standing by the bay doors to open them. He tapped a code into the keypad embedded in the wall. Slowly, the giant doors slid apart. Jaden followed the colonel into the cavernous space inside. The colonel gasped audibly: the hangar was empty.

"You sure you have the right building?" Jaden asked with a grin.

"I don't understand it," the man said, shooting Jaden a confused look. "They were here—I swear to you. We had six of them. Our teams spent a few months studying them, trying to crack their control systems. It was a total waste of time, though. Their technology was wildly advanced compared to ours. Hell, we couldn't even power the things. So we gave up on the research project, but those ships stayed *here*."

"Apparently not," Jaden muttered, striding away.

"Where are you going now?"

"I've got what I came for, Colonel. You've been very helpful."

Chapter Nine

Jaden returned to his saucer and flew high into the sky. Once he was confident that he was out of the base's range, he set his ship to hover and took another look at the Othali data. Sure enough, there were unidentified radar contacts leaving the area at extremely high velocity a few months after the Malor escaped. The track ended in the Amazon. But that didn't tell Jaden anything he hadn't already known.

This discovery did uncover new questions, however. How did the Malor manage to power their ships? And what were they doing between their escape from Guantanamo and their arrival at Wright-Patterson? Well, Jaden realized, one question probably answered the other. They must have been working on a way to provide power to their ships.

But it had been years now since they'd taken back their saucers. What had they been doing since then? Jaden sifted through the Othali data, looking for more recent contacts. He found one in Suriname from only a few months earlier. Laying in a course, he engaged the engines and took off. According to the Othali records, his destination was a bauxite mine. Jaden had no idea what bauxite was and had to look it up on the internet. A quick search revealed that it was the primary source of aluminum.

What did the Malor want with aluminum? It could be anything, Jaden thought. Humans used the metal for everything from aircraft parts to computer casings. He reached the mine minutes later. It was shallow compared to what he'd been expecting. But the article he'd found did indicate that bauxite was generally located close to the surface.

Jaden left the saucer and flew down to the ground. There were a couple of small buildings nearby. He approached the first of these and knocked on the door. Someone shouted something inside. It wasn't English, but according to his implants, the man had said, "What do you want?" Jaden opened the door and walked inside. It looked like office space. The room's sole occupant turned to look at him and said, "Who the hell are you?"

"My name is Jaden," he told him in a language his implants told him was Sranan. "I'm looking for information about the Malor—the aliens who attacked a few years ago."

The man became very excited, explaining that aliens had shown up here recently and extracted ore from his mine. He told Jaden that his cameras caught the entire thing. Jaden asked if he could see the footage, and the man brought him over to a computer in the back of the room. It took him a minute, but then he opened a video file. Sure enough, it showed a Malor saucer moving into the frame and hovering over the mine. A beam shone down from its center, and then chunks of rock floated up into the vessel. Apparently, the Malor had mastered the gravitational force, like the Martians.

"Have they returned since then?" Jaden asked the man.

He explained that the incident in the video was the only time they'd ever turned up here. Jaden thanked him for his help and left the building.

Jaden spent the next few hours flying around to different locations that had shown up in the Othali data. He visited an industrial equipment warehouse in southern California, but the foreman told him to get lost. Jaden used his implants to scan their facility and was able to access their camera system. They had flagged some footage from several months ago. It turned out to be a video of the Malor taking one of their saucers inside the warehouse and stealing several pieces of equipment. Jaden didn't know what any of it was, and a quick search of their inventory system didn't provide any help. But from what he could tell, the place stocked all different kinds of manufacturing devices used to construct automobiles.

Jaden found another facility from which the Malor had stolen a dozen supercomputers. In addition, they had taken hundreds of parts from a plant that assembled rockets. And a factory in Venezuela reported that aliens had broken into their building and made off with millions of dollars of sophisticated radio equipment.

But none of this was leading Jaden any closer to finding the Malor. He could say for sure that they were up to *something.* Trying to build some sort of machine or ship or weapon. But he was much more interested in their location than their activities. And toward that goal, he was finding nothing but dead ends.

Jaden finally gave up for the day and headed toward Savannah's house. This whole situation was so frustrating. His mom had to be out there *somewhere.* People didn't just vanish into thin air. They knew for sure that Melissa was in that building before the attack and that she wasn't after the collapse. And they had hard evidence that someone transported something out of the building immediately before the attack using transdimensional technology.

It was difficult to imagine who else but the Malor could have done this. And although Jaden hadn't located them yet, he did have the evidence now to show that they were actively developing something technological. So it had to be them. But where could they be? The Amazon basin seemed the most likely answer, but why wasn't there any sign of their presence showing up on Jaden's scans? He'd have to relay his findings to the warship and see if they could detect anything. But he realized it was also possible that the Malor had developed new technology to hide from them and that the Othali wouldn't be able to find them, either.

Thinking about the Malor sparked an idea. Jaden changed his course. Minutes later, he reached Washington, D.C.—or, at least, its former location. They'd erected a memorial right in the center of the area with parkland surrounding it. Gazing out the cockpit window, Jaden found it difficult to believe how much the land here had transformed. From the nation's capital city to utter devastation to neatly manicured grass and walkways. So many lives were lost on this very spot. But Jaden knew it would have been so much worse if they hadn't stopped them.

On a whim, he flew out to Marlton. Reaching his destination, he left his saucer and flew down to the street. Walking up to their old house, he felt tears welling up in his eyes. Melissa had sold the place not long after they defeated Isis. They couldn't move back here, and there had been no point holding onto it. There were two cars parked in the driveway, toys and bicycles in the yard. Some other family lived here now.

Jaden had so many memories here. Growing up with Malia, having no reason to believe they were abnormal in any way. Their mom and dad both looking after them. But now, Stephen had been dead three years, and Melissa was missing. They had to find her. And at this point, locating the Malor was paramount to that goal.

The front door of the house opened, and a woman gazed out at him suspiciously. Jaden hurried off. Once he'd moved out of sight, he flew back up to his saucer and took off for Savannah's house.

He walked inside a little before sunset. Savannah was busy preparing dinner. Jaden told her everything that had happened while she worked. She'd heard about the attack on the news, but he hadn't told her about his mom going missing. Savannah embraced him, holding him tight for a moment.

"You'll find her," she said. "I know you will."

He hoped she was right. But he wasn't feeling so optimistic just then.

Jaden woke before dawn and flew back to the compound. He couldn't find Malia or Griffin, so he went to eat breakfast on his own. But no sooner than he'd finished his food, the klaxon sounded an alert. Checking his implants, Jaden saw that the air patrol had found an intruder approaching the compound. They were towing a helicopter back to base. He hurried up to the hangar bay and found Salvatore. Brian walked in right behind him.

One of the saucers moved in through the bay doors moments later, a helicopter in its gravitational beam. The pilot set the chopper down on the tarmac. Members of the security force were waiting for them, weapons drawn. Jaden could see two men sitting inside the vehicle.

"Come out with your hands up!" the lead agent shouted.

The helicopter doors opened, and the two men emerged, hands in the air.

"Hey, hey, relax now," one of them said. "We come in peace."

Jaden recognized him by the dragon tattoo on his neck. "This is the weirdo I saw at Savannah's that night and snooping around the summit right before the attack!"

"I know you," Brian said to the man. "You're Ezra James."

"I am, indeed," the man said with a smile, dropping his hands and approaching Brian and reaching out for a handshake.

"Hold it!" the lead security agent said, pointing his weapon at the man. "You keep your hands on your head until *I* tell you otherwise!"

"Right, right—sorry, of course," he said, putting his hands back on his head.

"Who's Ezra James?" Jaden whispered to Brian.

"He's the founder and CEO of Ampere," Brian told him.

"Yes, among other things," Ezra confirmed.

"What's Ampere?" Jaden asked.

"It's a tech company," Brian explained. "They released a new kind of battery a couple of years ago that's revolutionized the industry."

"Never heard of them," Jaden said with a shrug.

"Well, maybe not directly," Brian replied. "But have you noticed how that shiny new iPhone of yours can go a whole month on a charge?" Jaden nodded. "That's because it's got an Ampere battery in it."

"What are you doing here?" Salvatore asked the man. "Your vessel violated our sovereign airspace."

"Oh, well, it's not *sovereign* yet, is it?" Ezra replied. "I mean, that attack interrupted the ceremonies, didn't it? You're not truly a nation until—"

"The treaty is signed," Salvatore told him. "I'm waiting for you to answer my question."

"Ah, well, congratulations are in order, then!" The others said nothing. "Yes, well, you see, Ampere is only one of my, ah, endeavors. I've got another startup called Starfire. We're building reusable rockets, space capsules, that sort of thing. Our first sub-orbital test is coming up—"

"What are you doing here?" Salvatore repeated impatiently.

"I was getting to that! You folks are providing the technical schematics for your gravitational propulsion to every nation on Earth, but in point of fact, the vast majority of them don't stand a chance of being able to *do anything* with that information. Most countries have never reached space, after all. But Starfire is on the cusp of doing exactly that. And it seems to me that it would only be fair to provide your data to us, too, seeing as how spaceflight has become largely privatized—"

"You mean like SpaceX and Blue Origin?" asked Jaden.

"Yes, yes, well, Elon and Jeff did have a bit of a head start, didn't they?" Ezra replied, rolling his eyes. "But don't you worry, Starfire is on their heels!"

"Never heard of it," said Jaden.

"Listen, kid," said Ezra, pointing a finger at him.

"Hey!" the security agent shouted, gesturing with his weapon.

"It's all right," Brian told the agent. "They can put their hands down, I think."

"Thank you," said Ezra, returning his attention to Jaden. "Amazon and Tesla have been around longer, but there's no denying the contribution Ampere has made to society—and continues to make. Hell, with the stuff we have in development right now, your iPhone will go a whole *year* on a charge. And EVs? How about ten thousand miles between charges, eh?"

"Sure, sure," said Brian, "but we haven't provided any information to SpaceX or Blue Origins, and they're already *in space*."

"Hmm, yes, well, perhaps they could be included, too," Ezra replied. "Look, the fact is that space travel is becoming less and less dependent on government agencies and more and more the domain of private industry. So excluding companies like Starfire from sharing your data is absurd. *We're* the ones driving humanity's expansion beyond Earth, so honestly, why would you share your technology with Monaco, or Lichtenstein, for God's sake, and not us?"

Brian replied only with a frown.

Salvatore shook his head. "I'm sorry, we've already signed the treaty, and there's no—"

"Now, hold on," said Brian. "He *does* have a point. It might make sense to include the major corporate players in the data sharing."

"That's what I'm talking about!" Ezra proclaimed with a grin.

"We'll need to bring this up with the entire council," said Salvatore.

"I'll wait," said Ezra. "I have all the time in the world. But hey, why don't you call them all together, and I'll make my case to them directly? The gang's all here, right? We could do this right now."

"Wait a minute," said Jaden. "Before anyone even thinks about giving this guy our technology, I'd like to know what he was doing at Savannah's house! And at the summit!"

"That's a fair point," said Salvatore. "Take him and his pilot to the brig," he added to the security agent. "I'll be there shortly to question him."

"Whoa, now just a minute," said Ezra. But the agent ordered him to put his hands on his head again, and then they escorted the two men out of the hangar bay.

"We should search the helicopter," Jaden suggested. "He had some sort of device at Savannah's that he used to blind me. And there was that hologram at the summit."

"My thought exactly," Salvatore agreed, moving toward the chopper.

"I'll get the rest of the council together," Brian said. "I'm not sure if Starfire deserves any special treatment at this point, but the other companies might."

Brian strode out of the hangar bay. Jaden and Salvatore went through the helicopter but didn't find anything interesting. They headed down to the brig.

"We patted them both down," the agent told Salvatore when they arrived, "but they had nothing on them but their phones."

"What was that device you used to blind me that night?" Jaden asked Ezra through the force field.

"You like that? I was eager to see if it would work on those implants of yours."

"How were you able to do that?" Salvatore demanded.

"It's simple, really. Essentially, it's a flashlight. Only orders of magnitude more powerful and spread across a much wider swath of the spectrum."

"And why did you use it on me?" asked Jaden.

"Testing purposes only," said Ezra. "Oh, I mean, I designed it to work specifically against Martian tech. Some segments of the intelligence community aren't so comfortable with your cozy relationship with our leaders. They want to be prepared in case they have to face you in a field of battle one day. So, I figured, hey, I'm pretty sure I can overwhelm your scanners and level the playing field a bit, at least. And it works. So they'll be paying me big bucks for that little device."

Jaden met Salvatore's gaze, giving him a frown.

"And what about the hologram you used at the summit?" asked Salvatore. "What was the point of that?"

"Testing again," Ezra said with a shrug. "And that worked, too, didn't it? The kid here fell for it. Oh, I know, it's not as advanced as *yours*, but I think we're off to a good start, right?"

"You had nothing to do with the attack?" Salvatore asked.

"Me?" Ezra said, a mixture of surprise and anger on his face. "Oh, come now, let's not jump to conclusions. I was merely doing a little R and D. Violence isn't my way. I had nothing to do with any of that."

"Jaden?" Salvatore asked.

Jaden reached out telepathically, penetrating Ezra's mind.

"Hey! Get out of my head!" Ezra yelled, looking alarmed.

Jaden probed his thoughts, and his memories of the summit rose to the surface. He'd been eager to try out his holographic emitter and see if he could fool someone. So when he happened to find Jaden there, someone used to interacting with holographic projections, he was thrilled. He couldn't hope to devise a better test. And it had worked!

Focusing on the night of their encounter at Savannah's house, Jaden found similar emotions. Ezra had seen television reports about Jaden's activity there and had sought him out to try his new invention. Jaden didn't detect anything more nefarious than that.

"I'm pretty sure he's telling the truth," he told Salvatore.

"Yes, thank you, of *course,* I am," said Ezra. "But I have to say, trespassing in my mind that way is a severe violation of my privacy! What does that treaty of yours say about that, eh?"

"Oh, shut up," Jaden muttered as he followed Salvatore out of the brig.

They set off for the conference room. The others were already there, and Brian was just finishing explaining the reason for the meeting.

"Oh, please," said Venus when he was done. "I don't see any reason for us to share anything with some crackpot billionaire."

"Yeah, we all know what happens when a crackpot billionaire gets his hands on alien tech," Jaden said, staring pointedly at Brian.

Brian chuckled. "Believe me, I'm not on the same level as Ezra James. At least, not since his battery breakthrough. Probably not before that, either. But his company hasn't actually reached space yet. So I'm not sure there's a reason to share anything with him, but we should consider the two big players."

"If we apply the same standard to this that we did to the treaty, then we should share the data with all of them, including Starfire," Salvatore suggested.

"That doesn't make any sense," said Vincent. Jaden bit down a retort; he just couldn't stand this man. "We agreed to include *every nation on Earth* in the data sharing. Would you have us do the same with every corporation? Even ones that have nothing to do with space exploration?"

"We could simply make it available to any entity that asks for it," said Brian. "There could be other uses beyond space travel. Anyone having to move heavy loads would surely have an interest in gravitational beams, for example."

"I think that's valid," Sydney agreed. "If someone's interested in developing a way to help advance humanity technologically, who are we to say no?"

Nobody objected.

"Very well," said Salvatore. "I'll have them bring in our guest."

A minute later, Ezra showed up with one of the security agents. Salvatore invited him to have a seat at the table. But at that moment, Venus got to her feet, a concerned look on her face.

"What is it?" asked Salvatore.

"Oh—nothing," she said distractedly. "I just have to look in on something. I'll be right back." She left the room.

"Well, Mr. James, I think we've got some good news for you," Brian told him. "We agree that the data should be made available to anyone who asks for it. So if you'd like to have your people make a formal request, we will provide the documentation."

"Terrific! I can't tell you—"

But at that moment, Commander Anhur, present via hologram, interrupted him. "I'm sorry—my people just informed me that they detected another transdimensional signal."

"Where?" asked Salvatore.

"Here in the compound," Anhur replied.

Salvatore's eyes lost focus for a moment. Jaden knew he was probably checking the control system to see if anyone else had gone missing. "Venus is gone," he reported.

"What?" said Sydney. "What do you mean, *gone*?"

Salvatore rose from his seat and headed toward the doors. The others followed. Out in the corridor, he held out one hand, sweeping it from side to side. Then he moved toward the hallway connecting the two wings and stopped at the corner, scanning that area more closely.

"What is it?" asked Malia.

"Transdimensional radiation signature, right here on the floor," Salvatore said. "Internal sensors show Venus walking out of the conference room to this spot and then disappearing."

"*Disappearing*?" asked Ezra. "Like completely vanishing from the spacetime continuum? Without a trace?"

"Yes," Salvatore said, fixing him with a stare. "Do you know something about this?"

"Well, uh... Have you people ever heard of the Anunnaki?"

Chapter Ten

"The Anunnaki?" Brian repeated. His eyes lost focus for a moment, and Jaden knew he must be using his implants to look up the term. "Ah, yes. I knew I recognized that name—they were the ancient Sumerian gods. What the hell do they have to do with anything?"

"Well, you know what they say," Ezra replied with a grin. "Any sufficiently advanced technology is indistinguishable from magic, right? They called them gods, but what if they were actually a highly sophisticated alien race?"

"This sounds familiar somehow," Jaden said sardonically.

"Huh?" said Ezra. "Oh, right. Yes, I suppose they weren't too different from you fine people, right?"

"I still don't follow," Salvatore said with a frown. "What would such beings have to do with our people disappearing?"

"That's just it, though. The entire Sumerian civilization vanished, didn't it?" Ezra said excitedly.

"Yes, due to drought," Brian told him.

"Hah! Drought and famine don't cause an entire people to disappear. They would just move to greener pastures. The Anunnaki were radically advanced aliens, and they were the ones responsible for removing the Sumerians from our plane of existence. They transported them to a different dimension! And it wasn't just them—the Mayans, the Anasazi, the Indus—the list goes on! So many civilizations that history tells us simply vanished were actually transported to the Anunnaki homeworld!"

"Wait, I've heard about this," said Sydney, her brow furrowed. "When I was looking into the alien abductions, I read about some ancient gods who were supposed to be aliens—"

"Yes, exactly!" said Ezra.

"Yeah, that was just a big conspiracy theory," Sydney replied with a frown.

"No, no, that's what some people say, but that's what they said about our Malor friends for decades, right? The Roswell crash was allegedly just *weather balloons*, for God's sake," Ezra said with a chuckle. "But we know better now, don't we? According to the Sumerians, the Anunnaki could come and go in a flash, moving between heaven and Earth. Only they didn't require spaceships to accomplish this. Ladies and gentlemen, the Anunnaki must have possessed implants similar to yours that allowed them to move transdimensionally. In the minds of the Sumerians, they were going to heaven. But in reality, they were simply going home to whatever planet they come from. And they could do so with a *thought*!"

"Listen, I'll confess, I've been wrong before about ancient aliens visiting the Earth," Brian said with a frown. "I *did* believe that the Roswell crash was weather balloons and that the inhabitants of Atlantis were human. Until new evidence proved otherwise.

Nevertheless, when it comes to these Anunnaki, I remain skeptical. What proof do you have of any of this?"

"Proof? I'll tell you what. You go out and search for their home planet. Then you'll find your proof. Your missing people will be there, among the Anunnaki, and the descendants of the Sumerians, the Anasazi, and all the rest. Living in the glory of—"

"Thank you, Mr. James," said Salvatore, cutting him off. A couple of security agents arrived then, and Jaden knew for sure that Salvatore had summoned them. "They've already brought your pilot back to the hangar bay. Once you arrive, our saucer will transport your helicopter beyond our border, and you'll be free to go. Don't forget to have your people submit a formal request for the data sharing."

"Yes, thank you, but—"

One of the agents grabbed him by the elbow and escorted him away.

"He might be on to something," said Jaden once Ezra was out of earshot. "All of us are living proof that aliens have been visiting Earth for centuries. So how do we know these Anunnaki *aren't* the ones taking our people?"

"It's a conspiracy theory, nothing more," said Brian. "I've looked into this before. And there's simply no proof that the Anunnaki ever existed. Well, they were the Sumerian deities, so they existed in those people's minds, but you know what I mean."

"At this point, the Malor are the most likely culprits," said Salvatore.

"Commander Anhur, did your people detect any Malor activity in this area at the time of Venus's disappearance?" asked Jaden.

"No, they did not," the commander replied, raising an eyebrow. "The visitor's helicopter was the only unidentified craft in the area."

"The Malor are definitely up to something," Jaden said. He told them about what he'd learned the previous day. "But I don't think we should just throw away this Anunnaki idea, either."

But nobody else agreed. They were all convinced the Anunnaki were nothing more than a conspiracy theory. The rest of them returned to their regular duties, but Jaden wasn't satisfied. He wanted to know more. And he knew just the person who could help him. Heading back to the hangar bay, he boarded his saucer and flew out of the hangar bay. Rising through the atmosphere, he accelerated until he matched the warship's orbit. He hailed them and requested permission to dock. Minutes later, he was heading up the corridor to Carl's quarters. But he wasn't there.

The Othali had outfitted their ship with Martian control consoles, and most of the crew had opted to have the nanobots injected into their bodies. Jaden accessed the system through his implants and located Carl. Heading up to the ship's bow, he entered the observation lounge. Giant windows along the front wall provided a beautiful view of the Earth below. There were only a few people here, and Jaden spotted Carl sitting in the corner, reading a book.

"Hey, Carl," Jaden said with a grin, taking the seat next to him.

"Ah, Jaden," the man said with a smile, putting his book down. "What brings you up here?"

Jaden took a few minutes to bring Carl up to speed with everything that had been going on down on the surface. The man's expression grew steadily grimmer as Jaden spoke.

"So, what do you think?" Jaden asked once he'd finished. "Are the Anunnaki real?"

Carl took a deep breath. "I honestly don't know. I did spend many years researching them. It's a compelling theory, for sure. But unlike what I found regarding the Malor and Othali, there's simply no proof."

"So you think they're just a conspiracy theory?"

"Oh, I wouldn't go that far. Just because we haven't found proof doesn't mean they're not real. Here's the thing. If they *do* exist, I suspect they're much more advanced than the aliens we've encountered so far."

"Why?"

Carl collected his thoughts for a moment. "Take the Othali. They achieved technological intelligence tens of thousands of years ago. We're infants compared to them—we've only had computers for about a hundred years! And the Malor developed advanced technology perhaps *hundreds* of thousands of years ago.

"But the universe is thirteen *billion* years old. Do you understand how large a number that is?"

"No, I guess I don't," Jaden said with a chuckle.

"Think of it this way," said Carl. "A million seconds works out to about eleven days. But a *billion* seconds comes out to roughly *thirty-one years*."

"Wow, okay," Jaden replied appreciatively.

"Now, consider this. It took about a billion years from the moment of the Big Bang before the galaxies as we know them today were fully formed. If a technologically intelligent species developed somewhere in our galaxy that long ago, can you even imagine the abilities they'd possess today? After twelve billion years of development?"

Jaden nodded, considering the ramifications. "I'd imagine they might have acquired the ability to transport people transdimensionally without the need for a spaceship."

"Bingo," said Carl, sitting back in his chair. "Now, again, there's no proof that such a species has ever existed. But when you consider the time scales involved, our little thought experiment at least allows for the possibility, wouldn't you say?"

"Yes, I sure would," said Jaden. "Thanks, Carl. I knew I could count on you. But, hey, don't you ever get tired of living up here in space? You don't miss Earth?"

"*Miss* Earth?" said Carl exasperatedly, staring pointedly out the window. "I believe I have the best possible view of our home from up here!"

Jaden ended up joining him for lunch. And they ran into Nadia and her husband, Awan, in the cafeteria. Before he knew it, Jaden had spent several hours catching up with his old friends. But finally, he bade them farewell and headed down to the surface. It was dinnertime, so he flew straight to Savannah's house. He walked in the front door and smelled the delicious aroma of whatever it was she was cooking.

"Hey, babe," he called out. "Indian again? I love it!"

But Savanah wasn't in the kitchen, even though things were cooking on the stove. Jaden checked the rest of the house, but she was nowhere to be seen.

"Savvy? You here?"

There was no reply. Jaden started to worry. He checked outside—her car was in the driveway. What the hell was going on? Where would she have gone in the middle of preparing dinner?

He accessed his iPhone with his implants. They had location sharing enabled with each other's devices, but the app wasn't coming up with any data for her. Jaden tried calling her phone, but it went straight to voicemail.

Hurrying outside, he swept his hand in a giant arc, scanning the area for any sign of her. There was none. She was just gone. Panicking now, he ran back inside and checked the cottage for transdimensional radiation signatures. There were none.

Jaden went back outside and was about to board his saucer when his phone rang. It was Savannah.

"Hey, where are you? I've—"

"Hello, Jaden," a male voice said, interrupting him.

"Who the hell is this?"

"Aw, you don't recognize my voice yet? It's me, kid. Ezra Brown."

"What are you doing with Savannah's phone?"

"Don't worry, Savannah is perfectly safe. And I'll return her to you if you'll spare me just fifteen minutes of your time."

"What the hell? You kidnapped her? You piece of shit—"

"Manners, Jaden. Here's the deal. I will send you my coordinates as soon as I hang up with you. Meet me here, and we'll talk. Just listen to what I have to say, and then I'll release Savannah to you, no strings attached."

"You son of—"

Ezra hung up.

"Shit!" Jaden yelled. But before he could do anything else, he received a text message. It was from Savannah's phone and included nothing but a set of coordinates.

Jaden boarded his saucer and loaded the coordinates into the navigation system. It was somewhere in upstate New York, out in the middle of the woods from the look of it. He engaged the engines and took off into the night.

Only minutes later, he reached the coordinates. It was too dark to see much, but his sensors showed a human male in the field below. He was alone. Jaden moved down to the main level and activated the gravitational beam, bringing the man up through the airlock. As he moved up through the floor to the main level, Jaden recognized him as Ezra. Reaching out with his mind, Jaden slammed the man into one of the pods. Grabbing him by the throat, he said, "Where is she?"

"Not so fast," Ezra said, his voice muted by Jaden's grip. "Hear me out first. Then I'll take you to her. I promise."

Jaden penetrated his mind telepathically. He tried to search his memories to see where Savannah was. But strangely, it didn't seem like Ezra knew her location.

"Yeah, that's not going to work," Ezra croaked with a grin.

Jaden let go of his throat. "Where the hell is she?"

"Well, you see, I knew about your telepathic abilities. So my men took her somewhere of their own choosing, without telling me where that might be. I don't have any idea where she is. But if you'll listen to what I have to say, I'll contact them and get the coordinates."

Jaden glared at him. He could just kill him now, but then he'd never find Savannah. Who knew what Ezra's men would do with her if Jaden murdered their boss. On the other hand, he could hear what he had to say, get Savannah's location, and *then* kill him. "All right. What do you want?"

"That's better," Ezra said, stepping down from the pod, straightening his shirt, and putting a little distance between him and Jaden. "So. Let me cut to the chase. You want your Mom back. That Martian lady, too, I assume. And I want... transdimensional tech. Help me find the Anunnaki, and we'll both get what we want."

"Wait, what?" said Jaden. "You're just after their technology?"

"I am," Ezra replied with a nod. "Think of it. Instead of spending hours on a plane to get from New York to London, you could just walk through a portal and get there in *seconds*. This technology would dwarf what we did at Ampere. If I could provide this to the masses, I'd be the richest man alive! Elon and Jeff would be shining my shoes!"

Jaden rolled his eyes. "It's just about the money for you. Another way to get even richer than you already are."

"And why not? I'll cut you in for a piece of the action if that's what you want. Say ten percent. I mean, if getting your people back isn't enough—"

"You piece of shit," Jaden said, moving toward him.

"Twenty percent?" Ezra offered, backing away. "I'm afraid I can't go much higher than that. There's going to be overhead, of course. Hell, the R and D alone—"

"Look, you're insane, all right?" said Jaden, shaking his head. "Nuts. Even if the Anunnaki are real, they were here *thousands* of years ago. They've got nothing to do with our missing people."

"Who else could have transported them *transdimensionally*, eh? They're still here, Jaden! They never left! And for all we know, time might not have any meaning for them. Perhaps they can cross the eons the same way they do different dimensions."

"Oh, you're saying they're time travelers, too?" Jaden said incredulously.

"Well, ah, I have no idea. I'm just saying it's *possible*."

"Right. Well, it sure has been nice chatting with you, but I'm afraid your time's up," Jaden said. "So go ahead and call your people and—"

"What if I can prove to you that the Anunnaki are real?"

"You can't. Now—"

"Oh, but I can. How quickly can you take us to Iraq?"

"*Iraq*?" Jaden repeated. "Why the hell would I want to go there?"

"Take us to these coordinates," Ezra said, tapping on his phone, then showing Jaden the display, "and you'll see."

Jaden scanned the coordinates with his implants and brought up a map. It was a location roughly two hundred miles from the Persian Gulf. "Why don't you just tell me what's there?"

"No way," said Ezra, shaking his head. "You've gotta see it to believe it."

Jaden heaved a heavy sigh. "You might be the most annoying human being I've ever met. All right. Let's go to Iraq. But if I take a look at whatever it is that's there, then you let me have Savannah back. No more bullshit."

"No more bullshit," Ezra agreed.

"I'm serious now. Even if I don't agree to help you, that's it. You'll let her go."

"You have my word," Ezra said solemnly.

Jaden held his gaze for a moment longer, then shook his head and said, "I can't believe I'm agreeing to this." But he laid in the coordinates and engaged the engines.

They moved up to the cockpit and sat down. Ezra stared out the windows at the lights passing by far below, his eyes wide.

"How fast are we going right now?"

"Mach twenty-two, more or less," Jaden told him.

"Incredible," Ezra muttered. "And my understanding is that it's gravitational propulsion? How does that work, exactly?"

Jaden heaved a sigh. "The engines emit gravitational waves. They make us go."

"So, they're actually, ah, *pulling* you toward your destination, then?" Ezra asked, his brow furrowed.

"No," Jaden said, rolling his eyes. "I guess technically it's antigravity."

"But that's impossible..."

"Look, man, I don't fully understand it myself. But the Martians mastered the gravitational force millions of years ago. So, maybe ask one of them next time you see them."

"I certainly will."

They reached their destination twenty minutes later. Jaden kept the shields up but took them lower, only a hundred feet off the surface. Below was what looked like an archeological excavation site. A pit had been dug in the ground, exposing a giant, four-sided, three-tiered structure, with long steps leading up to the front. It was the middle of the night here, but enormous floodlights lit the area.

"What is that?" Jaden asked.

"Only one of the most significant archeological finds in the last century, at least," Ezra replied.

"Uh-huh. So what is it?"

"That is a ziggurat. And unlike most of the ones we've found, it's almost perfectly preserved, thanks to some peculiarities in the chemical composition of the sand around here."

"You do realize that I have no idea what that word means. Ziggurat, did you say?"

"Yes, yes," Ezra confirmed impatiently. "This is the site of the ancient city of Nippur. It was the religious center of Mesopotamia for thousands of years. They built temples on the tops of these structures, and they believed their gods lived inside of them."

"Mesopotamia? I thought you said the Sumerians were the ones who believed the Anunnaki were gods?"

"Mesopotamia is the name of this region. The Sumerians were the people who lived here. But they weren't the only ones who worshipped the Anunnaki. So did the Akkadians, Assyrians, and the Babylonians. But let's go down there. The things I want to show you need to be seen close up."

Jaden scanned the area. Sentries were guarding the perimeter of the site, but nobody was inside. "All right. Come on."

Jaden led him down to the airlock. He activated the gravitational beam and lowered them to the top tier of the structure. There was a rectangular temple, open to the elements. Jaden followed Ezra inside.

"How old is this thing?" Jaden asked. "It looks new."

"Yes, remarkable, isn't it? In truth, it's about four thousand years old. Every other ziggurat they've found in this region has been horribly eroded. They've reconstructed a few of them. But the Iraqis found this one a couple of years ago, perfectly preserved. They're keeping it a big secret, though. I've been researching the Anunnaki for ages, so I have a couple of local contacts who told me about this place. But they have not announced this find to the larger archeological community."

Jaden walked around the space, marveling at the figures and symbols carved into the walls.

"Look at this one," Ezra said, pointing out a scene in the center of one wall. There were four figures on the left, with abnormally long bodies. Their eyes were unnaturally large, almost as if they'd been wearing goggles. To their right were several smaller figures, kneeling or bowing to the giants.

"Are the big ones the Anunnaki?" Jaden asked.

"Precisely. The smaller ones are the Sumerians worshipping their gods. Now, come over here and check *this* out."

Jaden followed him to the opposite wall. This scene depicted only three Anunnaki, no humans. They appeared to be standing inside this very structure. But one of them seemed to be stepping through a rectangular portal. His right arm and leg had disappeared inside the rectangle.

"You see that?" asked Ezra. "It's supposed to show the Anunnaki returning to their home in heaven. But what does that look like to you?"

"Looks like some sort of portal," Jaden said skeptically.

"Exactly. They weren't going to heaven. No, they were transporting themselves transdimensionally. Back to their home planet, or some other place, perhaps. But their technology looked so incredible to the people who lived here that it must have seemed like magic, its practitioners like gods."

His curiosity piqued, Jaden held out one hand and took thorough scans of the area. And he could hardly believe the results. There were transdimensional radiation signatures here. But not just a few. They covered the chamber as if people had delta-shifted hundreds or perhaps thousands of times from this spot.

Chapter Eleven

"I don't believe it," Jaden muttered.

"What is it?" Ezra asked eagerly.

Jaden told him what he'd found. "The signatures are faint as if they were left here an extremely long time ago. I'll have to ask Salvatore to look at the data; I don't know how to determine the exact age."

"Well, the place was underground for a millennium or two, so it had to be before that. But... I was thinking. Is there any reason you have to show any of this to the others? I'm just saying, the two of us make a pretty good team, right? I've got the knowledge, you've got the... uh... well, frankly, the technology. The gadgets to properly investigate the evidence."

"Nah, man, this is interesting, but you haven't *proven* anything. I'll show Salvatore, and we'll see what he thinks."

"Jaden, now, listen to me," Ezra said with a frown. "This is only the tip of the iceberg. There's a lot more I can show you."

"These radiation signatures are *ancient*. Whoever left them hasn't been here in thousands of years—you admitted as much yourself. This doesn't help. Someone's taking our people *now*. I'm not going on some wild goose chase with you, looking for some aliens who may or may not have been here in the ancient past."

"But Jaden—"

"No way. Forget it. I did what you asked. I took us to Iraq to see what you wanted to show me. Now, order your people to free Savannah."

"Jaden—"

"*Now*!" Jaden told him, reaching out with his powers and lifting the man a couple of feet into the air.

"Right, yes, okay," said Ezra, pulling Savannah's phone out of his pocket. He examined it for a moment, then said, "Uh... I don't seem to have a signal here..."

"For the love of God," Jaden muttered. He strode out of the temple, pulling Ezra along behind him. Then he activated his saucer's gravitational beam, and they flew back up to his ship.

Moving up to the cockpit, Jaden laid in a course back to the United States, and they flew into the night. He brought them to a hover directly over New York City, and Ezra tried the phone again. Finally, he reached one of his men, got his coordinates, and relayed them to Jaden. Plugging them into the system, Jaden realized it was only ten miles from the field where he'd met Ezra. They arrived there only seconds later.

Scanning the area below, Jaden realized it was an abandoned farm. Savannah was inside an enormous barn with three armed men. Reaching out telepathically, Jaden knocked the men unconscious. Then he contacted Savannah and let her know he'd be right there. Her sense of relief was palpable.

Moving them down to the airlock, Jaden used the gravitational beam to lower them to the ground. He escorted Ezra to the barn. Savannah was tied to a chair; she'd managed to tip it over but couldn't free herself. They'd covered her mouth with duct tape. She was trying to say something, but her words were muffled. Jaden was pretty sure she was probably swearing at Ezra.

"Seriously?" Jaden said to the man, shooting him a disgusted look. "Duct tape?" Ezra shrugged but looked mildly embarrassed. "Untie her, man. Hurry up."

Ezra righted Savannah's chair, untied her arms and legs, and ripped off the duct tape.

"Ow!" Savannah shouted, covering her mouth. Then, getting to her feet, she kicked Ezra between the legs. He yelped, toppling to the floor in a heap, and lay there groaning.

Jaden hugged Savannah and said, "Let's get out of here."

"Wait—he's got my phone," she replied.

"Oh, right," said Jaden. "Hand it over, and we'll be on our way."

Ezra moaned. Holding up one hand, he held out the iPhone. Savannah snatched it from him, and they headed out of the barn.

"Wait!" Ezra called out. "How do I reach you? There's so much more to show you!"

"You don't," Jaden told him. "If I decide I'm interested, I'll call you."

Jaden flew up to the saucer with Savannah. She grabbed him in a hug when they reached the cockpit and broke into sobs.

"Everything's all right now," he assured her, holding her tight.

"I know," she said with a sniffle. "I kept my composure the whole time. I was scared, but I knew you'd find me."

"Listen, you should probably come with me and stay at the compound, now," Jaden told her.

"Nah, that's not necessary," she said, taking a seat. "It was my fault—I forgot to lock the door again," she added, rolling her eyes. "Stupid of me, I know. But I won't forget again."

"Yeah, but what if they're waiting for you when you get home? They could grab you again on your way into the house. Or when you're leaving in the morning."

"I don't know," she said with a sigh. "I've got school."

"Come on. A few months ago, you were practically begging to come live with me at the compound. You said then that you could do your classes online."

"That's true," she admitted.

It took a few more minutes, but he finally convinced her it would be safer, for the time being, at least, for her to relocate. They stopped at her cottage so she could pack a bag, then they flew to the compound.

Jaden was exhausted, but it was almost dawn now. He helped Savannah settle into his quarters, then went to find Salvatore. The control system showed him still in his apartment. He was just leaving as Jaden arrived. He filled him in on what Ezra had shown him. Salvatore took a look at the data from his scans and showed Jaden the algorithms to use to date the radiation signatures.

As it turned out, there were over three thousand different signatures, ranging in age from two thousand to four thousand years old. The oldest ones were extremely faint, though, and Salvatore suggested that there might have been more that had faded out of existence over time.

"So, what does this mean?" asked Jaden. "Is that whacko right? Were the Anunnaki really aliens traveling to and from the temple transdimensionally?"

Salvatore took a deep breath, letting it out in a sigh, and considered this for a minute.

"I don't know," he said finally. "I've called a council meeting this morning. Let's discuss this with the others."

Jaden went back to his quarters, then headed to the cafeteria with Savannah. They joined Malia and Griffin for breakfast, and Jaden and Savannah took turns telling them what had happened overnight. After that, the twins bade their friends farewell and went to the conference room for the council meeting. Once everyone had arrived, Jaden updated them on his findings, calling up holograms of the scans he'd taken.

"I have to admit, this is remarkable," Brian said once he'd finished. "It seems pretty clear that *someone* was indeed making regular visits to ancient Mesopotamia. But the question is who?"

"And why?" Sydney added with a frown. "Why would a super-advanced species run around an ancient civilization masquerading as gods? What were they getting out of it?"

"I've been thinking about this since Jaden's arrival," said Salvatore. "And I believe it had to be the Malor."

"But the Malor travel on ships," said Vincent. "We've

seen no other evidence that they possess the ability to travel transdimensionally independent of their vessels."

"Consider the carvings the people of Nippur made of these beings," said Salvatore. "The enormous heads and protuberant eyes. The resemblance to the Malor cannot be ignored."

"But the aliens in the carvings were giants!" Sydney pointed out. "The Malor are smaller than us."

"That is true, but we don't know how accurate these carvings might be," Salvatore replied. "The people who made them believed the aliens to be gods. So they might have increased their size in their representations as a sign of deference. There is evidence of other ancient peoples doing that when depicting their rulers, for example."

"Intending to show them as large in power and importance, not necessarily in physical size," said Brian. "That makes sense. If you ignore their height for a moment, they do bear a striking resemblance to the Malor."

"Hold on, now," said Jaden. "I'm not sure if I buy that, but Vincent is right. The Malor travel in ships. Not through transdimensional portals."

"Perhaps they were delta-shifting across only a short distance," said Salvatore. "They could have had a ship in orbit, and used the portals to move back and forth from the surface."

"Beaming down like Star Trek?" asked Sydney. "That could be."

"We've seen their scout ships," Jaden pointed out. "They used those to fly to the surface. Why would they do that if they could just step through a portal? And besides, they didn't take their mother ship to a planet until its inhabitants achieved industrialization, right? They used the natives' technology to harvest the world's resources. Once they realized how primitive humans were back then, why would they have kept coming back over and over again for millennia? It doesn't add up. There had to be some other species doing this."

"Could there be more than one faction of Malor?" asked Malia. "We're making an unspoken assumption here that their entire civilization is monolithic. Maybe there's a separate group that helps cultivate primitive societies, kind of like the Othali did. They could be the ones who were visiting Mesopotamia."

"Perhaps," said Brian. "But the data the Othali were able to extract from the Malor databanks did indicate that their entire civilization traveled on that mother ship. It sounded like they *were* monolithic in that regard."

"Listen," said Jaden, shaking his head. "I've gotta be honest with all of you. This is the best lead we have. And Ezra says it's only the tip of the iceberg. It couldn't hurt to follow up with him and see what else he's got. Mom is out there somewhere. So is Venus. We can sit here all day debating which aliens did what, but at the end of the day, does it matter? Whoever took them did it using transdimensional technology. Let's follow this wherever it goes. I already checked on the known Malor contacts, and that's nothing but a dead end."

"That's not entirely true," Commander Anhur said through his hologram. "We've conducted additional scans of the Amazon River region, and we believe we've found something. It's going to take a closer investigation to confirm, but it looks like a settlement."

"A Malor settlement?" asked Sydney.

"Correct," Anhur confirmed. "Jaden established that they possess at least a handful of saucers. So we'd like to conduct further reconnaissance before we send a team down there. Make sure we know what we're getting into. But there's a good chance that's where they're holding our people—if it was indeed the Malor who took them."

"Very well," said Salvatore. "Please keep us posted, Commander."

"What, that's it?" asked Jaden incredulously. "Meeting adjourned? What about Ezra's info? Why don't I go see what else he's got while the warship's checking into that settlement?"

"I don't think so," said Salvatore. "While your findings are intriguing, they are ancient history. There is no evidence that the beings who visited that city so long ago have any relevance to our situation today."

"I agree with Salvatore," said Brian. "I want to find Melissa and Venus as much as you do, but Ezra's a crackpot. A rich one, maybe, but he's no archeologist. We should focus on this Malor settlement, and we'll need your help with that. If we come up empty there, then it might be time to follow up with Ezra."

"That man is also a scumbag," said Sydney. "He *kidnapped* Savannah! Why would you trust him?"

"Look, maybe those Malor have Mom and Venus, or maybe they don't. But I say let's follow the radiation signatures. That's hard evidence! I'll take my saucer and go check out his info on my own.

It won't take away from the warship's investigation in any way. What harm could there be in that?"

"Given the circumstances, I can't blame you for acting on your own to comply with Ezra's demands to secure Savanah's safe return," said Salvatore. "But enough is enough. You do not have clearance to pursue this any further. If you do so, I will ground you and revoke your flight privileges."

Jaden stared at him in disbelief for a moment, then shook his head and sighed. "All right. You're the boss."

The meeting adjourned, and Jaden stormed out of the conference room. He went straight to his quarters, but Malia caught up with him before he got there.

"Hey, promise me you're not going to do anything impulsive, all right?" she said.

"Yeah. Sure. Whatever, Malia."

"I'm serious. Trust Anhur and Salvatore. They know what they're doing."

"It doesn't make sense not to pursue all leads," Jaden said. "I found the same radiation signatures in that temple that we found near the disappearances. That can't be a coincidence."

"No, probably not," Malia conceded. "But the activity at that temple happened *thousands* of years ago. So you have to admit, that seems pretty far removed."

Jaden opened his mouth to retort but then thought better of it. They were beating a dead horse at this point. He only nodded in response.

"Just be patient, okay?" she pleaded. "Give me your word you won't go running off on your own to see Ezra. Please?"

"Yeah. All right."

Malia held his gaze a moment longer, then went on her way. Jaden entered his quarters. Savannah was asleep in his bed. He lay down next to her, holding her with one arm and going over everything they'd learned in his head.

Savannah woke up a little while later, and Jaden talked to her about what they'd discussed in the council meeting. She agreed with Malia and begged Jaden not to go off on his own. It was almost like they both expected him to go see Ezra.

Well, they were right. That's what Jaden wanted to do. He didn't believe for a second that the Malor were behind these disappearances. There was no denying that Ezra was a nut job. But those radiation signatures couldn't be explained away. Just because they were thousands of years old didn't mean that the beings responsible for making them weren't still here. Maybe they'd moved on to other societies after Sumer fell. And perhaps now, for whatever reason, they were targeting the Collective. Jaden had to know.

He waited until Savannah logged into the console he'd set up for her to take her classes online, then kissed her goodbye, and left. Jaden went straight to the hangar bay. He boarded his saucer, went up to the cockpit, and issued the command to open the bay doors. But as he laid in a course for New York, Salvatore contacted him through his implants.

"Jaden, this is Salvatore. Where do you think you're going?"

"To find Mom and Venus."

"That's it. I'm revoking your flight status. Disembark immediately."

"Sorry, I can't do that."

Jaden felt bad defying Salvatore like this. He'd been almost like a father to him these last several years and had saved his life on more than one occasion. But Jaden had made up his mind. He switched off the saucer's transponder, locked out all communications from the compound, and left the hangar. Once he'd cleared the threshold, he shot into the sky.

Chapter Twelve

Jaden accessed the internet and started the process of finding Ezra James. But as he flew over the Atlantic, a thought occurred to him. Maybe he should take a look at this Malor settlement for himself first. If they were the ones who had their people, it could save everyone a bunch of time.

The trouble was that he'd need to get his hands on the new Othali data. And given the way things had gone down with Salvatore, contacting Anhur probably wasn't the best idea. He could access the warship's systems through his implants, but that would alert them to his activities, and they might try to stop him. Maybe if he interfaced with their processors telepathically? But, no, then they'd know for sure it was him. Nobody else possessed that ability.

Jaden had a better idea. Reaching out telepathically, he contacted Nadia.

"*Jaden? Is that you?*" she asked in his thoughts when he touched her mind.

"*Hey, yeah, it's me. Listen, I need to ask you for a huge favor. You're not going to like it, and I have to ask you to keep this a secret.*"

Melissa had saved Nadia's life after Bomani tried to kill her on

Mars. And with Malia's help, they'd managed to bring her out of her coma. Jaden was pretty sure she'd be willing to help him out.

"*Sounds serious. What do you have in mind?*"

Jaden told her what he was planning to do. "*The only problem is that I don't have the coordinates for this Malor settlement. And if I access your ship's systems, they'll realize what I'm up to.*"

"*Jaden, this could be dangerous. Let Anhur do his thing. Once the recon's done, he'll get a team in there. You know he will.*"

"*Don't want to wait that long. They might have my mom in there.*" Jaden could sense her letting out the mental equivalent of a long sigh. Then she sent him the coordinates.

"*I wouldn't do this for* anyone *else. But promise me you won't take any unnecessary risks. If there's any chance they're going to overwhelm you, wait for Anhur's team. All right?*"

"*Yeah. Fair enough. Thanks for this, Nadia. I owe you one.*"

Jaden changed his course to the new coordinates. Once he'd reached the Amazon region, he flew in low and stopped about a hundred miles away, keeping his shields up. His scans showed the location in the middle of the rainforest. There was something there for sure. It looked like some sort of underground structure. There were several enormous pools on the surface. It looked like they were farming algae for food.

But then, Jaden spotted what looked like a hangar hidden below the trees. Unfortunately, passive scans weren't picking up much. So he risked a quick active scan.

"Uh-oh," he muttered. Sensors showed more than two dozen Malor saucers inside. They certainly had been up to something.

Suddenly, his implants warned him that half a dozen ships were moving in his direction, coming from the Malor settlement. Jaden's heart jumped into his throat until he noticed that he was getting transponder signals from the vessels. With a sigh of relief, he realized that it was Anhur's recon team on its way back to the warship. He was still off the grid, so they went on their way without any sign of having noticed him.

Jaden returned to his scans. It seemed like the underground structure was their center of operations. If they had his mom and Venus, that's where they had to be. He risked another quick pulse with the active scanning beam. The main entrance to the compound seemed to be located in a squat, concrete building on the surface. An elevator led down from there. But he spotted a tunnel that came out next to a small tributary that fed into the Amazon. It looked like little more than a ventilation shaft. But that was probably his best way inside.

Staying low, Jaden flew his saucer to the end of that shaft. He grabbed a plasma cannon and his emitter from the weapons locker, then made himself invisible and went down to the surface. Creeping along by the edge of the stream, he found the entrance to the shaft in the side of a ridge. It was covered with a metal grate. Jaden ripped the grate out of the way using his telekinesis, then crawled inside.

The tunnel was too narrow for Jaden to stand or even crouch. So instead, he used his telekinesis to fly through it. He went slow, scanning the area ahead to make sure he wasn't heading into an ambush. But strangely, he wasn't showing any life signs inside.

Reaching the opposite end of the shaft, he found another grate. Peering through it, careful not to make a sound, he saw a massive concrete chamber, empty except for a derelict Malor saucer in the middle. Where was everyone? He scanned the entire area again, but there was nobody here.

Could the Malor be using their shields to stay invisible? It was certainly possible. He knew they possessed the technology for that but didn't know how it worked. It was unlikely such equipment would have the same radiation leak as the Martian emitters, but Jaden checked anyway. There was nothing to detect. How else could he tell if there was anyone here?

If they were moving about or breathing, they'd create small air currents. Jaden ran an active scan to check for any such airflow but found none. Convinced the chamber indeed was empty, he popped the grate and jumped through the opening, hitting the floor twenty feet below and scanning his surroundings one more time.

From this position, he could hear a humming noise in the distance. Moving cautiously across the chamber, he left through a doorway in the far corner. There was a long corridor with a series of small rooms. This place looked like it had been an old military bunker or something; it reminded him of places he'd seen in old movies.

At the far end of the corridor, he found the source of the noise. It was an equipment room hosting two large machines. Scanning them, he realized one was some sort of power generator. He detected a narrow shaft running deep into the ground and figured it must have been a geothermal system, similar to what they had at their compound. The other machine appeared to be a holographic emitter system of some kind. What were the Malor doing with this?

Returning to the corridor, Jaden scanned the compound again and found the elevator shaft leading to the main entrance. Creeping over to the elevator doors, he realized they had no electricity. It looked like the only thing the generator was powering was the holographic system. Using his powers, he forced the doors open. The carriage was in bad shape. There was water damage and mold growing on the walls, and the ceiling was almost completely rusted out, exposing the shaft above.

Jaden flew up to the surface, reaching the small entry building. The steel doors were locked, but daylight was seeping through little holes in the walls. Confident now that there were no Malor here, Jaden used his plasma cannon to blast a hole through the doors.

As he moved away from the building, its appearance changed. From this vantage point, it looked brand new. He stepped closer to it, and it looked dilapidated again. Jaden flew over to the hangar he'd seen earlier. But as he stepped up close to it, the entire thing disappeared, including the saucers inside. Once he'd moved away from it, the structure reappeared. He checked the algae pools, but they were nothing more than holographic projections, too. The holograms weren't solid, nor were they shielded. Their purpose wasn't to keep people out, only to trick them into thinking the Malor had a settlement here.

What the hell was going on here? Why did the Malor want them to think they had a base of operations here? Or was it even the Malor who had created this ruse?

Jaden didn't have any answers. He returned to the underground bunker to get a closer look at the derelict saucer. This was real. But someone had stripped most of its systems. It was barely more than a hollow shell. There were a couple of computer cores still inside, but the control systems were gone. It had no engine, and there was a gaping hole in the rear of the hull.

This was a waste of time. There was nothing more to discover, and it was clear that neither his mom nor Venus had been taken here. Jaden headed back up to the surface and boarded his saucer. Once he'd reached the cockpit, he did a quick search and found an address for Ezra James on Long Island, New York. Jaden laid in a course and took off into the sky.

Taking a look at the satellite data, Jaden spotted a sprawling mansion at that address. He had no way of knowing if Ezra would be there at this time, but it was worth a shot.

But suddenly, a thought occurred to him. Opening communications to the compound, he let Salvatore know what he'd found at the phony Malor settlement and sent him his scans. Salvatore tried to order him back to base, but Jaden immediately cut off communications. Minutes later, he reached Long Island.

Jaden scanned the home and found two people inside, one male and one female. The man might be Ezra; his height and weight were about the same, but he couldn't tell for sure. So he went down to the ground and walked up to the front door. He knocked, and moments later, a butler answered.

"You're not Ezra," Jaden said with a grin.

"No, sir, I'm afraid not," the man replied. "May I ask who's calling?"

"Salesman," Jaden said. "I'll try again some other time," he added, walking off as the man closed the door behind him. Jaden returned to his saucer and did another search.

Ampere leased office space in the upper levels of a building near Grand Central. Jaden flew there. He set the saucer to hover outside Ampere's offices, high above Forty-second Street and scanned the interior. A few people were inside, but again, he couldn't confirm Ezra's presence here. Leaving the ship, Jaden flew to a small balcony. The door was ajar, so he opened it wider and stepped inside.

The room was surprisingly bare. There was a large mahogany desk in the far corner and nothing else. Sitting behind the desk was Ezra James, reclining in his chair with his feet on the desk, talking on his phone.

"Listen, Jerry, no more excuses, okay? It's not rocket science—no, scratch that, *of course,* it's rocket science," he said, chuckling at his own joke. "But dammit, we're already two weeks behind schedule, get—"

Jaden made himself visible. Ezra let out a little scream, nearly fell out of his chair, and dropped his phone.

"Jaden, my boy! It's so nice to see you," he said, jumping to his feet. "How did you get in?"

"Your door was open," he replied, nodding toward the balcony.

"Ah, right, of course," Ezra said distractedly, staring at the door. But then he remembered his phone. Squatting down for a moment to retrieve it, he straightened up and said, "Jerry, I'll call you back." Then, pocketing the device, he said, "To what do I owe this pleasant surprise?"

"I'm in," Jaden said. "I need to find these Anunnaki and get our people back."

"Great!" said Ezra, patting him on the shoulder. "I knew you'd come around eventually!"

"Yeah, so tell me what else you know, and I'll be on my way."

"No, no, no, that doesn't work for me at all," Ezra replied, shaking his head. "I'm going with you."

"Forget it. Just tell me everything, and I'll find them."

"Why would I do that, Jaden? There's nothing in it for me that way. I'll do everything I can to help you find your people, but in return, I want that transdimensional tech. So take me with you, and together, we'll both get what we want."

"You do know I could take the information directly from your mind, right?" Jaden asked, stepping toward him menacingly.

"Yes, yes," said Ezra, backing way. "Sure you could. But what happens if you find something that you can't explain? I don't know where the Anunnaki are *now*; I can only tell you places I know they've been in the past. You can follow those breadcrumbs only so far. Your abilities are formidable, but you're going to need my knowledge to follow this trail to its end, my boy."

Jaden sighed. He was probably right. Even if he took every bit of knowledge the man had about the Anunnaki, it probably wouldn't be enough to find them. And if he reached a dead end, he'd have to find Ezra again to get past it, and by then, he'd probably have gone into hiding. Jaden couldn't afford to waste that kind of time.

"All right," he finally agreed. "Let's go," he added, turning toward the door.

"Oh, well, I can't go *now*," said Ezra.

"Yes, you can," Jaden retorted, reaching out with his mind and lifting him off the floor.

"Whoa, now hold on! God only knows where this quest might take us or for how long! I need to get my affairs in order, tie up some loose ends—"

"Those people have my mom and Venus, and who knows what they might be doing to them?" Jaden said. "We need to go *now*!"

"Give me three hours," Ezra pleaded. "I'll wrap up a few things and turn the rest over to my assistant." Jaden eyed him skeptically. "Have you ever run a billion-dollar company before, kid? Never mind two of them. I can tell you, an operation like that doesn't run itself. If I just disappear, there's no telling what—"

"All right, all right," Jaden muttered, returning him to the floor. "Three hours. Then we go."

"Yes, perfect, thank you," said Ezra. "So, uh... I'll meet you back here, then?"

"Yeah," said Jaden, moving to the balcony. He dove off the edge, flying back up to the saucer.

He had to admit he could use a nap. It felt like ages since he'd last slept. So he moved his saucer to a position high above the Atlantic, put it in sentry mode, then stepped into one of the pods. He set a timer for three hours and fell asleep almost instantly.

Chapter Thirteen

Back at the compound, Malia was in the hangar bay, in the middle of a heated argument with Salvatore.

"It's *Jaden*," she shouted at him. "You're going to take a squadron of saucers to try and bring him back to base? Seriously? He'll resist. And then what? You're ready to shoot him down?"

Several other saucer pilots were standing nearby, including Griffin, observing this debate while trying not to be obvious about it.

"If he were anyone else, he'd already be in the brig," Salvatore said calmly. His lack of emotional display frustrated her. This would be easier if he didn't seem so rational. "He may be your brother, but he's also a member of our security force. And as such, he is part of the chain of command. He violated a direct order and—"

"Yes, he *is* my brother. And together, we've been at the center of everything that's happened these last few years with the Malor, and with Majestic, and now with whoever is behind these disappearances. That's our *mother* they took!"

"And we will do everything in our power to rescue her—"

"And so will Jaden! Look, he's got abilities that nobody else in your chain of command possesses. Hell, he figured out singlehandedly that the Malor settlement was a ruse when the entire

Othali recon force concluded otherwise. That one action saved us who knows how many hours."

"But therein lies the problem," said Salvatore. "He continues to exhibit impulsive behavior. If that *had* been a Malor stronghold, what then?"

"But it wasn't! And yes, he may be impulsive, but he was only putting himself in danger, not the rest of us."

"That's incorrect. If the Malor *had* been there, they surely would have overwhelmed him. And then they'd have *three* of our people, and it would be that much more difficult for us to mount a rescue. And as you rightly point out, Jaden possesses abilities that the rest of our force does not. By going off on his solo mission, he's robbed us of our most valuable asset—"

"He's not an *asset*!" Malia shouted. "You can't just use him as another one of your weapons. Maybe you don't feel emotions, but we do. So why can't you just let Jaden do this his way? Sure, Ezra's probably full of crap. So let Jaden prove it. In the meantime, we can continue pursuing the Malor, and by the time we find them, Jaden will probably have returned, ready to devote his full attention to that effort. Until then, it doesn't hurt to allow him to eliminate the possibility that Ezra is right."

Salvatore considered this for a moment. The pilots looked on in silence. "All right. We'll do it your way. I'll let Jaden be. Instead, I'll take a few people to the phony Malor compound and see what we can find. If you hear from Jaden, and he's done with Ezra, please ask him to meet us there."

"I'll tell him, but I'm coming with you."

"Malia, no. I need you to remain here in case Isis or the Malor turn up in our absence."

"Not a chance. Our entire saucer fleet is here, and the warship maintains a constant watch over the compound. So I'm going with you. I've got the same abilities as Jaden, and you might need me."

Salvatore let out a sigh. "You win. Let's go."

Just then, Brian Kwan hurried into the hangar. "What's going on?" he asked. "I heard there was shouting in here?"

Malia glanced over at Griffin; he shrugged apologetically.

"We were debating tactics," Salvatore told him. "But we've reached an agreement. So Malia and I are heading out to the phony Malor base. We'll report back with our findings."

"I'm going with you," said Brian. Salvatore stared at him; Malia thought she caught the faintest trace of exasperation in his expression. But he only nodded and headed off toward his saucer.

Malia boarded with Salvatore, Brian, Griffin, and two other security agents, Jasper and Selena. They left the compound and flew off toward South America. Malia and Brian joined Salvatore in the cockpit. When they reached their destination, Salvatore took them in low, displaying a hologram of the area in the cockpit's center console.

"That sure looks real," Brian noted. "They went to a lot of trouble to make us believe they were here."

"Yes," Salvatore agreed. "But Jaden's scans are conclusive. Their emitter technology is impressive. I can find no evidence from here that we're not looking at a real Malor base."

Salvatore took them to the small building housing the elevator. They disembarked and floated down to the ground. The guards were armed with their service pistols, but the others didn't bother taking weapons. As they approached the structure, its appearance suddenly changed. Malia could see that it was old and rundown. Salvatore told Griffin and Jasper to stay above ground and stand guard. Malia blew Griffin a kiss as she went by; he winked at her.

Brian had the Martian neural implants and nanoparticles now, like everyone else in the Collective, so he could fly down the shaft with Malia, Salvatore, and Selena. They reached the bottom and stepped into a long corridor.

"I'm not sure I'll ever get used to that," Brian said with a grin.

"What, flying?" asked Malia. Brian nodded. "Oh, come on. That little elevator shaft is nothing. I'll take you skydiving later, and then you'll get used to it real fast."

"Thanks, but no thanks," he replied with a grimace.

Malia thought this place looked like an old military compound, perhaps from the 1950s or 1960s, certainly not like anything the Malor would build. They took a quick tour of the facility, confirming everything Jaden had sent them in his scans.

"We should take the holographic emitter with us," Brian suggested when they reached the equipment room. "Could learn a thing or two from this."

"Good thinking," said Salvatore. "If we get Venus back, she should be able to reverse engineer it and use what she gleans to improve our emitters."

"*When* we get Venus back," Malia chided. "Not 'if.'"

They reached the main chamber, and Brian made for the derelict saucer. "There are a couple of computer cores still in here. Let me see if I can crack these. Might be some interesting data on here."

Selena stood guard while Malia surveyed the rest of the area with Salvatore, but there was nothing else here. "I wonder how they got the saucer in here," she said. "It's too big for the elevator shaft."

"That's a good question," Salvatore agreed. "Let's go see if we can disable the holographic system." She followed him back to the equipment room. He took a minute to examine the setup more closely. "Fascinating. The system can also project solid holograms as well as highly advanced shielding. The geothermal generator supplies power to nothing but the emitter," he noted. "It is remarkable how quickly they regained their technological prowess."

"Well, they operate with a hive mind. They're nothing if not efficient."

It took a few minutes, but Salvatore was able to disconnect the emitter from the power system.

"I'd like to take the emitter up to the saucer, but it's bolted to the concrete," he said.

"Where?" asked Malia.

Salvatore pointed out six separate connections. Malia went to work. Reaching out with her mind, Malia focused on the first bolt. The whole room began shaking as she used her telekinesis to remove it. She had to tap into the Earth's magnetic field, but once she'd done that, the bolt shattered.

"They did *not* want anyone taking this thing out of here," she commented before moving on to the next bolt. A few minutes later, she'd removed all six connectors.

"We'll have to take it up the shaft to get it to the saucer," said Salvatore.

"I've got it," said Malia.

Using her telekinesis, she lifted it off the floor. But a moment later, they realized that it wouldn't fit through the door.

"They must have built it in this room," said Salvatore.

Malia used her powers to blast a hole in the wall, doubling the size of the opening. Next, they moved the emitter through the corridor and up the elevator shaft. Once outside, Salvatore brought his saucer closer and opened the cargo hold. Malia set the emitter down on the ground. Then Salvatore engaged the ship's gravitational beam to move the equipment into the hold. After that, they returned to the bunker. They moved into the big room, and Malia saw that a giant section of the ceiling had disappeared.

"Now we know how they got the saucer in here," Salvatore observed.

Malia nodded. "It's interesting that all those radar signatures came from this area. But they didn't converge on this location the way you'd expect if this were a real base."

"They probably spent a lot of time coming here to leave those signatures in an effort to reinforce their ruse," said Salvatore.

"Yeah, maybe," Malia agreed pensively. "They must know that we have access to the radar data. But that still doesn't explain why the signals don't converge here."

"They probably didn't want to make it *too* easy for us to find it."

"Unless this *was* their real base at first," said Malia, trying to fit the pieces together. "If it were, then they'd surely obfuscate their exact location. Hang on. I'm going to take another look at that radar data."

Salvatore nodded and went to check on Brian's progress. Malia used her implants to access his saucer and called up the Othali data. Sure enough, the radar contacts in this area had stopped a few months earlier. However, they'd occurred quite regularly before that.

But there was something else. The trails all ended within a hundred miles or so of the base. Why would that be? The Othali data included only objects exceeding Mach ten or so. Were the Malor flying out of their compound at top speed, then slowing down below that velocity for the remainder of their flights? What purpose would that serve?

She checked the places Jaden had investigated. Sure enough, there were high-speed radar contacts leading to each of those locations. That was how Jaden had found them. Malia cross-referenced those with the activity around the base. They matched. In each instance, a radar contact had departed from the area before disappearing about a hundred miles out. And only seconds later, a new one had appeared within range of the destination. But how could they have traversed the intervening miles so quickly?

Malia gasped. She told Salvatore what she'd discovered.

"That can mean only one thing," he observed.

"They must be delta-shifting across the distances in between," said Malia.

"Yes," Salvatore agreed. "This all but confirms that they have restored their transdimensional capabilities."

"But if that's true, why haven't we detected the radiation signatures anywhere around here?"

"It appears they're making their jumps once they're already airborne," Salvatore pointed out. "They're not near any physical structures when they do it, so I wouldn't expect to find those signatures."

Malia nodded. "But they're making the jumps with their saucers. We don't have any evidence that they can travel that way without them."

"Yet," said Salvatore.

This did make it seem like the Malor had to be the ones behind the disappearances, Malia thought. If they'd managed to construct transdimensional drives for their saucers in so short a time, anything was possible. They could very well have found a way to build personal transport devices that they could use to remove Melissa from the summit and Venus from their compound.

But that also meant that they could be *anywhere* at this point. As far as Malia knew, there was no limit to how far they could travel by delta-shifting. So they could have taken their people to any location on Earth or beyond.

But this still begged the question, why? What could the Malor possibly want with Melissa and Venus? It wasn't like this was a hostage situation—they hadn't demanded any ransom. And with their delta-shifting capabilities, they could infiltrate the compound at any time and take anything they wanted.

Malia could come up with no answers. She went to check on Brian's progress. He was having trouble breaking into the Malor computer cores. He could access them through his implants but couldn't crack their security. Malia knew that Jaden could probably get in telepathically, but she didn't want to point this out in front of Salvatore. It would only add more fuel to his fire. But finally, Brian said, "Well, this is odd."

"What is it?" asked Malia.

"I just found a backdoor. It should only take me a minute to get in this way."

"Why is that odd?" asked Malia.

"Because someone else has already hacked the thing this way. Only a few days ago, from what I can tell."

"Who would have done that?" asked Malia. "The Malor wouldn't need a backdoor to get onto their own computer, would they?"

"No, this wouldn't have been the Malor. Whoever did this was breaking into the core."

Malia suddenly got a bad feeling about this place. Who else could have come here? Were they still here somewhere? Holding out one hand and turning in a slow circle, she scanned the entire facility but found no sign of anyone else here with them. She wondered if someone was using an emitter to stay invisible, so she passed an active scanning beam across the area, looking for any unexplained air currents. If someone invisible were moving or even breathing, they would displace some of the atmosphere. But there were no such disturbances.

Malia tried accessing the saucer's system again with her implants. Maybe the ship's more powerful sensors would detect something she couldn't. But she wasn't able to make a connection. She alerted Salvatore.

"Strange," he said after a moment. "I can't access the saucer, either. Let me go check on the ship."

"I should go with you," Malia suggested, following him toward the corridor.

"No," said Salvatore, gazing around the chamber. "I want you to remain here with Brian. And... stay alert. You, too," he added to Selena, who was standing guard by the door.

Malia felt a shiver run down her spine as he moved into the corridor. Despite the negative scans, she couldn't help feeling like someone else was here, watching them. Reaching out with her mind, she tried to sense any unwelcome guests, but couldn't find anyone this way, either.

"How's it going?" she asked Brian.

"Just another minute," he said, his brow furrowed in concentration. Then moments later, he added, "Hah! I'm in!"

Chapter Fourteen

Jaden woke with a start. He felt like he'd only been asleep for a few minutes. But his saucer was alerting him that it had detected the telltale radiation of a Martian emitter. Jaden initiated an active scanning beam that revealed an incoming ship.

"Oh, shit," Jaden muttered, jumping out of his pod. Only one vessel matched the size and speed his scans were detecting: Isis's chariot. Jaden left the saucer and flew back to Ezra's office. He found him walking around the room, yelling at someone on his phone.

"We gotta leave *right now*," Jaden told him.

"Ah—sorry, Frank, hold on," Ezra said into his phone with an annoyed expression. "I told you three hours," he added to Jaden. "It's only been about fifteen minutes. I'm not ready yet."

"We've got company," Jaden told him impatiently. "It's time to go."

But at that moment, the balcony doors creaked open a little wider. Jaden didn't see anyone there, but scanning the area, he detected an emitter.

"Get down!" Jaden yelled, tackling Ezra and dropping him to the floor. A second later, a plasma shot blew a hole in the opposite wall, directly across from where Ezra had been standing.

"Holy shit!" Ezra shouted, looking wide-eyed at the damage.

Reaching out with his mind, Jaden found a hybrid in the room with them. Taking control of his implants telepathically, he rendered him visible. An instant later, he knocked him unconscious. The hybrid fell to the floor.

"Come on!" said Jaden, standing up and helping Ezra to his feet. He rushed over to the balcony, but Ezra balked.

"We can't go that way! There's nothing but a five-hundred-foot drop out there!"

"You'll be fine—let's go!"

But at that moment, someone invisible pushed Jaden aside. He stumbled a step but reached out with his mind and shoved Ezra aside a moment before another plasma shot went hurtling past him. Jaden found the second hybrid telepathically, made him visible, and knocked him out. The hybrid dropped.

"You're right. We'll go this way," Jaden said to Ezra, grabbing him by an elbow and escorting him out to the corridor. Glancing over his shoulder, Jaden saw the balcony doors being thrown wide open. "Hurry!"

"The elevator's this way," Ezra said, running down the hallway, knocking two of his staffers out of the way.

Jaden followed him to the end of the corridor. Ezra frantically jammed his finger against the call button. "No time for that," said Jaden. Then, grabbing Ezra telekinetically, he focused on the window and blew it out of its casing. He dove through the opening, taking Ezra with him. Jaden left them in freefall for a moment as he summoned his saucer. Ezra screamed at the top of his lungs. But then Jaden flew them into his ship's airlock, immediately using his implants to fly them out over the ocean.

Letting out a long sigh, Jaden led Ezra up to the cockpit. "You wanna tell me why Isis showed up at your office?" he asked as he plopped down in one of the seats.

"Isis? That insane Martian who tried killing everyone with her virus?" Ezra asked, pacing nervously. "How the hell should I know?"

Jaden felt suspicious. "Are you working with her?"

"What? In case you didn't notice, her people tried to *kill me*!"

Jaden didn't trust him. He penetrated his mind, trying to find any memories of Ezra interacting with Isis or her hybrids. But the only thing he sensed was fear and surprise. Ezra felt even more bewildered by the attack than Jaden did.

"All right, now you listen to me," said Ezra once Jaden had left his mind, pointing at him with one finger. "If you and I are going to work together, then you've got to stop doing that. It's a violation of my person, and I will not tolerate it!"

"Sorry, man," Jaden replied. "I wasn't sure if I believed you."

"I have done nothing to earn your distrust," Ezra said with an expression of hurt and disbelief.

"Oh, yeah, except for kidnapping my girlfriend, showing up that night and using that device to blind me, and lurking around the summit," Jaden replied, rolling his eyes. Ezra opened his mouth to retort, but Jaden held up one hand. "Never mind. Forget it." He checked his ship's sensors, but there was no sign of pursuit.

"There's no way they could have tracked me here. My own people can't even find me right now. Someone at the compound must have tipped them off."

"Why would they do that?" Ezra asked, sitting down across from Jaden.

"Don't worry about it," Jaden muttered. He was pretty sure it had to be Vincent. But there was no point suggesting this to Salvatore. He would dismiss his accusation out of hand and add it to his list of Jaden's offenses. "All right. Tell me what else you've got on these Anunnaki."

"Yeah, of course," Ezra said with a nod, collecting his thoughts for a moment. "Have you heard of the Anasazi?" Jaden shook his head. "I'm sorry, that term is frowned upon these days. I should call them the Ancestral Puebloans."

"I still haven't heard of them," Jaden replied impatiently. "Why can't you call them Anasazi?"

"That's what the Navajo called them, and it means 'ancient enemies.' Highly offensive to their descendants. Anyway, they were a group of Native Americans who lived in the Four Corners region of the southwestern United States starting as long as nine thousand years ago, give or take a millennium."

"Uh-huh," said Jaden. "And what have they got to do with the Anunnaki?"

"Well, why don't I *show* you?" Ezra said with a grin. "Take us to Sego Canyon. It's off Route 70 in Utah."

Jaden found the location using his implants, laid in a course, and engaged the engines. They took off into the sky. Reaching the canyon minutes later, he set the saucer to hover. "We're here. What now?"

Ezra got to his feet, gazing out the cockpit windows and looking around. Finally, pointing to the south, he said, "Over there. That parking lot. You see it?"

"Yeah," Jaden replied. "You're taking us to a *parking lot*?"

"Trust me, my boy," he said, patting Jaden on the shoulder.

Jaden sighed. He moved the saucer directly over the parking area. They moved down to the airlock, then used the gravitational beam to lower themselves to the ground. A few people were getting into a car; they froze, staring at Jaden and Ezra with their mouths wide open.

"Hi, there," said Ezra, waving to them.

"Just ignore them," Jaden muttered. "Why are we here?"

"Follow me," Ezra said, wandering off. Jaden followed him to a rock wall just beyond the short driveway leading to the road. "There you go," Ezra said with a big grin, nodding toward the rock wall.

Jaden moved in closer. There were figures painted on the wall. They were unnaturally tall, with elongated heads and huge eyes. "They kind of look like those figures we saw carved into the walls in Iraq," he said to Ezra.

"Precisely! The Ancient Puebloans drew these petroglyphs thousands of years ago."

"So the Anunnaki visited them, too? Did the Puebloans think they were gods?"

"Unfortunately, we know very little about the people who drew these. These drawings are some of the only records we have of them.

We've found plenty of archeological artifacts, but the pictographs appear to have been their only form of written communication."

Holding out one hand, Jaden scanned the area. He found no evidence of transdimensional radiation signatures. "Well, this is pretty neat, but it doesn't look like the Anunnaki ever came here. At least not by delta shifting."

"Oh, really?" Ezra said, looking crestfallen.

"Please tell me you've got more than this," Jaden replied, "because this is looking like a dead end to me."

"I know!" Ezra said, perking up again. "Come on!" He hurried back to the parking lot. Jaden followed him, and they boarded the saucer. "Set a course for Mesa Verde in California," Ezra told him, retaking his seat.

"This had better be good," Jaden muttered. He set a course, and they took off. Reaching the destination, Jaden gazed out the window and saw what looked like a small city embedded in the side of a cliff. "I know this place. Salvatore took Malia and me here right after we first met him. Those were dwellings down there, right?"

"Exactly right," Ezra said with a grin. "Let's go take a look!"

They went down to the ground and approached the complex. The last time Jaden was here, they'd had a battle with the hybrids. The place made him nervous. But he scanned the structures and found no evidence of anyone else here but them.

"This is where some of the Ancient Puebloans lived," Ezra told him, "but this complex is nowhere near as old as the Sego Canyon drawings. We believe it was constructed in the late 1100s or so. There is evidence that this functioned as the heart of a larger society that included nearby communities."

"Yeah?" asked Jaden. "So what happened to them?"

"The Ancient Puebloans vanished in the late 1200s. By 1300 at the latest, this complex was abandoned. Their people disappeared from the entire Four Corners region."

"Where did they go?"

"Nobody knows," Ezra said with a shrug. "But are you, ah, picking up any signs of delta shifting here? Because I believe the Anunnaki took these people away."

Jaden held out one hand and scanned the complex again, this time looking for transdimensional radiation signatures. "There's something... It's faint. And I can't pinpoint it. But it's coming from somewhere inside the complex."

"Well, let's go take a look!" said Ezra, climbing a set of steps to an elevated terrace.

Jaden followed him up. They wandered through the complex, having to climb ladders in some places, but Jaden still couldn't find where the signatures were located. Finally, they returned to the first terrace, and Jaden passed an active scanning beam through the structure. "This is weird."

"What is it?" Ezra asked eagerly.

"There's some sort of chamber or cavity farther inside the cliff face. It's about fifty feet behind the rest of the complex, but I don't see any way to get there."

"I've never heard of anything like that," Ezra said with a frown. "Are you sure?"

"There's definitely something back there," Jaden confirmed. "It's strange, though. It's almost like there's something in the rock that's shielding it from my scans. Wait here. I'm going to go back up to the saucer and see if I can blast through the rock and create an access tunnel."

"What? No! This site is a historical treasure! You can't do that!"

"Look," Jaden said with a sigh. "So far, you're leading me on some kind of wild goose chase. Some old pictures on a wall, and now this place. Maybe these radiation signatures are coming from that chamber. But even if they are, it doesn't get us any closer to finding the Anunnaki. If they ever existed, and if they're even still around." He shook his head. "I'm starting to think Salvatore was probably right. The Malor must be the ones who took Mom and Venus."

"No, no, no—just wait a minute," Ezra pleaded. "If the Puebloans built a chamber back there, then they must have had a way to access it, right? You give up too easily, my boy! Why don't you do some more scans and see if you can find a way in there, huh?"

Jaden was starting to feel stupid. It seemed like the others were right about Ezra. He was just a crackpot who believed in some unfounded conspiracy theories. Nothing more. But Jaden wanted to be sure. So, he went back inside the complex, as far back as he could go, and started looking for some sort of hidden tunnel. But after searching from one end of the structure to the other, he came up empty.

"What about this?" Ezra called out.

Jaden went to see what he was talking about. He was standing at the edge of a round pit in the ground. "Yeah, they've got these circular chambers all over the place," Jaden commented. "So what?"

"It's called a 'kiva'," Ezra told him. "They served some sort of ceremonial function. Of course, there would have been a roof over this space back in the day. But I'm wondering about the firepit in the middle there."

"What about it?" Jaden asked, taking a closer look. "Looks like a firepit to me."

"Maybe," Ezra said, sitting down on the pit's edge and using the ledges in the walls to climb down to the bottom. He squatted by the firepit. "Can you see if there's anything underneath this with your scanners?" he asked, staring up at Jaden.

"Underneath it?" Jaden asked skeptically. But he held out one hand and checked. Oddly, he couldn't detect *anything* beneath the area. He tried an active scanning beam, but it couldn't penetrate the ground. "This is weird." He jumped into the pit, using his telekinesis to land softly next to Ezra. Looking more closely at the firepit, he realized that it did look like it could be covering something. Reaching out with his mind, he tried lifting the firepit off the ground. And sure enough, it turned out to be the cap of a cylinder embedded about a foot into the earth. Setting it aside, Jaden peered into the opening. There was a shaft delving deep into the ground.

"I'll be damned," Ezra said, grinning at him. "Let's go see what's down there!"

Jaden could see indentations in the shaft's wall and suspected that wooden rungs must have been embedded there to provide access. But those must have rotted away a long time ago. Jaden lowered himself into the hole using his telekinesis, taking Ezra along with him. It grew very dark as they descended. Jaden used his hand implants to emit a beam of light. They flew down about twenty feet or so, emerging in a space about the same size as the kiva above. The ceiling was so low that Jaden had to crouch. Shining his beam around the area showed tunnels extending in every direction.

"There's an entire subterranean complex down here," Ezra said, his voice brimming with excitement. "This could be the find of the century, my boy!"

"It's strange that I couldn't detect this from above," Jaden said with a frown, scanning the ceiling. "There must be some kind of shielding in the ground."

"Must be something the Anunnaki installed," said Ezra. "The Puebloans certainly wouldn't have possessed that kind of technology."

"I'm not sure it's technological," Jaden replied. "Could be a naturally occurring compound in the rock." He checked for transdimensional signatures again and found the signal was stronger down here. "Come on. This way," he said, heading down one of the tunnels that seemed to lead toward the back of the complex.

They walked for a minute, then reached another underground kiva. Jaden led the way across that and into another tunnel. This one was longer. It passed beyond the location of the rear wall above.

Soon, they emerged into a small chamber. On the opposite side, there were steps leading up.

Jaden proceeded cautiously, scanning the area ahead. He started feeling anxious that they might run into some hybrids or Malor or something, but it seemed to be empty. Finally, they reached the top of the steps. There was another kiva here, larger than any of the others they'd seen so far. At the far end stood a stone table that looked like it could have served some ceremonial purpose. Scanning the space, Jaden found hundreds of faint transdimensional radiation signatures.

"This is it," he told Ezra. "Someone delta-shifted in and out of this room over and over again. But the newest signatures are about a thousand years old."

"The Anunnaki," Ezra whispered. "I knew it."

"Yeah, but this is just another dead end," Jaden muttered, scanning the chamber to make sure there was nothing else here. But then he spotted something in the far corner. It looked like it was a rock about the size of a man's head. But he went over to pick it up and gasped. It was a human skull carved from milky white crystal.

"What is it?" Ezra asked, moving to his side.

Jaden handed him the skull. "A creepy souvenir. But nothing that helps us."

Ezra examined the object for a moment, turning it over and over in his hands. "This is a clue! Only one civilization in the history of the Earth made crystal skulls. I'm not sure I understand how this got here, but I can tell you for sure who made it."

"Yeah? Who?"

"The ancient Mayans, my boy," Ezra replied, clapping him on the shoulder. "Let's go!" he added, taking the skull and heading back down the steps.

Chapter Fifteen

Salvatore flew up the elevator shaft. Reaching ground level, he spotted one of their guards lying face down in the dirt. He drew closer to him and realized that he had a gaping hole in his back. Squatting down, he turned the body over on its back.

"Jasper," Salvatore said sadly. He was dead. The plasma shot had incinerated his heart. Isis and her hybrids had to be nearby somewhere. Standing up straight, Salvatore scanned the area but didn't detect anyone else. "Griffin, this is Salvatore," he said through his implants. "Report."

There was no reply. Salvatore tried accessing his saucer again but still couldn't. Prowling cautiously away from the elevator building in a giant arc, he kept up a constant scan, searching for Griffin. Finally, he found him, unconscious on the ground. There were no apparent wounds.

"Griffin?" he said, squatting down and shaking him by one shoulder. "Wake up, son." Griffin sat up with a start, eyes wide with fear. "What happened?"

"Hybrids," he whispered, scrambling to his feet and looking around frantically. "They showed up out of nowhere. There had to be a dozen of them. One of them hit me with a laser before I could alert you. Where's Jasper?"

"They took him out with a plasma cannon," said Salvatore. "I'm sorry." He knew the two had been friends for a long time. Griffin only stared at him in stunned silence. Salvatore still couldn't detect anyone nearby. "Malia, this is Salvatore," he said through his implants. "We've got a problem up here. It's time to go." There was no response. "Malia? Brian, this is Salvatore. Can you hear me?" No answer. Suddenly, Salvatore realized why he couldn't detect anyone. Someone was jamming his implants.

"Quickly, back down to the bunker!" he said to Griffin, setting off at a run. But as they reached the elevator shaft, a dozen hybrids materialized outside the building entry, pointing plasma cannons at them.

"Well, the Malor were here, all right," Brian told Malia. "The data on this machine shows that they made this place their base of operations until a few months ago. At first, they were working on independent power supplies for their saucers."

"That explains how they were able to take their ships back from Wright-Patterson," Malia observed.

"Yes," Brian agreed. "They flew them under their own power and brought them here. After that, it seems like they were trying to build a transmitter."

"Trying? Shouldn't that be easy for them?"

"Luckily not," said Brian, fixing her with an ominous gaze. "They were working on a *transdimensional* transmitter."

Malia gasped. "But... that's only necessary for communicating across vast distances. Who were they trying to contact?"

"There's no information about that in the data," Brian said with a shrug. "But anyway, a few months ago, they packed up and moved out."

"Where did they go?"

"I'm afraid there's no record of that, either."

Suddenly, a chill ran down Malia's spine, and the feeling that someone was in here with them returned in full force.

"Malia!" Selena called out, drawing her laser pistol and pointing it into the main corridor. "I've got emitter telltales over here!"

"Shit," said Malia, hurrying over. But as she reached the doorway, a plasma blast slammed into the frame, spraying the two of them with dust and debris. Reaching out with her mind, Malia sensed three people moving up the passage toward them. She penetrated one of their minds, forcing a young hybrid woman to become visible. Selena fired her weapon, hitting her in the chest. The hybrid slumped to the floor. "Two more coming in fast," Malia told Selena. The woman fired two more shots up the corridor, but another plasma blast hit her in the hip an instant later. She fell down screaming, dropping her pistol.

Picking up Selena's weapon, Malia penetrated the next hybrid's mind telepathically, forcing him to become visible. The moment she could see him, she fired the laser, hitting him in the abdomen. The man dropped to the floor.

A plasma shot tore through Malia's stomach, leaving a gaping hole in its wake. Malia screamed, dropping to her knees and forcing herself to remain conscious. She could already feel her body healing the wound. But at that moment, an invisible foot connected with her face, knocking her flat on her back.

"Die, you little bitch!" a female voice cried out.

Focusing on the source of the sound, Malia lifted the invisible hybrid off her feet, then penetrated her mind and forced her to become visible. The woman was hanging a few feet in the air, staring daggers at Malia. She pointed her plasma cannon for another shot, but Malia used her telekinesis to rip it out of her hands and into her own. Getting to her feet, she aimed the weapon at the woman's face.

"How many more of you are there?"

The woman clamped her mouth shut, giving her an icy stare.

"Fine," said Malia, penetrating her mind again. Memories surfaced in the woman's mind, showing a dozen hybrids floating down to the ground using the chariot's gravitational beam, then hurrying toward the bunker. "Shit," she said, disentangling herself from the woman's thoughts. She fired the plasma cannon, blowing her head off.

"Selena," Malia called out, dropping to her knees next to the woman.

Brian rushed over, taking in Selena's condition. "Can you help her?"

Malia nodded. Selena was unconscious now. Malia's wound had fully healed; she found it easier to focus without the pain. Reaching out with her thoughts, she penetrated Selena's mind. Luckily, the plasma shot had cauterized the wound; otherwise, she would have lost too much blood by now for Malia to heal her.

Malia took a deep breath and focused on transferring her energy into Selena's body. She didn't understand how she could do this; according to both her mother and Venus, it shouldn't be possible. But Malia had discovered the ability more than a year ago, and since then, it had worked every time.

She focused on Selena's wound. It was slower than healing her own body, but the damaged and missing tissue began reconstituting itself. Bone, muscle, connective tissue, blood vessels, nerve cells—they all rebuilt themselves until finally, new skin grew over the area. Malia focused on returning Selena to consciousness. The woman gasped, opening her eyes and taking in her surroundings. Then she looked from her hip to Malia, shock in her eyes.

"You... you healed me?" she stammered.

"I did, but we've gotta get out of here. There are at least nine more hybrids above ground. Can you stand?"

Malia helped her to her feet, but Selena seemed fully mobile.

"I tried reaching Salvatore, but there's no response," Brian said.

Malia tried contacting Salvatore, Griffin, and Jasper through her implants but had no more luck than Brian. Reaching out telepathically, she found Salvatore.

"Three hybrids just attacked us down here. We couldn't reach you with our implants. Where are you?"

"There are more hybrids up here. They killed Jasper and captured Griffin and me."

Salvatore showed her what he was seeing. They were marching them away from the bunker, plasma cannons trained on them. Up ahead, the chariot was hovering fifty feet in the air.

"*I'll take care of your captors,*" Malia told him. "*The moment I do, fly your ass back down here.*"

"*I will. But I have no way to warn Griffin.*"

"*I'll take care of it.*" Malia reached into Griffin's mind next. "*Hey, babe.*"

"*Malia! I'll never get used to you doing this.*"

"*I told you I'll only do it in emergencies.*" She let him know the game plan. Once he'd acknowledged her, Malia took a deep breath. Using Griffin's sight to focus on the nine hybrids surrounding them, Malia lifted them off the ground, hurling them as far away as she could. Salvatore and Griffin had implants and nanoparticles just like everyone else in the Collective, so it wouldn't take them long to fly back. "*Hurry! Get down here*!"

But Salvatore and Griffin were already moving into the elevator shaft. Malia, Brian, Selena ran up the corridor and met them as they reached the bottom.

"What now?" asked Malia.

"We've got to find a way back to our saucer," said Salvatore. "The chariot is jamming our implants; that's why we've lost communication."

"Can you use your powers to bring the saucer down here through the opening in the roof?" Brian asked Malia.

"I think so," said Malia, taking a deep breath. But at that

moment, there was an explosion in the large chamber. It shook the floor beneath them and sent a wall of fire hurtling up the corridor. No time to think, Malia reached out with her mind and created a barrier of stillness between them and the flames, stopping the superheated air from reaching them. But they could still feel the intense heat.

"Good thing you're here," Brian told her, as most of the flames dissipated.

"We need to leave before they fire again," said Salvatore.

"They'll probably target the elevator next," said Malia. "We should go out the other way!"

"It's too hot in there," said Salvatore. "Let's go!"

They flew up the elevator shaft. As they shot out of the little building at the top, the chariot dropped a plasma charge. It incinerated the structure on its way down, and moments later, flames spewed out of the shaft.

They stopped a hundred feet away. Reaching out with her mind, Malia found the saucer hovering right where they'd left it. Focusing with all her might, she pulled the saucer toward them. The chariot fired on its previous position, missing it by only a few feet.

"They're flooding the area with active scanning beams," Salvatore told them. "Fly!"

Usually, the saucer sent a signal that allowed them to see it with their implants even when its shields were raised, as they were now. But with their implants jammed, they were flying blind. Only Malia could sense where the ship was, so they followed her. She flew into the airlock, the others right behind her, and hurried up to the cockpit with Salvatore and Brian. Luckily, the shields blocked the hybrids' jamming signal, so Salvatore had no trouble accessing the saucer's control systems. But as Salvatore piloted the saucer high into the sky, the chariot fired on them. "Direct hit," he reported. "Shields are down to thirty percent. One more shot like that, and we'll lose them completely."

"How are they tracking us?" Brian asked.

"Active scanning beams," Salvatore explained.

"What about that Malor equipment we're carrying?" asked Malia. "Its holograms are good enough to fool our sensors, so they should be effective against the chariot, too, right?"

"Yes. It should be able to hide us from their scanning beams," Salvatore confirmed. "But we have no way to access its control system from here."

"I'll go down to the cargo hold and see if I can patch it into our system," said Brian. He dropped through the floor.

"In the meantime, I'll try to slow down the chariot," said Malia.

Salvatore continued flying the saucer evasively as the chariot fired on them repeatedly. Staring out the cockpit windows, Malia reached out with her mind. She could see only tiny sections of the chariot when its weapons fired, but that was enough. She tapped into the magnetic field and used her telekinesis to arrest the massive ship's motion. But suddenly, she felt someone else pushing back against her, neutralizing her powers.

"Isis is aboard that ship," she told Salvatore. "She's working against me!"

Salvatore returned fire. Venus had equipped all of their ships with high output plasma cannons, but it wasn't enough to get through the chariot's shields.

"Keep trying," Salvatore encouraged her as they flew over the Atlantic. "Any little advantage you can get us will help." But then he said, "We're slowing down. This shouldn't be. Engines are still engaged."

"Isis must be using her telekinesis against us," said Malia. Reaching out with her mind, she could sense their nemesis pulling their saucer toward her. Malia fought her with all her might and managed to repel her.

"We're back to full power," Salvatore told her. "Nice work."

Malia continued to focus, trying to slow down the chariot again. But Isis resisted. It was a battle of wills, each trying to overwhelm the other. Meanwhile, Salvatore continued flying erratically and hitting the chariot with multiple plasma shots. But then the chariot hit the saucer again, knocking out their shields.

"We're in trouble," Salvatore said through his implants. "How's it going with the Malor emitter?"

"I think I've got it," Brian replied. "You should have control of this thing now."

"Yes, I can access its systems," Salvatore confirmed. "Stand by."

He dove toward the ocean and brought them to a standstill twenty feet above the water. Accessing the saucer's sensors, Malia could tell that the chariot had shot past them and was now flooding the area with active scanning beams, trying to find them.

"I think it's working!" Malia said. The chariot opened fire, shooting lasers far into the distance. "What are they doing?"

"They've calculated our likely position based on our previous trajectory, and they're firing on that location."

Malia chuckled. "They have no idea where we went."

But at that moment, another vessel appeared out of nowhere. It fired on the chariot, ripping a gaping hole in its hull. The chariot sped away, and the newcomer changed course, heading directly toward Salvatore's ship.

"That's a Malor saucer!" said Malia.

"Yes," Salvatore agreed. "And they can see through their own emitter."

Chapter Sixteen

Jaden and Ezra left the cave dwellings and returned to the saucer.

"Listen, man," said Jaden, sitting down in the cockpit, "this is it. I'm done. We're wasting our time out here."

"What? How do you figure?" Ezra demanded. "This is *huge*! We found an ancient Mayan crystal skull inside a heretofore undiscovered subterranean tunnel complex beneath the Ancestral Puebloan Cliff Palace!"

"So what?" Jaden said with a shrug.

"You want to find the Anunnaki, right? We have here further evidence that they were behind the disappearance of yet another ancient civilization, as I always believed. And what was this skull doing here, eh? The Anunnaki are the connection! This must mean they interacted with the Mayans, too."

"The Mayans vanished?"

"Not all of them," Ezra replied. "At its height, the Mayan civilization had forty cities and a population of at least ten million people. But then, in the eighth and ninth centuries, their southern territories fell into rapid decline. It was the heartland of their civilization, but entire cities were completely abandoned.

"We have to investigate this! If we were to find evidence of transdimensional radiation in an ancient Mayan city—"

"It would only mean that the Anunnaki were there *a thousand* years ago! Who cares? This whole thing is a dead end. If the Anunnaki were a more advanced alien species, they're long gone now. There's no evidence that they're still around today."

"Of course, there is," Ezra insisted. "You found the same transdimensional radiation signatures in Iraq and here that the Othali found where your people disappeared. That cannot just be a coincidence! These things have to be connected!"

"Yeah, they probably are," Jaden conceded. "Because it must have been the Malor all along. I should go back to the compound and help them find *those* aliens."

"Jaden, my boy," Ezra said with a chuckle. "How do you expect to get anywhere in life if you keep giving up so easily? *This means something*," he added, holding out the crystal skull. "I'll tell you what. Humor me a little longer. Let's investigate the Mayans. And if we don't have some sort of breakthrough there, then we'll call it a day. You're off the hook, and I'd ask you only to return me to my home before you go back to your people."

Jaden fixed him with a stare, letting out a long sigh. "All right," he said finally. "But this is it. End of the line." Ezra nodded. "Okay. Where are we going?"

"Well... that's a good question."

"What, don't you know where they were?" Jaden asked incredulously.

"Oh, I do, but their civilization occupied well over a hundred thousand square miles in present-day Mexico, Guatemala, and Belize," Ezra explained, his expression pensive. "Well, Tikal would be my first choice. It was the beating heart of the Mayan Empire at its peak. But this skull... It has me second-guessing myself. Perhaps the Temple of the Skull in Palenque..."

"I'll just be here waiting while you debate with yourself," Jaden said impatiently.

"Tikal. It's in Guatemala. We should definitely check there first."

"All right," Jaden said, laying in the course.

They took off into the sky. Minutes later, they reached the ruins of the ancient Mayan city of Tikal.

"We'll want to go to the temples," Ezra said, gazing out the cockpit windows. "There—you can see them in the trees," he added, pointing toward the west.

Jaden took them to a position directly above the temple complex. There were two large pyramids. He scanned the area and found faint signals coming from beneath the western pyramid. "There's something down there all right," he said. "Hang on," he added. His scans showed a subterranean chamber, far below the temple. And there was a shaft leading down to it that looked like it had been dug quite recently. Jaden brought up a holographic image of his scans in the center console to show Ezra. "It looks like someone's already been down there. There must have been some other access tunnel in the past, but that's long gone. Whoever came here before us made their own."

Ezra stared at the image for a few moments, his brow furrowed. "Who could it have been?"

"I don't know, but I'd guess it was Isis and her hybrids. I'm going to go down there and get a closer look."

"Great! Let's go!" said Ezra, getting to his feet.

"Uh... you should probably wait here this time," Jaden told him. "There's a bunch of people down there, and they've got security guards stationed around that shaft. I'll take scans and show you whatever I find."

Ezra reluctantly agreed. Jaden moved down to the airlock. Using his emitter to make himself invisible, he flew down to the ground, right in the middle of the plaza. Tourists were moving about, and they'd roped off the area in the center around the shaft. Jaden flew over the guards' heads, landing by the entrance. Taking a quick scan, he confirmed that someone had blasted this hole using lasers. They'd vaporized solid stone to get to that chamber; it had to be either Isis or the Malor.

Jaden dropped into the shaft. It descended at a steep angle and was completely dark inside. He used his hand implants to project a beam of light. Reaching the bottom, he took in his surroundings. The chamber was roughly twenty feet to a side, and there was a stone table in the middle, just like the room they'd found under the cliff dwellings.

The stone walls were bare, with no carvings or paintings. But a square section of one wall was missing, exposing the dirt beyond. It looked like someone had cut it out with a laser. Jaden scanned the chamber and found hundreds of transdimensional radiation signatures. The newest ones were over a thousand years old. There was nothing else to see here.

Jaden returned to the surface and flew back up to his saucer. He told Ezra what he'd found and brought up a holographic image showing the interior of the chamber. "This one section of the wall was missing," he said, pointing it out to Ezra.

"How strange," he observed, taking a closer look. "The rest of the walls are plain. I wonder if there was something drawn or carved on the missing area."

"My thought exactly," Jaden agreed. "But we'll never know."

Ezra nodded and frowned, retaking his seat. "We should check the Temple of the Skull."

"I don't know, man," Jaden said with a sigh.

"Jaden, please! There was *something* here, but whoever made that shaft took it before we could see it! We've got to check Palenque! There could be crucial evidence there!"

Jaden took a deep breath. This seemed like a wild goose chase. Part of him felt like he should stop wasting his time, return Ezra to New York, and help Salvatore find the Malor. But... *Someone* had visited this temple before them and removed something from the wall. And that someone was almost certain to be Isis. Even if this didn't lead them to their missing people, Isis's interest in these ancient beings was reason enough to investigate further. She would only be pursuing them if she had something to gain. And anything advantageous to her was bound to be detrimental to the Collective. "All right," he said finally, laying in a course.

They shot into the sky, reaching Palenque very quickly. The archeological site was a little farther west. Jaden brought them into position above the complex.

"The Temple of the Skulls is that smaller building there by the trees," Ezra said, pointing it out.

"And why do they call it that?"

"Oh, well, the sole surviving carving on the wall is a skull," said Ezra. "But there are skulls on the Temple of the Inscriptions, too. That's the larger structure there."

Jaden scanned the complex. "I'm not detecting any transdimensional signatures here. There is a chamber inside the Temple of the Inscriptions—looks like that's a tomb."

"Yes, that's well known," Ezra confirmed. "No hidden chamber anywhere?"

"Wait... Yeah, there is one underneath the Temple of the Skulls. But I don't see any way down there. There must have been a tunnel leading to it at one time, but that's long since collapsed. If you want me to go take a look, I'm going to have to blast my way in."

Ezra considered this for a moment, then sighed and nodded. "Do it."

There were a handful of tourists walking around the grounds, but none of them were too close to the Temple of the Skull. Jaden calculated the frequency necessary to create a shaft through the earth above the hidden chamber, then fired his laser. It took several seconds to clear a hole large enough for him to pass. But once he was done, he said, "Wait here. I'll be right back."

Jaden made himself invisible, left the saucer, and flew down the shaft. Shining his light beam on the area, he realized this was a tomb. The chamber was only large enough to hold the sarcophagus lying in the middle. The rock walls were completely bare, but there was a stone tablet leaning against the wall behind the head of the grave. Some sort of writing was carved into it, but Jaden didn't recognize the language, and his implants weren't offering a translation. He scanned the area again but still couldn't find any sign of delta shifting occurring here.

Jaden was about to leave when he noticed engravings along the base of the sarcophagus. It was probably nothing important, but he took scans of it anyway. The writing wrapped around the base. Standing back, Jaden realized how large the sarcophagus was. It wasn't any wider than he'd expect, but it was over twelve feet long. Curious now, Jaden scanned the interior. And the results startled him. The skeleton inside didn't look human. The being had been about ten feet tall, its skull elongated and its eye sockets much larger than a human's.

Jaden's heart started beating a mile a minute. Could this be an Anunnaki? Only the skeleton remained, but he was able to get a DNA scan from the bone tissue. He was no geneticist and had no idea how the DNA compared to a human's. But Salvatore or Malia would probably be able to glean some information from it.

Returning to the surface, he flew up to the saucer. He sat down in the cockpit, brought up a holographic image of the chamber to show Ezra, and told him what he'd found.

"Incredible," Ezra muttered. "We hit the jackpot, my boy," he said more loudly, slapping Jaden on the shoulder.

"Yeah, this is something," Jaden replied and couldn't help grinning.

"Whoa—wait a minute," said Ezra, leaning in to get a closer look at the image. "Can you zoom in on that tablet?" Jaden enlarged the area. "I'll be damned."

"What does it say?" asked Jaden.

"I have no idea. The Mayans developed a writing system that used syllabic glyphs, similar to modern Japanese writing. But this isn't that."

"Huh? What do you mean? What is it, then?" asked Jaden, taking a closer look as well.

"It's written in the Harrapan script. That's the language of the Indus Valley Civilization."

"Yeah? Well, what does it say?" Jaden asked again.

"Couldn't tell you. Nobody's managed to decipher their language."

"Seriously? When did they exist? I don't remember hearing about them before."

"They abandoned their cities and fell into decline around 1800 B.C. Which makes this find extremely strange."

"There's a dead Anunnaki down there," said Jaden. "This find was already strange."

"Well, yes, point taken. But the Mayans didn't come to this place until roughly 200 B.C. Which means that the tablet is not only from a different place but a different time."

Jaden stared at the inscription on the tablet. Venus had found a way to adapt the Othali translation algorithms to their implants. He tried applying the matrix to the tablet, but it came up empty. There wasn't enough here for it to build the underlying language. "Can you read the inscription on the sarcophagus?"

"No, I'm afraid not," said Ezra with a shake of his head. "I know enough to recognize it as Mayan script, but that's about it."

Jaden ran the script through the translation matrix. "Here lies Babajide of the sky dwellers. He left his people to live with ours. His life was long beyond reckoning, but we could not cure him when he fell ill. The sky dwellers could have healed him, but he refused to go back."

"That's what it says?" Ezra asked skeptically. Jaden nodded. "But... how can you know that?"

Jaden told him about the Othali translation algorithms.

"I'll be damned," said Ezra. "They must have called the Anunnaki the 'sky dwellers.' Can you read the tablet?"

"There's not enough material there for the algorithm to formulate their language."

"Hm," Ezra said with a nod. "Well. It would seem this Babajide left the Anunnaki to settle down with the Mayans. How odd. The tablet would seem to suggest that the Anunnaki had some involvement with the Indus Valley Civilization. I wish I knew what it says. Its presence in Babajide's tomb would seem to indicate that it held some personal significance for him."

"Where did those people live?"

"The Indus River is near the Indian border in eastern Pakistan."

"Are we going there next?" Jaden asked with a grin.

"Oh, but aren't you taking me back to New York now?"

Jaden shook his head. "We still don't have much. But that's no Malor buried down there. There was definitely some other alien species hanging out on Earth back then. So let's go see what we can find in Pakistan."

"That's what I like to hear!" said Ezra, pumping his fist in the air.

"Yeah, yeah. Well, what's our destination? Specifically, I mean. Pakistan's a pretty big place."

"That's a great question," Ezra said with a frown.

"Wasn't there a central city like the Mayans had?"

"We don't know," Ezra said with a shrug. "Nobody's been able to translate their script, so we have no written record of them. We've got plenty of archeological findings that help us establish their achievements and how they lived. Their cities were planned in grid patterns, for example. Highly organized. But we have no historical record. And at its peak, their lands extended from the mouth of the Indus River about nine hundred miles inland. There may have been as many as a thousand cities and settlements, but we know almost nothing about the political structure of their society. Anunnaki activity could have been centered anywhere in that region."

"These transdimensional signatures are awfully faint," said Jaden. "It could take weeks if we've got to scan that whole area for a signal. Oh, shit," he added, suddenly realizing something. "Isis's people removed that section of wall from the chamber underneath

Tikal. And that was where the Anunnaki were delta shifting. They must have been looking for them, too... What do you want to bet there was some sort of inscription on that wall that they didn't want anyone else to find?"

"There could have been something there pointing to the Anunnaki involvement with the people of the Indus Valley," Ezra replied.

"Let's get going," said Jaden. "I'll take a look at the radar data on the way there and see if I can find any signs of hybrid activity in the region." He set a course for Pakistan, and they shot into the sky.

Chapter Seventeen

Salvatore took them high into the sky again, shooting off to the east. Malia lost sight of the Malor saucer but could see it on sensors; it was falling far behind. But suddenly, it disappeared.

"Where did they go?" Malia said out loud. But before Salvatore could answer her, another Malor vessel appeared out in front of them, closing fast. "Oh, no—now there are two!"

"I don't think so," said Salvatore, as he took them into a steep dive. "There was a flash of transdimensional radiation when that ship appeared. I think it's the same one."

"It delta shifted to get in front of us?" Malia asked. Salvatore nodded. "So they've managed to build a transdimensional drive."

Brian returned to the cockpit. "What's going on now?"

Malia brought him up to speed.

"But they can't see through *our* shields, right?" asked Brian. "Even at thirty percent, they should hide us."

"Yeah, but Isis knocked out our shields with her final strike," Malia explained.

"They could still track us with active scanning beams, just like Isis did," said Salvatore. "We can outrun him again, but he'll just leap frog ahead of us. But he outguns us, so there's not much else we can do."

They pulled far ahead of the Malor again, but sure enough, the vessel delta shifted out in front of them. They fired, but Salvatore shot high into the sky. They flew fast and erratically for the next several minutes, trying to shake their pursuer. But every time they gained a significant lead, the Malor delta shifted out in front of them again.

"I can't seem to lose him," said Salvatore.

"He's nothing if not persistent," Brian commented.

"Why does he want to shoot us down so badly?" Malia wondered out loud.

"Maybe they want their emitter back," Brian suggested. "Might make sense to jettison it. The thing doesn't work against him anyway."

"Perhaps," said Salvatore. "We've got scans, so we could always reverse engineer it. But I'm going to try engaging him."

"Are you sure?" asked Brian. "He doesn't just outgun us—their shields are stronger, too."

Salvatore didn't reply. But a moment later, the Malor saucer delta shifted out in front of them again. This time, instead of taking evasive maneuvers, Salvatore flew toward it, firing weapons. The Malor adjusted course repeatedly to avoid being hit, but one plasma shot made a direct impact. "His shields are down to seventy percent."

"That's it?" said Brian.

The Malor returned fire. Salvatore banked hard to avoid it, but the shot grazed their hull.

"We've lost shields," Salvatore told them. "One more shot, and we'll lose engines. Or worse. I'm signaling the Othali for assistance."

"It'll take them a few minutes to get here," said Malia. Checking sensors, she spotted a volcanic island chain not too much farther ahead, off the western coast of Africa. "Take us in closer to those islands," she suggested to Salvatore. "I'll try to crash him into the land."

Salvatore nodded. Only a minute later, they reached the islands. The Malor appeared out of nowhere directly in front of them, firing weapons. Salvatore dove, flying them around the volcanic cone of one of the larger islands.

Gazing out the cockpit windows, Malia focused on the Malor ship, using her telekinesis to push it into the mountain. She thought she had it—the saucer increased power to its engines in an attempt to avoid impact. It wasn't enough, but the ship only grazed the edge of the caldera.

"Crap!" said Malia. "Take us around the next one, and I'll try again."

They shot toward the next island, but the Malor delta shifted right in front of them again. Salvatore changed course, going the other way around. He brought them closer to the volcano this time, and the enemy gave chase, firing weapons. Malia focused with all her might, pushing the saucer into the mountain.

At that moment, the Malor scored a direct hit on Salvatore's ship. But Malia had succeeded in slamming the enemy saucer into the island. It began flipping end over end and crash-landed on a small, uninhabited island.

"We've lost engines," said Salvatore. The saucer was racing

skyward, but they'd be in trouble once they lost momentum. "And navigation," Salvatore added moments later.

"I've got it," said Malia. Reaching out telekinetically, she took control of the saucer.

"See if you can land us on that little atoll where the Malor crashed," said Brian. "If I can access his computer, we might be able to locate their new base."

Malia nodded. She moved them toward the island, setting them down on the opposite shore from the Malor ship. Just in case his weapons were still active, she wanted to keep the rocky peak between them.

Salvatore, Brian, and Malia went down to the main level.

"The Othali are on their way, but I'll see if I can repair the engines while we wait," Salvatore told them.

Brian grabbed a plasma cannon from the weapons locker and moved toward the airlock. "Wish me luck!"

"I'll go with you," said Malia. "Even if you can't crack the computer, I might be able to get in the Malor's head."

She followed him out through the airlock. Even without engines, their saucer could hover several feet above the ground using gravitational thrusters. Malia followed Brian, passing under the ship and moving along the shore. On the far side, they found the Malor ship. It was sitting at an odd angle, one side sticking up in the air. The lead edge had crumpled on impact, and there was a plume of black smoke rising high into the sky.

"Looks like his engines are down," Malia said, scanning the

ship. "Weapons are still online, but I don't think he's got sensors. I'm detecting one life sign—" At that moment, a laser shot hit the rocky ground in front of them, blasting out a crater, throwing Brian and Malia into the air, and spraying them with debris. Malia caught Brian and herself using her powers before they crashed, returning them to the ground safely, behind a large boulder to give them some cover.

"What were you saying about his sensors?" Brian asked with a grin.

"Yeah, yeah," she said, failing to suppress a smile of her own. "Give me a second." Closing her eyes, she reached out telepathically. She could sense the Malor's consciousness and penetrated his mind. His thoughts were so foreign, Malia realized. Highly visual, much more so than the humans, Martians, or Othali. She could sense the Malor trying to push her out of his mind. But she focused with all her might and managed to knock him unconscious. "He's out. Let's go. But let's be careful—I'm not sure how long he'll *stay* out."

Brian nodded. They moved out from behind the boulder and hurried the rest of the way to the saucer. Malia identified the hatch in the center, but they couldn't find a way to open it. Finally, Brian fired his plasma cannon at it. With the ship's shields down, this worked. They climbed through the opening.

The odor inside assaulted Malia's senses. It was like stale vomit. She remembered smelling this on their mother ship, but it was stronger here. They found the Malor strapped into a seat in the center of the ship. But as they approached, he turned, drawing a weapon.

"Look out!" Malia shouted, diving for the floor and taking Brian down with her. The Malor fired. There was a metallic crackling sound, and the energy blast hit the wall behind them. Aiming his plasma cannon, Brian fired. The shot ripped a hole through the Malor's abdomen. His eyes closed, and his head dropped onto his shoulder.

Malia reached out with her mind, trying to penetrate his thoughts before it was too late. The Malor was unconscious, but his brain wasn't dead yet. She tried to find memories of their new base. Images of an enormous underground bunker surfaced, but then the Malor died before Malia could determine its location.

"Damn," Brian said with a sigh when Malia told him what she'd found. "Well, let me see if I can access the computer. Hopefully, we'll have better luck there."

"I'll see if I can find their transdimensional drive," said Malia.

Brian furrowed his brow, and his eyes lost focus. Malia knew he was using his implants to infiltrate the Malor control system. Moving through the rest of the ship, Malia looked for access panels to the hardware. She found one, but upon removing it, found what she believed were the main engines. Malia didn't think the Malor used gravitational propulsion, but neither was she sure how their ships flew.

Malia found a smaller access panel. Removing that, she found what she thought must be the transdimensional drive. She'd seen the one on the Othali warship before. It consisted of two giant metal cylinders with long fins protruding from them. This device looked similar, although it was nowhere near the same size. Malia tried to locate the connectors to remove the drive but couldn't find a way to do it without severing the power lines. She decided she should probably wait until the Othali arrived. Their engineers would be able to figure it out. She went to check on Brian's progress instead.

"I used the same backdoor we found on the ship in their bunker," Brian explained. "But the system has taken heavy damage. I'm pretty sure the data is still here, but I can't seem to access it."

In the end, Brian decided to remove the data storage unit. And he was able to help Malia disconnect the transdimensional drive. Devices in hand, they left the saucer.

"We shouldn't just leave the Malor ship lying here like this, should we?" asked Malia.

"It wouldn't be a bad idea to destroy it before we leave," Brian agreed. "But we're going to need more than this plasma cannon for that. The warship can take care of it once they get here."

They returned to Salvatore's saucer. He was still working but didn't think he'd be able to restore power without replacing some parts. But minutes later, the sensors detected a massive ship headed directly toward them. For a moment, Malia wondered if it was the chariot returning for the kill. But then she realized it was the Othali warship.

Chapter Eighteen

Jaden rechecked the Othali radar data on the way to Pakistan. There were a handful of high-velocity contacts crisscrossing the area, but they seemed random, without any two of them converging near the same spot.

"What about scanning for Martian energy signatures?" Ezra suggested. "I can't imagine they're using the same power frequencies that we do."

"Their ships' shielding would block that," Jaden said with a sigh. "Let me check in with Nadia."

"Who's Nadia?" Ezra asked.

Jaden ignored him. He felt terrible asking her for yet another favor, but there was no other choice. It would take him a long time to scan the entire region, and meanwhile, he had no idea what these aliens might be doing to his mom and Venus. Reaching out telepathically, he made contact with Nadia.

"Jaden! I hear that Malor settlement was a dead end, huh?"

"Yeah, sure was. But I've got a lead on another group of aliens that have been here on Earth for centuries. I need a little help, though."

Jaden asked her if she might be able to scan for transdimensional signatures in the Indus region. He could sense Nadia's unease.

"If I run the scan myself, Anhur will know, and he's sure to ask about it."

"That's no good. He'll tell Salvatore where I'm going."

There was a slight pause.

"Let me check with one of the guys in engineering," Nadia said finally. *"He might be able to run it as a hidden process to prevent the bridge from noticing. This is going to take a little while; check in with me in about thirty minutes, and I'll let you know how it goes."*

"Awesome, thanks, Nadia."

By the time Jaden checked in with her again, she had a set of coordinates for him.

"We had to wait until our orbit took us over that part of the world," she told him. *"But my friend was able to take the scans without alerting the bridge. Jaden, this is by far the strongest transdimensional signature either one of us has ever seen on a planet surface. This location had a lot of traffic to build up such a strong signal."*

"Perfect," Jaden replied. *"I don't know how I'm ever going to repay you for this."*

"I'll think of something. Be careful out there."

Jaden adjusted their course to take them to Nadia's coordinates. They arrived only minutes later. Jaden set the saucer to hover over the area while he scanned the surface. It was the middle of the night here, and they were in a mountainous region near the Afghanistan border. There were very few lights nearby.

"There's some sort of subterranean complex down there," he reported to Ezra. "I'm not detecting any life signs... But there is telltale radiation from at least a half dozen Martian emitters. The hybrids must be down there."

"I don't see any other ships," Ezra noted, gazing out the cockpit windows.

Jaden chuckled. "It's dark out here. You probably wouldn't see them even if they were on top of us. But they're out there somewhere. Those hybrids didn't fly here on their own. They must have their shields up, though; I'm not detecting them on sensors. But Nadia was right. The radiation signature here is ten times stronger than it was at any of the other sites."

"Well... are we going down there, then?"

"*We* aren't, but I am. You're going to stay right here. I'll make myself invisible."

"I'd love to go with you this time," Ezra said with a frown. "What if you give me one of those fancy emitters of yours, and then I could become invisible, too."

"Nah, man. You need the neural implants to make that work. Sorry."

Jaden grabbed his plasma cannon, made himself invisible, then left the ship through the airlock. The hybrids had blasted out an access tunnel; Jaden landed near the opening. He wasn't detecting any emitters on the surface or in the shaft, so he flew in, getting to the bottom as quickly as possible.

It was pitch dark down here, but he didn't dare risk a light. He had to rely on his implants to scan his surroundings. He was in a long passage that seemed to be part of the original structure. The walls were lined with a strange material. Scans showed that it was fibrous, and he could detect individual cells as if it had been alive at one time. He touched the wall, and it felt like smooth tree bark.

The corridor extended in one direction only another twenty feet or so. There was a large chamber at the end that appeared to be empty. Scanning the other way, he found what seemed to be the central hub for the complex. The other tunnels extended away from it like spokes on a wheel. But that's where the hybrids were, too. Jaden proceeded as quietly as possible.

Moments later, he detected two hybrids headed toward him. Pressing himself against one wall, he held his breath until they'd passed. Then he let out a quiet sigh of relief: they hadn't noticed him. He continued toward the central hub.

Jaden stopped at the edge of the area. Scans showed three hybrids inside. Reaching out telepathically, Jaden knocked them out one at a time. Then he moved inside. There were thick pillars in the center that resembled tree trunks. But unlike the walls, these seemed like they might still be alive. His scanners weren't showing life signs per se, but there was some sort of energy emanating from the trunks, and there was a fluid of some kind moving slowly through microscopic conduits.

Growing from the trunks were oval structures that reminded Jaden of eggs. Scanning them, he realized that they were comprised of cells, too. It seemed like this entire complex was built from living tissue of some kind. But the pods' cells were packed with DNA, much more densely than the walls.

Jaden remembered learning about human scientists using DNA for data storage and wondered if this central structure was some sort of organic computer. But at that moment, he detected another hybrid moving quickly toward the central hub. Jaden froze, his plasma cannon at the ready.

"Who's in here?" a voice called out as a deep red light flooded the area.

The hybrid was only a few feet from Jaden now. Reaching out telepathically, he penetrated his mind and forced him to become visible. Next, he ripped the plasma cannon out of his hands, tossing it aside, and pinned the man against the wall, holding him there telekinetically. With a thought, he forced the hybrid's mouth wide open to prevent him from closing his jaw. The hybrids all had a cyanide capsule embedded in a fake tooth.

Focusing on the hybrid's thoughts again, Jaden accessed his implants and disabled communications. "*What is this place*?" he demanded.

The hybrid glared at him. "*I already summoned the others before you ambushed me. They'll kill you if they find you in here.*"

"*Fine. We'll do this the hard way.*"

Jaden focused on his memories of this complex. Thoughts and images rose to the surface. Isis had found this place using information she acquired from the Mayan site. But this hybrid didn't know what that might have been. He confirmed Jaden's suspicion that the central core was some sort of computer system. Isis and her people had tried accessing it but couldn't get very far.

However, she found something that led her and her primary team to leave in a hurry. But this hybrid didn't know what they'd found or where they went. Isis had tasked this group with trying to crack the computer core.

Just then, Jaden detected three more hybrids hurrying toward his location. He rendered his captive unconscious, letting his body drop to the floor. Then he reached out telepathically and knocked out the three newcomers, too. They must not have been members of Isis's Omega Group; Jaden knew this would have been much more difficult if they had been. But Isis probably hadn't expected the Collective to find her people here.

Moving toward the central core, he tried accessing it with his implants but had no luck. He reached out telepathically instead. Sure enough, this was an organic computer. It seemed like a hybrid of a neural processing network and an actual brain. But it was clear that this technology was radically more advanced than anything he'd encountered before, whether it be human, Martian, Othali, or Malor.

"*Jaden Kwan*," a voice said in his head, startling him. "*What are you doing here*?"

For a moment, Jaden thought it was Isis. His scans showed no other hybrids nearby, but perhaps she was on one of the ships they had here. But it was not her voice. In fact, Jaden couldn't tell if the voice was male or female.

"*Who is this?*"

"*I am the sentry.*"

"*Yeah? Sentry for what?*"

"*The place you occupy.*"

Jaden realized this it was the computer core. It must be some sort of AI.

"*And how did you know who I am?*"

"*I read your name from your mind.*"

Telepathic AI. Great, Jaden thought to himself. "*Where are the people who built you?*"

"*I do not know. They left over a hundred revolutions ago and have not returned.*"

"*Revolutions? Oh, you mean years. They've been gone that long, huh? And you have no idea where they went?*"

"*I'm afraid not. I wish I did.*"

"*They were telepathic, too?*" Jaden asked.

"*Yes.*"

"*What was this place? Did they live here?*"

"*This was their Earth outpost. Why did you come here? You're not with those others.*"

That last part wasn't a question. Somehow, this sentry *knew* Jaden wasn't with the hybrids. "*No, I'm not with them. You read that in my mind?*"

"*You're seeking my people,*" the sentry replied, ignoring his question. "*The others were, too. They wanted to obtain their transdimensional technology.*"

"*And did you give it to them?*"

"*No. Part of my mission is to protect my people's knowledge.*

Providing such primitive beings with technology so advanced would be disastrous. They are not ready yet."

"Well, that's good, at least," Jaden muttered out loud. "*They found something here, though. That's why their leader left. Do you know what it was?*"

"*Nothing that will help them.*"

"*You won't tell me what it was?*"

"*No.*"

"*I think your people might have abducted a couple of* my *people. Do you know where they might have taken them?*"

Jaden sensed an emotional reaction coming from the sentry. It was sadness. The sentry missed its people.

"*I do not.*"

"*Can you tell me anything else about your people that might help me find them?*"

After a slight hesitation, the sentry said, "*No.*"

Jaden couldn't help but feel that if he only asked the right questions, he might get some helpful information out of this system. Isis had found *something*, after all. Jaden tried accessing the computer's storage units, but the security protecting the data was incredibly complex. He'd learned how to crack the human and Martian systems and could do it in less than a minute. But he didn't even know where to start with this.

"*I'm sorry, you are not authorized to access our records.*"

"*Yeah, yeah, I know.*"

This was incredibly frustrating. While there was no denying

that this was a huge find, it did little more than confirm that the Anunnaki were real. Something he already knew for sure from the evidence he'd found at the Mayan site. But their own computer didn't know where they'd gone. Assuming it was telling the truth.

Jaden scanned the rest of the complex, hoping to find some sort of clue. Six corridors extended out from this central area, spaced evenly. Each led to nothing but an empty room. Between the corridors, behind the walls, were what appeared to be mostly open cavities. Jaden approached one. His scans showed small objects inside, lying on shelves.

He ran his hand along the wall, wondering if there was some sort of control system present that wasn't registering on his scans. But when he touched it, the wall became transparent. There were old-looking bowls and pitchers inside, as well as trinkets that might have been jewelry. It seemed like this was nothing more than a display, like something one would expect to find in a museum.

Jaden recorded the contents with his implants, then went around to the rest of the compartments and took scans of the items they contained, too. Maybe Ezra would recognize something helpful. Jaden found another crystal skull in one alcove and a statue of a man with a lion's head in another.

As he was finishing with the last compartment, Jaden received an alert from his saucer. Someone was flooding the area outside with active scanning beams. The hybrids were looking for his ship; it was time to get out of here.

Jaden issued a command to move his saucer to a location a few miles away. He flew back up the access tunnel and out to his ship. Once he'd boarded, he engaged the engines and took them high into the atmosphere, far away from the hybrids. After that, he went up to the cockpit and told Ezra what he'd discovered.

"Their own AI didn't know where they went?" he asked with a puzzled look once Jaden had finished. "And it wouldn't tell you what Isis found?"

"No," Jaden said with a shrug. "But I think it was... embarrassed. Or something. It said that it wouldn't help Isis, whatever it was. But based on that hybrid's memories, Isis felt differently."

"Hold on now; you think the AI felt *embarrassed*?" Ezra asked with a disbelieving grin.

"Don't look at me that way," Jaden said. "The thing definitely had emotions. But yeah, it seemed like it didn't want to admit that it had made a mistake. Oh, but check this out." He brought up a holographic display and showed him the relics he'd found stored in the alcoves. "I don't know what most of this stuff is, but I'm guessing they collected souvenirs from the places they made contact with humans. Look—they have a crystal skull."

"Yes, yes," Ezra said, examining the collection with interest. "A Mayan calendar stone... an Ancestral Puebloan jar... well, well, what do we have here? Hold that image, my boy."

Jaden froze the display. It looked like a bracelet. "What is it?"

"That is a Viking arm ring," Ezra told him. "Look at the intricate carvings on the surface. This is made of ivory. Walrus tusk, to be specific," he added, giving Jaden a pointed stare.

"Yeah? So what?"

"This could have come from only one place. Greenland," he added in response to Jaden's blank expression.

"There were Vikings in Greenland?"

"For hundreds of years. Care to guess what happened to them?"

"They disappeared?"

"Indeed, they did. I'd say that's our next stop, wouldn't you?"

Jaden shook his head. "Screw Greenland. We found their command center or whatever this place was. That computer's gotta have some information that would help us, but the AI won't let me in."

"That AI told you it doesn't know where its people went. Don't get me wrong; I'd love to find out what else it *does* know. But it's not talking, and it seems like those boys you took out down there called in the cavalry, no?"

"Yeah," Jaden said with a sigh. "But we've got a ton of evidence now. I'm sure I could convince Salvatore to investigate. We could come back with a whole fleet and drive the hybrids away. I'll find a way to get through that AI."

"Maybe you will, maybe not. But it couldn't hurt to go take a look at Greenland first. Just to be thorough."

Jaden considered it for a moment. Maybe whatever Isis had found had led her to Greenland, too. And if it had, then Jaden wanted to know what was there. "All right. Let's do it."

Chapter Nineteen

They took off for Greenland. Once they'd arrived, Ezra guided Jaden to the ruins of the Viking settlement. Jaden scanned the area for transdimensional radiation signatures.

"There," he said, pointing to the ruins of an old building. "It's faint. Doesn't seem like they came here as much as the other places. But the signal's coming from the surface. There's nothing underground here."

"No sign of your hybrid friends in the area?" Ezra asked with a frown.

"Nah, they're not here. I don't know what Isis found, but this wasn't it." Jaden ran one more scan of the surrounding area to make sure there wasn't anything else interesting. Then he spotted it. There was evidence of an impact crater to the north of the settlement. And in the ground below it, he was detecting metallic debris. Jaden gasped.

"What is it?" Ezra asked.

Jaden told him what he'd found. "The metal is an alloy I've only seen used in one place."

"Where?"

Jaden held his gaze for a moment. "Malor ships."

"You're telling me there's a Malor vessel down there?"

"No. I'm telling you there's a debris field from a Malor vessel. The thing was completely destroyed. And it looks like it's been down there for a thousand years or so."

"How can that be? The Malor weren't here back then... were they?"

"They were sending scout ships back then. Judging from the mass of the debris, this must have been one of those."

"But I'm pretty sure the *Vikings* couldn't have shot down a Malor ship," Ezra said.

Jaden scanned a wider area. There was nothing else within a twenty-mile radius, so he expanded his search to fifty miles. It took a few minutes, but he still came up empty. Deciding to give it one more shot, he extended his scans to one hundred miles. This gave him an area of more than 30,000 square miles.

"We're gonna be here a while," he said, sitting back in his chair. "That's a lot of—wait." The scan had detected something. "There's an enormous metallic object buried under the ice about seventy miles north of here. It's the same alloy as the debris."

"Holy shit," Ezra muttered.

Jaden set a course. Once they'd reached the area, he initiated a more detailed scan. "There's a Malor ship down there. It's mostly intact, but it's missing one section. Looks like someone took a bite out of it."

"Another scout ship?"

"Nah, this is way bigger."

"Surely not a mother ship like the one in the invasion?"

"No, not that big. Not even close. It's about twenty times larger than their saucers. It's under about three hundred feet of ice. I'm not detecting any life signs. It's been down there about the same amount of time as that debris. Looks like it's still got power, though."

Jaden calculated the frequency he'd need to blast a hole through the ice. Then he fired the saucer's lasers, cutting a shaft down to the damaged section of the ship. It took a few minutes to go that deep, but once there was a clear path, he told Ezra to stay put and left through the airlock.

It was freezing outside. Jaden flew through the shaft he'd dug, wishing he had one of the Othali spacesuits for this excursion. Reaching the ship, Jaden moved inside. It was utterly dark down here; he used his implants to provide some light. He scanned the damaged section. There were no signs of any kind of energy weapon impacting the area. It looked like someone had just grabbed on and ripped off a chunk of the ship.

Scanning the rest of the vessel, he found what had to be the bridge. He flew through the passages, finding his path unobstructed. The bridge was undamaged, but there were no bodies. It was so cold that he'd expected to discover the Malor corpses perfectly preserved, but there were none. Scanning the rest of the ship, he found no signs of any remains. How could that be?

Jaden tried accessing the Malor control systems with his implants but, as expected, couldn't get in that way. He knew Brian could probably manage it, but Jaden didn't have his hacking skills. But he was still able to infiltrate the neural processors telepathically.

Checking the data storage system, he started with the most recent record.

It was a holographic video showing the ship's final minutes. They were flying low, moving toward the Viking settlement. Based on the timestamp, Jaden calculated that this had taken place in the Earth year 997. Suddenly a figure appeared on the ice sheet below them. He stood ten feet tall with an elongated head and huge eyes. It was an Anunnaki. The Malor stopped, hovering above the alien to conduct scans.

But suddenly, the Anunnaki raised one hand and clenched his fist. The Malor control system issued an alert: hull breach. Their sensors showed that the Anunnaki had somehow ripped off a piece of the ship.

Jaden realized he'd been holding his breath and forced himself to let it out. The Anunnaki opened his hand again, moving it slowly downward. He pointed toward the ice sheet directly beneath the Malor ship with his other arm. Their sensors showed that he was melting an enormous hole in the ice, large enough to contain their vessel. The Malor tried to flee, bringing their engines to full power. But it was no use. They couldn't escape the Anunnaki's telekinetic grasp.

The Anunnaki lowered their ship into the water but kept the missing section of the hull above the surface. Then he refroze the water, locking the vessel into the ice sheet. The Malor tried to use their engines to move out of the ice, but the ship wouldn't budge. They attempted to signal their mother ship, but the Anunnaki was blocking their transmission.

The Malor fetched their weapons and headed out to confront the alien. But as they reached the hull breach, they found him coming for them. A couple of them managed to fire their weapons, but this did not affect the Anunnaki. And then the alien swept his arm in a giant circle, and the Malor vanished. He left the ship as the recording ended.

That was it. That was the last record in their system. The ship had sat here ever since, the long passage of time covering it with an ever-thicker sheet of ice.

Jaden tried going further back in their records. He found images showing their departure from their mother ship. It looked like the one that had invaded Earth. One of their scout ships had reported detecting some kind of technologically advanced being living among the Greenland Vikings. It had gone in closer to get more detailed scans, but the being had destroyed it. The Malor had decided to send this ship to investigate.

Suddenly, a giant portal in space opened up ahead of the vessel. The Malor moved through it, and on the other side, Jaden recognized Saturn by its rings. They navigated around Jupiter, using its gravity well to accelerate toward Earth. Then, using the Moon's gravity to slow down, they detected some sort of alien structure on the far side, buried beneath the surface. None of their scout ships had ever found that, but they'd always focused their surveillance on the planet. The Malor decided they'd come back to get a closer look once they'd finished on Earth. But then they encountered the Anunnaki and never got the chance.

Jaden could hardly believe what he'd just witnessed. One Anunnaki had possessed the power to take out a Malor ship, and it seemed effortless. Granted, he and Malia together had managed to take down their mother ship, but only after they'd destroyed one of its engines. And they had help from the Othali. And it had *not* been easy—far from it. Jaden had passed out from the exertion.

But this Anunnaki had overpowered the Malor ship with a wave of his hand. Their people possessed telepathy and telekinesis... just like Jaden and Malia. Only they were vastly more powerful. And the Anunnaki had made those Malor disappear. Jaden moved back up to the damaged area of the ship and scanned for transdimensional radiation signatures. Sure enough, they were there. The signal was faint, but it was conclusive. The Anunnaki had transported those Malor by delta shifting them without the aid of any kind of engine or device. How the hell was that even possible?

Malia had unknowingly delta shifted her brainwaves before the Othali showed up, Jaden reminded himself. The Anunnaki must be able to do something similar. Except they could transport *matter* that way.

They *had* to be the ones responsible for taking Melissa and Venus. Jaden had just witnessed them doing the same thing to the Malor. But where did they take them? Could it be to that structure the Malor had detected on the far side of the Moon? If they'd left their outpost on Earth, maybe that's where they'd gone.

There was only one way to find out. But he wasn't about to go to the Moon on his own. There was a good chance *this* was what Isis had learned from the AI in Pakistan. Jaden had to contact Salvatore now and call for reinforcements. There was no way he could refuse him with all the evidence he'd collected.

Jaden hurried back up to his saucer and brought up a holographic display to show Ezra everything he'd found. While he was watching that, Jaden reestablished communication with the Collective and contacted the compound. But they informed him that Salvatore was not there. He was aboard the Othali warship. So Jaden tried reaching Salvatore there instead.

"This is Salvatore," he said through his implants. Jaden tried explaining what he'd learned, but Salvatore cut him off. "Jaden, I need you to report to the Othali warship immediately. We've located the Malor base, and we're going to need your help getting inside."

"No, you don't understand. I found the Anunnaki, and you're not going to believe—"

"We can discuss that later. You have your orders. Salvatore out."

He cut the transmission. Jaden couldn't believe it. He wouldn't even *listen* to what he had to report? Well, to hell with him, then. Jaden could at least do some recon and see what they were up against.

"Jaden, this is... *astonishing*," Ezra said as he reached the end of the recording. "The Anunnaki were able to delta shift matter using nothing more than their body and mind. How... what's wrong?"

Jaden told him about his conversation with Salvatore. Then he laid in a course for the Moon and engaged the engines.

"Where are we going?" Ezra asked, staring out the cockpit windows. But then, as they left Earth's atmosphere and entered the blackness of space, he added, “We’re going to the Moon?” Jaden fixed him with a stare but said nothing. “Oh hell, yes!” Ezra shouted, jumping to his feet and pumping both fists in the air.

Chapter Twenty

The Othali sent a saucer to take Malia, Brian, Salvatore, Griffin, and Selena up to the warship. But Anhur objected to Salvatore's plan to destroy the Malor saucer. Instead, he wanted to bring it aboard so his people could tear it down and see what other upgrades the Malor might have made to it. Salvatore agreed. Once they'd boarded the saucer, the pilot activated a gravitational beam to transport the enemy vessel up to the warship.

Lieutenant Malik, the chief engineer, greeted them on the docking platform with Nadia. Brian headed off to engineering with Malik; they took the Malor transdimensional drive and computer core with them. Nadia escorted the others to the bridge. Anhur greeted them when they arrived. He told them they'd be returning to orbit until Brian and Malik could recover the Malor data and determine the location of their new base.

But at that moment, the klaxon sounded an alert. It startled Malia; what was wrong, now? She shot Nadia a questioning look, but she only shrugged.

"Ensign, what's happening?" Anhur said, taking a seat.

"Sir, the chariot just appeared off our bow. They're hailing us."

"Raise shields," said Anhur. "And put that ship on the viewscreen."

"They took heavy damage in the Malor attack," Salvatore told him. "Surely they haven't had time to make repairs yet?"

"Ensign?" said Anhur.

"Scans do show a significant breach in their aft hull, sir. They've got a force field in place to seal it. But there are no signs of repair efforts having begun."

"Very well," said Anhur. "Let's see what they want. Put them on the viewscreen."

The image changed. Gone was the exterior view of the chariot. An Indian woman sitting on a golden throne took its place. She wore a red sari and an elaborate headdress with a cat figure above her forehead. Malia knew this was Isis in one of her many guises. She called this one "Durga." But Malia could not explain why she was bothering to disguise herself this way anymore, now that they all knew who she was.

"Greetings, my friends," she said with a slight accent. Her smile was more of a smirk. "It's good to see you again, Nephthys," she said to Malia. That was the name she'd used for her when she held Malia in captivity. "And you, Salvatore."

"Someone broke your ship, Isis," he said to her.

"What is it we can do for you?" Anhur asked.

Isis glared at Salvatore for a moment, then smiled again, saying, "I'll be blunt. We want that Malor saucer you retrieved."

"I don't know what you're talking about," Anhur replied. "We don't have a Malor saucer."

"Of course, you do. We observed you taking it aboard your ship on long-range sensors. Hand it over, and we'll be on our way."

"Close the channel," Anhur said. Then, the exterior image of the chariot returned to the viewscreen.

"Sir, they're raising shields and powering weapons."

"Get us out of here," Anhur ordered. "Set a course for low Earth orbit."

But as Malia watched, the chariot fired on them. The impact rocked the warship; Malia had to grab onto a console to keep her balance.

"Target that ship and fire plasma cannons!" said Anhur.

But the chariot shot away before the plasma shots made impact and returned fire.

"Launch fighters," said Anhur.

Moments later, Malia spotted more than a dozen saucers streaking away from the warship and firing on the chariot. Isis's ship tried to flee but couldn't outrun the smaller vessels. She launched her own fighters. The battle devolved into chaos as the saucers engaged in individual dogfights.

The warship closed in and opened fire on the chariot again, but it disappeared from view before impact. Reaching out with her mind, Malia was still able to locate it.

"Commander, the chariot is still nearby," Malia told him. "I can sense it. May I help with the battle?"

Anhur nodded. "Yes, go ahead."

Malia focused on the saucers but found it difficult to tell which were theirs. "Can you highlight our ships on the viewscreen?" she asked the commander. Malia knew they'd be able to use their transponders to identify them.

"Make it so, Ensign," said Anhur.

Green crosses appeared superimposed over their saucers. Malia chose one of the enemy saucers and reached out with her mind. Then, concentrating with all her might, she hurled it into the chariot. The saucer went up in a giant explosion, and the chariot became visible.

The warship fired on the chariot again, but it shot out of the way. Malia crashed another one of their saucers into it, then the others withdrew. Moments later, all the enemy craft fled the area, and they lost sensor contact with them.

"Interesting that Isis chose to risk a battle with her ship already damaged," a voice said. Turning, Malia realized that Brian had arrived on the bridge with Lieutenant Malik.

"My thought exactly," Anhur agreed, getting to his feet. "Ensign, take us into orbit. Lieutenant Malik, any progress?" Malik nodded. "Very well, let's meet in the conference room. You're welcome to join us," he added to Griffin and Selena.

They moved into the large chamber behind the bridge. The group of them took their seats, Anhur at the head of the table. "That was fast," he said. "What have you got?"

"To begin with, these rogue Malor did *not* build or design that transdimensional drive," Malik told them. "It's the same model we've encountered on their saucers before."

"Those of us from this solar system never realized the saucers had that capability," Brian added. "Our attention was focused on the mother ship during the invasion."

Anhur nodded. "They equip their scout ships with them primarily for emergency evasions in battle," he explained. "We discovered this when we explored the world they'd destroyed. The units don't have much power. Not enough to escape the Earth's gravity well, certainly. And I'm not aware of their saucers delta shifting during the invasion. We didn't detect them doing it, at least."

"Isis must have been after the saucer's transdimensional drive," said Malik.

"And she would have been disappointed if she'd managed to retrieve it," Brian noted with a grin. "Based on what she said to Jaden, she's looking to move her people to a new world. But that thing would never get them there. Although I suppose her people could probably reverse engineer it and build a larger one."

"It does explain why she was willing to risk a battle despite the chariot's damage," said Anhur. "This is probably the first chance she's had to get her hands on such a device."

"I didn't realize that kind of drive had a range limit," said Malia.

"It's more complex than that," Malik explained. "Delta shifting requires an enormous amount of energy no matter how you're using it. The scout's drive could transport it to any location on Earth, but this close to such a massive body, it lacks the power to escape. But if it used its regular engines to escape Earth's gravity, then it could go quite a bit farther with the transdimensional drive."

"How far?" asked Malia.

"We'd have to run tests to determine that for sure, but my guess is that it could jump as far as Mars or Venus."

"How far can the warship go?" Brian asked.

"Our maximum theoretical limit is about a thousand light-years," said Anhur. "But nobody's ever tested this class of drive that far. Our trip here was the farthest jump our people have ever made with it."

"What about the Malor mother ship?" asked Malia.

"We weren't able to analyze their drive before the fire destroyed it," said Malik. "But based on the information we've been able to glean from our encounters with them, we believe they've got an operational limit of roughly twenty thousand light-years."

"So they could make it across the galaxy in five jumps," Brian said, nodding appreciatively. "Impressive. What would it take to travel to another galaxy?"

"Theoretically impossible," said Anhur.

"Again, if you could escape the galaxy's gravity well using normal propulsion, then a drive like the mother ship's could get you pretty far," Malik added. "But there are engineering limits. The more mass you're trying to move, the more power you need. But the mass of the drive increases as a function of power output. You'd need a drive like the one on the mother ship to get a small saucer to Andromeda, for example."

"And I'm betting the mother ship's drive alone is many orders of magnitude more massive than a saucer," said Brian.

"Exactly," Malik agreed. "And a ship that size couldn't carry a drive so large."

"But you're assuming the drive has to be attached to the ship," Malia observed. "I know it would make it a one-way trip, but could the mother ship's engine be used to launch a separate saucer that far away?"

Malik shook her head. "Not with any technology we possess. Our transdimensional drives and the Malor's work much the same way, and they're unable to delta shift any matter without going along for the ride themselves."

"Our engineers theorized about doing that," said Anhur. "But our people lacked the technology to achieve it."

"And it was fraught with danger," Malik added. "The drive is the thing keeping the path through the other dimensions open as you travel. If you don't take it with you, the portal could collapse on you midway to your destination."

"And then what happens?" asked Brian.

"It's hard to say. You could find yourself shunted to an alternate universe or trapped inside a transdimensional bubble."

"I'm sorry—an alternate universe?" asked Malia.

"Yes," Malik confirmed. "Are you familiar with the concept of quantum superposition?"

Malia nodded. "It means that a particle or photon can exist in multiple states simultaneously, with each state representing a different possible outcome."

"Care to translate that for me?" Griffin said with a grin.

"You've heard of Schrodinger's cat, right?" Malia asked him.

"Sure... There's a cat in a box, along with some radioactive material. If a single atom of that material decays, then poison is released, killing the cat."

"Right," Malia agreed. "But the decay is a quantum event. So the atom exists in both the decayed and non-decayed states until someone *observes* it. Then the quantum superposition collapses, and one outcome or the other becomes reality."

"Meaning the cat is both dead and alive until someone opens the box to check," Griffin said. "And then it's one or the other."

"That's correct," Malik confirmed. "Multiverse theory states that *both* outcomes become reality, but not in the same universe. In our world, the cat is alive. But there is another world in which it is dead."

"And so, you're saying that if a transdimensional portal were to collapse as you were moving through it, you could travel from the universe where the cat's alive to the one where it's dead?" asked Malia.

Malik nodded. "You've got it."

"I've never been too comfortable with that theory," Brian said with a frown. "It's based on what our people call the Copenhagen interpretation of quantum mechanics. But it doesn't stand to reason. The superposition of states applies only to quantum systems, not the macrocosmic world in which we live. In the Schrodinger's cat experiment, that superposition collapses the moment the decaying atom interacts with the rest of the world. If it decays, then the particle it emits interacts with the machine that releases the poison. One outcome for the atom, and one for the cat, without any human observer required. It's the interaction that determines the outcome, not the observation of it."

“No multiverse for you, then,” Malik said with a grin.

“No,” Brian agreed.

“Well, in multiverse theory, the alternate universes arise from the quantum superposition, not anything macrocosmic,” said Malik. “So it could still hold true without your Copenhagen interpretation.”

“Perhaps,” Brian conceded. “But you also mentioned the possibility of a transdimensional bubble. How does that work?”

“Well, using our transdimensional drive, we create a portal from our location to the destination,” Malik explained. “But we’re moving through the extra spacetime dimensions that are usually curled up to do it. The drive forces them to uncurl, just briefly, as we pass through them. So, in essence, it’s creating a little bubble of our reality inside those other dimensions, then letting it collapse once we’ve reached the other side. But without the drive moving through the portal, the object you’re transporting could get stuck there, in that bubble of our reality, cut off from the rest of our world.”

“But we can say for sure that the Malor aren’t any more capable of jumping to alternate universes or creating transdimensional bubbles than we are, right?” asked Malia.

“That’s correct. And like I said, these particular Malor did not build the transdimensional drives in those saucers,” said Malik. “The saucers already had them. Now, that’s not to say that they haven’t developed a personal, portable drive unit. Using such a device, an individual Malor could delta shift into your compound, grab one of your people, and then jump away again. And right now, that’s our working theory.”

"Which brings us back to their new base," said Anhur. "*Where* are they taking them?"

"Yes," said Malik, calling up a holographic display above the table. It showed the Earth, then quickly enlarged an area of northern Siberia. Looking closely, Malia could see nothing but a rocky ridge surrounded by forest. "Here, according to the data we recovered from the Malor computer."

"Based on what I could find on the internet, there was an old Soviet weapons bunker at that location," Brian added. "Chances are they were using it to store nukes."

A new image appeared on the holographic display. "This is what archival satellite imagery shows," Malik told them. It was a closer view of the bottom of the ridge. Malia could see a couple of massive steel doors embedded in a concrete façade in the face of the cliff.

"But the only thing we can see on our scans," Malik added, "is this." The image changed. It showed the cliff face extending all the way down, only a rock wall where the steel doors used to be as if those had never existed.

"What do scans show inside?" asked Anhur.

"Nothing," Malik said with a shrug. "We can see the ridge and the trees and those doors, but our scanning beams cannot penetrate the ground in that area. Based on what we found in the Amazon, I believe this entire area is being holographically projected. Or at the very least, they're using that system to shield everything on the inside from our scans, along with the doors."

"Meaning there's no way to tell from the outside if our people are in there," Malia observed.

"Precisely," Brian confirmed.

"So, how do we get in?" asked Anhur.

Malik shook her head. "Short of blasting through the doors and going in with guns blazing, I don't know."

"And that could work," said Brian. "Except that their saucer fleet is probably inside. And there's a good chance they've built weapons around the perimeter that are hidden by their holographic system."

"Without doing some recon first, we'd have no idea what we're up against until we get there," Malik concluded.

"We can take care of the recon," said Salvatore. "If you can let us borrow one of your saucers."

Anhur considered this for a moment. "Very well. Let us know what you find. We'll provide whatever support you require."

Chapter Twenty-one

Jaden knew he mustn't use the saucer's engines to achieve escape velocity from the Earth's gravity. Doing so would enable Isis to detect them. Instead, he tapped into the planet's magnetic field, reached out with his mind, and accelerated them. Once they'd achieved escape velocity and moved out of orbit, Jaden checked the ship's control system. Adjusting their course to keep them on target for the Moon, he kept the engines just below the detection threshold. With their velocity increasing continuously, he'd have to reverse the engines halfway there to insert them into a lunar orbit.

"All right," he said to Ezra. "We should get there in twenty minutes or so."

"What? It took the Apollo missions *days* to get there! We must be going, what, ten percent the speed of light?"

"Nah, man, not even close," Jaden said, rolling his eyes. "And you own a rocket company?"

"I'm the CEO, not one of the engineers," Ezra told him.

"Well, we're not even going to hit one percent the speed of light."

Ezra proceeded to chew Jaden's ear off about how badly he'd always wanted to go to space. The 1960s Moon missions had inspired him.

"To be honest, my childhood dreams of going to space were a large part of my decision to found Starfire," he told Jaden. "And I'll confess watching Jeff go up on one of his own rockets made me more than a little jealous."

"You do know they accept tourists on those flights, right?" Jaden said. "I know it's pricey, but I'm sure you could afford it. Cheaper than trying to get there yourself."

"No, no, my boy," Ezra replied with a grimace. "I wouldn't give those guys one penny. And besides, I'm one-upping them pretty good on this trip, eh?"

They reached the Moon, and Jaden completed one orbit to help bleed off some of their velocity. He'd been able to calculate the exact position of the Anunnaki base from the Malor data, so when they reached the far side the second time, he took them in close. But there was nothing but an impact crater at those coordinates. Jaden scanned the area repeatedly but could find no evidence of any technology at all, much less an alien base.

Then he had an idea. Maybe the whole thing was concealed beneath a holographic projection. The Malor sensors were more advanced, so they must have seen through the hologram. Jaden reached out with his mind to see if this base had an AI like the one on Earth. Sure enough, he could sense an underground structure. It was shaped like a wheel, much like the one on Earth, but bigger, with a central core and large chambers at the ends of the spokes. Focusing on the central core, Jaden tried to tap into the control system.

"*What are you doing here, Jaden Kwan*?" a voice said in his head, neither male nor female.

"*We're trying to find the people who build this place,*" Jaden replied, taken aback by its knowledge of his name, despite having expected it.

"*You'd better come inside. There's something here for you.*"

Jaden's heart skipped a beat. "*For* me *specifically*?"

The AI didn't answer. Instead, the center area of the crater changed, revealing a tunnel inside, with a force field covering the opening.

"*I've altered the frequency of the barrier to allow your ship to pass. Please, come in.*"

Ezra asked him what was going on. Jaden explained. "Well, what are you waiting for?" the man asked. "Take us in!"

Jaden's stomach tightened, a sudden wave of apprehension washing over him. This could be a trap. What if Isis was already here, and she'd managed to reprogram the AI? But reaching out with his mind, he sensed nobody else inside. And besides, the AI on Earth hadn't tried to trap him. Taking a deep breath, Jaden guided the saucer through the force field and into the tunnel.

After about a hundred feet, they reached an enormous chamber that looked like a hangar bay, except that the walls and floor were made from the same wood-like material he'd seen on the Earth base. He set the saucer to hover near the center of the area.

He scanned the interior using the ship's sensors to confirm what he'd detected himself. Scans agreed that there were no other life signs inside. And the space had a breathable atmosphere, as well as gravity similar to Earth's. So these Anunnaki must have possessed the same ability as the Martians to control the gravitational force artificially.

"All right," he said to Ezra, getting to his feet. "I'm going to take a look around. You wait here."

"Not a chance! We're on the *Moon,* for God's sake! I'm going with you—this gives me the chance to one-up those other guys!"

"You already have," Jaden replied, rolling his eyes. "They've never been to the Moon."

"Sure, sure, but I don't want to be the guy who waits in the ship while Neil Armstrong takes one giant leap for mankind! Look, there's nobody else here," he added, gazing around the hangar bay through the cockpit windows. "What could possibly go wrong?"

"Fine," Jaden said with a sigh. "Let's go."

They disembarked, using the saucer's gravitational beam to float down to the surface. Jaden couldn't shake the feeling that they weren't alone in here despite the negative scans. Gazing up the entry tunnel they'd used, he took one more scan, but there was nobody there.

The two of them set off across the hangar, moving into the passage that led to the central hub. This area was enormous compared to the Earth base. The tree-trunk-like structure in the center was more than twice as thick and had many times more pods growing off of it. Jaden tried accessing the data banks telepathically but couldn't get in.

"*I'm sorry, I lack the authority to grant you access to our control system,*" the AI told him telepathically.

"No worries. So, what is it that you have for me?"

Suddenly, a holographic image appeared only a few feet away from them. It startled Jaden; Ezra squealed, nearly tripping over his own feet.

The image was an Anunnaki. He towered over Jaden and Ezra. He turned his head and seemed to be gazing directly at them. His head was elongated, with enormous eyes that felt like they were staring into Jaden's soul.

"Greetings," the Anunnaki said. "I left this message in the hope that someone would find it one day. Someone who could help my people."

"What happened to them?" Jaden asked. He wasn't sure if this was just a static message or interactive like the AI.

"As I record this, it is the Earth year 1908. My people have lived among the various civilizations of the planet for thousands of years. But now, our enemies have found us. We've been hiding from them for eons. I don't understand how they finally located us; we took measures that should have prevented it."

"Who are they?" Jaden asked.

"They rounded up my people and imprisoned them." Either the alien was ignoring him, Jaden decided, or it was a static message. "I alone managed to escape. But, although I have tried everything to free my brethren, I have failed. Our enemy's technology is too advanced. I have not been able to crack it. And it is only a matter of time before the enemy finds me and incarcerates me with the others.

"My sincere hope is that the people of your planet will one

day grow technologically to the point that *you* can liberate us. Or, perhaps, another spacefaring species will arrive in this system and possess the ability to do so. Therefore, I am including a map showing the location of the prison."

The hologram changed, showing the Earth instead. It zoomed in rapidly, centering on an area in Algeria. Then it froze, and a red circle appeared over an area Jaden knew very well. "No... I don't believe it," he muttered.

"What is it?" Ezra asked.

But the Anunnaki reappeared before he could respond. "Please. If you could find this base and access this message, you may soon achieve the ability to break us out of our prison. But if—"

The Anunnaki inhaled sharply, suddenly staring off at a point beyond Jaden and Ezra. Jaden turned, expecting to see someone behind them, but the area was empty.

"They've found me," the Anunnaki said. Then, he vanished behind a flash of light. The hologram continued a moment longer, showing only the empty control room, but then ended.

"This can't be," Jaden said, feeling bewildered.

"What is it?" Ezra asked.

"That location for the Anunnaki prison... That's where our compound is!"

"I don't suppose you've found it there?" Ezra said with a confused look.

Jaden's head was swimming; this new information gave him more questions than answers. "You saw what that single Anunnaki did to the

Malor. What kind of aliens could overpower them like that? And if the Anunnaki are in some sort of jail, they can't be the ones who took my mom and Venus. So maybe these enemy aliens were behind it?"

"We should go see if we can find that prison," Ezra suggested.

Jaden had to agree. But he had more questions. "*Why doesn't the AI on Earth know about this* message?" he asked the Moon AI. "*It doesn't know your people were imprisoned.*"

"*How could it? The last of our people came* here *for refuge before being captured himself.*"

"*You never bothered telling the other AI about this*?" Jaden asked.

"*I wish I could. Unfortunately, I have no way to reach it.*"

"*What? Couldn't you send a radio signal or... something*?"

"*Our people did not need radios. They communicated with each other and with us telepathically, as you're doing.*"

"*Then you could have told the other AI that way.*"

"*Unfortunately, not. The entire Moon lies between here and there. Not even my people could pass a signal through so much mass. But perhaps you could let it know next time you're there*?"

"*Yeah, sure, if I ever end up in Pakistan again. Well, thanks a lot.*" Jaden was about to head back to his saucer when he heard a buzzing sound coming from that direction. "What the hell was that?" Ezra only shrugged. Jaden scanned the area: three more saucers had arrived inside the hangar bay. A dozen hybrids were headed toward the central hub. "Oh shit!" he said out loud. "*Why did you let* them *inside*?" he asked the AI.

"*They were here before. I saw no reason to deny them entry.*"

"*The hybrids were already here before us?*"

"*Yes. I played the message for them, too.*"

"Shit," Jaden said again.

"You keep saying that—what's wrong?" Ezra demanded.

"Hybrids. A dozen of them headed right for us."

"Oh... well, perhaps we should leave now?"

"Yeah, obviously. And I'm sure I could sneak past them on my own, but we don't have any way to conceal *you*."

"What the hell are we going to do, then?" Ezra said, a note of panic in his voice.

"Quick—get behind the computer core," Jaden told him. There was nowhere else to hide.

"The what? Where?" said Ezra, looking around frantically.

"That tree-trunk-looking thing," Jaden said. "Hurry!"

Ezra scurried around the core, ducking out of sight. Jaden turned his attention to the approaching hybrids, using his emitter to become invisible. He couldn't see them; they were using their emitters, too. His implants could detect their presence using their radiation leaks, but there wasn't enough data to track them. But he was able to sense them telepathically. Reaching out with his powers, Jaden penetrated the first one's mind, knocking her unconscious. She fell to the floor, dropping her plasma cannon.

Jaden put the second one under, then, reaching out telekinetically, launched their plasma cannons into his arms. Hurrying around the core, he made himself visible and tried handing one to Ezra, but the man jumped when Jaden appeared out of nowhere.

"You're going to give me a heart attack doing that," he muttered. "How the hell do I use this thing?" he added, taking the weapon.

Jaden gave him a crash course.

"Great, but those guys are invisible! How can I shoot them if I can't see them?"

"Just aim up that corridor," Jaden told him. "They've got to come through there to get in here. But make sure you don't shoot *me*!"

"Obviously, I'm not going to do that—I can't fly that spaceship of yours, and that's my only way home!"

Returning his attention to the incoming hybrids, Jaden realized that three more had made it to the hub. Aiming his cannon, he shot one; as the hybrid became visible, Jaden could see that he'd blasted a hole through his abdomen, vaporizing his emitter. Ezra fired a shot but missed the corridor, creating a crater in the wall instead. The hybrids returned fire. Ezra screamed as one of their shots hit the core next to him.

Jaden shot one of the others but missed the second. And at that moment, the remaining seven hybrids rushed into the command center. Jaden could sense that they were spreading out around the perimeter; Jaden and Ezra wouldn't be able to hide behind the core much longer.

"Listen to me," Jaden said in Ezra's ear. "We've gotta make a run for it. They're all in here with us, now. I'll take out the two standing guard by the passage back to the hangar bay. Then I'm going to fly us out of here."

"But they'll shoot us!"

"I'll heal—"

"*I won't*!"

"I'll keep you in front of me," Jaden assured him. "My body will shield you."

Just then, one of the hybrids fired at them. Jaden grabbed Ezra, pulling him to the floor; the shot hit the core directly above them. Jaden returned fire but missed.

It was time to go. Reaching out with his mind, Jaden knocked out one of the hybrids standing by their exit. Peering around the core, he shot the other one. Then, grabbing Ezra telekinetically, he flew out of the command center and up the passage as fast as possible.

One of the hybrids fired at them as they departed, just missing. Another hit Jaden in the leg; he gritted his teeth against the pain but could already feel the wound healing. But the next shot grazed his arm and hit Ezra. The man screamed.

Reaching the hangar bay, Jaden accessed his saucer's control system, issuing a command to fly up the tunnel to the surface the moment they were aboard and head back toward Earth. He flew them into the airlock and up to the main level. Lying Ezra on the floor, he realized he'd passed out. Then he spotted his wound.

"Oh, no," he muttered, his eyes welling up. The plasma shot had left a deep gouge across his chest. Reaching out telepathically, Jaden penetrated his mind. He tried to get Ezra's system to heal the wound, but the damage was too severe. Part of his heart was burned away. Jaden knew Malia could channel her healing energy into a patient, but he didn't understand how she did it. He tried to focus on doing this, imagining Ezra's wound repairing itself. But nothing happened. "Shit," he said out loud, leaving Ezra's mind and slumping on the floor. Tears streamed down his cheeks as the realization hit him: Ezra was dead.

Chapter Twenty-two

Malia returned to the warship's docking port with Salvatore, Brian, Griffin, and Selena. The Othali had granted Salvatore command access to one of their saucers while their people went to work repairing Salvatore's. Once they'd boarded, Malia headed up to the cockpit with Brian and Salvatore. They moved out of the docking port and returned to Earth. Salvatore took them in low over Siberia, about a hundred miles from the bunker. They approached from the south, which was the direction the doors faced. Once they were within three miles, he locked the saucer into a hover ten feet above a small river.

"Sensors still show nothing but the ridge, even from this close range," Salvatore reported.

"They won't detect us out here?" asked Malia.

"Only if they use active scanning beams," Salvatore replied. "And they'd have no reason to do that unless they already suspected our presence."

"They've gone to great lengths to keep this base hidden," Brian added. "Active scanning beams would give away their location, so they're not likely to use them unless absolutely necessary."

"Malia, can you tell if our people are in there?" Salvatore asked.

"Give me a moment." Reaching out with her mind, Malia tried to sense Melissa or Venus inside the bunker. But all she could feel inside was solid rock. "I can't get through their shielding telepathically, either."

"That probably shouldn't be surprising," Salvatore noted. "The Malor are telepathic and also aware of your abilities."

"The mother ship didn't obstruct our telepathy, but they didn't know about us then," Malia agreed.

"Malik's probably right," said Brian. "We should ask Anhur to assemble a strike force. Those doors must still be there. If we blast our way through them and go in with a hundred Othali soldiers, we should be able to overwhelm the Malor and recover our people."

"That's risky," said Salvatore. "They might have upgraded the doors to something we can't penetrate. And there are probably shields in place as well. If I were them, I'd have weapons mounted around the perimeter, too. So if we show up in force and can't get inside, our people would be sitting ducks at that point."

"Not only that, we don't know for sure they've got our people in there," Malia reminded them. "We've got to find another way inside. It's the interior we need to reconnoiter. Jaden got inside the Amazon facility through an air vent. Is there anything like that here?"

"There must be," said Salvatore. "But it's hidden by their hologram."

"That might hide the opening, but we should be able to detect any air current beyond it," Brian suggested.

Salvatore nodded. A moment later, he said, "There." A holographic image of the ridge formed in the center console. The view centered on an area the top, about a hundred feet back from the southern edge. A red circle appeared. "Sensors are detecting air flowing out of the rock at this spot."

"That's it, then. We can use that to get inside," said Malia.

"We've still got to get through the hologram," Salvatore replied. "It will feel solid to the touch. But our weapons might not be able to penetrate it."

"And firing weapons is sure to alert the Malor to our presence," Brian added.

"I might be able to get us through it," said Malia. "Can you take us directly over that vent?"

Salvatore kept them low, flying around to the west of the ridge, where the incline was the shallowest. Then he took them to the top, hovering only feet above the ground. "This is it. The vent is directly below the airlock."

Malia moved down to the main level and entered the airlock. Opening the outer hatch, she focused on the ground below, reaching out telekinetically. She could sense nothing but stone. But knowing it had to be a hologram, she imagined blocking the projection in this area. Slowly, her sense of what was there began to change. Malia could feel the energy flowing over the surface like water. She imagined damming the flow. It started to work. At first, it was nothing more than a flickering in the projection. But slowly, the part of the hologram directly beneath her began to deteriorate, until finally, she could see the air vent beneath. Using her powers, she removed the grate and brought it up inside the saucer.

"We're in," she told Salvatore through her implants. "But we'd better hurry. I don't know how long I can hold this."

"Understood," came his reply. "We're on our way."

Moments later, Salvatore, Brian, Griffin, and Selena entered the airlock, each toting a plasma cannon; Salvatore had an extra that he handed to Malia. They used their emitters to become invisible, then descended into the ventilation shaft one by one. Once they were all in, Malia followed. She closed the saucer's hatch, then allowed the Malor hologram to reconstitute itself.

Reaching the bottom of the shaft, Malia found herself looking through a giant grate into what appeared to be a storage area. Salvatore popped the grate out of the opening, setting it aside on the floor. They crept out of the shaft, then Salvatore replaced the grate.

"The Soviets were definitely storing nukes in here," Brian told the others through his implants. "Scans still show some residual radiation. It's well within safe levels but unmistakable."

"I am detecting a few dozen Malor life signs in the complex," Salvatore reported. "But no human or Martian ones."

Malia felt her heart sink. Reaching out telepathically, she tried locating her mother or Venus but also came up empty. She felt crestfallen. There had been little doubt in her mind they'd find them here. "They're not here," she confirmed to the others through her implants.

"We should have a look around anyway," Brian suggested. "They could be keeping them in cells with the same shielding they have over the exterior of the complex. Or they could be keeping them elsewhere. If I can tap into their control systems, we should be able to find a record of their whereabouts."

They moved across the storage area, Salvatore leading the way. Passing through the doors, they entered a long corridor. Malia's scans showed her an enormous hangar bay at the other end. But halfway there, several Malor walked into the passage, heading directly toward them. They flattened themselves against one wall to let them pass. Malia breathed a sigh of relief: the Malor couldn't see through their emitters.

Reaching the end of the corridor, Malia peered around the corner. There were five Malor saucers inside. They had assembled fuselages for four more, but scans revealed that those didn't have engines or weapons yet.

In the center of the hangar was an enormous, metal-framed tower. It reached the ceiling and had thick cables running up the middle. Malia couldn't say for sure, but it looked like an antenna.

"I'm not detecting any cells in there," Salvatore told the others. "But we went by a couple of smaller rooms. I'm going to take Griffin and go check those."

"There are a few smaller areas on the other side of the hangar," Brian replied. "We'll take a look over there."

Salvatore and Griffin headed back up the corridor. Malia and Selena followed Brian, carefully making their way to the rear of the hangar. The Malor were busy working on their new saucers and the antenna and making lots of noise with their tools. This allowed the three of them to move quickly without being heard.

They made their way across the space, sticking close to the rear wall. They found a few more rooms that the Malor were using as labs on the other side. They had large glass windows, making it easy to see inside. In one of them, two of the aliens were working on what looked like a new transdimensional drive, like the one they'd found on the crashed saucer. Inside the next room, there were two Malor assembling a computer core. It looked identical to the one they'd pulled from the wrecked ship. Finally, they found a Malor strapped to what looked like a surgical table in the last room. There were two others in the room, and they had a device positioned by the patient's head. Malia had no idea what they were doing in there. But it was evident they weren't holding Melissa or Venus in this area. Malia's scans showed no other chambers beyond these.

Brian led them back across the hangar to the corridor, where they regrouped with Salvatore and Griffin. They hadn't found any signs of their missing people, either.

"Let me see if I can tap into their control system," said Brian.

"Be careful," Salvatore told him. "If they detect you, they'll realize we're here."

Brian nodded. "I'm going to try using the same backdoor we found on the two saucers' computers. If that exists here, it shouldn't alert them to my presence."

Brian's eyes went unfocused, and Malia could tell he was accessing the Malor system. But suddenly, something went horribly wrong. A klaxon blared through the complex. Brian fixed Salvatore with an alarmed stare.

"It would seem they've been alerted," Salvatore noted.

"I don't understand... this should have worked!" Brian said.

"We'd better get out of here," Malia suggested.

They hurried down the corridor, but before they'd moved very far, a spiderweb of lasers crisscrossed the passage. Malia didn't understand their purpose; they passed through them unharmed.

"Well, being invisible isn't going to help us anymore," Brian told the others. "They're using those beams to track us!"

Sure enough, several Malor emerged from the nearby rooms pointing weapons at them. Selena and Griffin fired their plasma cannons at them, but the Malor were wearing energy shields of some kind. The plasma shots hit their surfaces without affecting the aliens.

Suddenly, Salvatore vanished in a bright flash of light. "Salvatore!" Malia shouted. "What did you do with him?" she demanded. But it was no use; the Malor couldn't understand her. They didn't use spoken language, so the Othali translation algorithms were useless.

Malia tried ripping the weapons out of the Malor's hands, but their shields blocked her telekinesis, too. She was going to try penetrating their minds, but the Malor fired on them. There was a metallic crackling sound, and something hit her in the chest. The weapon was different from the one they'd wielded in her encounter with them in the desert. This one stunned her, and she found herself struggling to remain conscious.

The others passed out, hitting the floor and becoming visible. One of the Malor pointed his weapon at Malia again. Making herself visible, she set her plasma cannon down on the ground and held up both hands in a gesture of surrender. They removed the others' emitters, and one of them pointed at Malia's with his weapon. She took it off and set it on the ground.

Several more Malor showed up. Each carried a device that projected some kind of energy beam that they used to lift Malia's companions off the floor and move them into the hangar bay. While they were doing that, Malia quickly scanned the area and confirmed her suspicion. There was a transdimensional radiation signature where Salvatore had disappeared.

The Malor who had shot her approached Malia, prodding her in the back with his weapon. He wanted her to follow the others; Malia complied.

She didn't know what she was going to do yet. Her powers didn't work against their shields. But by yielding, she'd at least managed to remain conscious, giving her some small hope of finding a way out of this.

The Malor took them to the back of the hangar bay. There, they shackled each of the others' hands together behind their backs. They used the same kind of handcuffs they'd used on Malia and Jaden in the desert; instead of metal, there was an energy field binding their wrists together. Finally, they propped them up against the wall in sitting positions.

One Malor grabbed Malia's arms, shackling her wrists behind her back, too. Then the one who'd shot her gestured with his weapon for her to join the others. Malia sat down against the wall next to Griffin.

They left two Malor to stand guard, and then the others went back to whatever they'd been doing before. Taking a deep breath, Malia tried contacting the Othali warship telepathically. But it was no use. She couldn't get through the bunker's shields, and her implants couldn't penetrate the barrier, either.

Malia sat there for a few minutes, trying to figure out what to do. But suddenly, the klaxon sounded again, and the hangar bay doors began to open. Malia was curious if she could get a signal through the opening. She tried using both her implants and her telepathy but had no more success than before. She wondered about this until she realized that there was a force field in place beyond the steel doors.

Several Malor boarded two of the saucers, and moments later, they passed through the energy field and took off toward the sky. The metal doors close again after them. Malia wondered where they were going, but she had more pressing concerns to address first.

Chapter Twenty-three

Jaden moved Ezra into one of the medical pods to keep his body in stasis until he had a chance to deliver it to his family. Then he hurried up to the cockpit.

The saucer was accelerating away from the Moon, and there was no sign of pursuit. The ship's sensors wouldn't be able to detect the hybrids' ships anyway, but Jaden checked back along his path telepathically and couldn't sense anyone. Still, he wasn't about to take any chances. He accelerated his ship telekinetically. Without the Earth's magnetic field, he didn't have nearly as much power as he had on the way out here, so he kept it up longer and still managed to exceed the engines' top speed.

Next, he tried contacting Salvatore through his implants. But there was no response. He tried Malia and Brian, too, but couldn't reach them. This was concerning. He was still too far from Earth to connect with any of them telepathically, so he contacted the compound through his implants instead, reaching Sydney.

"Hey, this is Jaden. Everything all right down there?"

"As far as I know," she said with a note of apprehension. "Why?"

"I'm on my way there now. Just put everyone on alert until I get there."

"Jaden, what's going on?"

"Do you know where Salvatore and the rest of them went? I can't reach them."

"The last I heard, they were on their way to Siberia. They found the Malor base. But that was a while ago, now, and nobody's contacted me since then."

Jaden took a deep breath. He wanted to go see if they were in trouble. But if the Anunnaki prison was anywhere near their compound, that could spell *bigger* trouble. "All right. I'll see you soon."

Jaden tried reaching Salvatore, Brian, or Malia telepathically as he moved closer to Earth but still had no luck. Now he was really starting to worry. There were many situations that could prevent a radio signal from reaching them, but far fewer that would obstruct telepathy. And none of them were good.

Once Jaden had reached the compound, he took his saucer inside the hangar bay and disembarked. He found Sydney waiting for him, along with Vincent.

"Will you *please* tell us what's going on, now?" Sydney pleaded.

Jaden gave them a quick update.

"But that's rubbish," Vincent said, shaking his head. "Isis must be behind this. It's an elaborate ruse, I'll grant you that, but how can an alien prison be *here*? Surely we would have detected it."

"Yeah, well, I would have thought so, too," Jaden muttered. Then, accessing the compound's control systems, he initiated a full scan of the facility and the surrounding area. "How did Salvatore and the others track down the Malor?" he asked Sydney. She brought him up to speed.

"Salvatore was planning on grounding you upon your return and quite possibly throwing you in the brig for insubordination," Vincent told him with a gloating expression.

"Oh, is that so?" Jaden demanded, stepping toward him. Vincent backed away, his expression changing to alarm. "You want to tell me how the hybrids found our people in the Amazon? They couldn't have traced them there without inside information. Remind me—what's our penalty for treason?"

"That's enough, both of you," Sydney said, stepping between them. "We're in a crisis here. Let's figure out a plan before we go pointing fingers at anyone. All right?"

Jaden glared at Vincent a moment longer before backing off. "Yeah," he said with a sigh. Just then, the control system notified him that the scans were finished. "Our sensors can't detect anything out of the ordinary here in the compound or the surrounding area."

"Of course, they can't," Vincent replied. "That's because there is no *Anunnaki prison*, especially not here."

"The alien in the hologram said their enemy's technology was much more advanced than theirs. And we know for sure that the Anunnaki were way beyond us. So just because we can't detect anything doesn't mean it's not here. I'm gonna check with the warship."

"You're wasting your time," Vincent said, shaking his head.

Jaden contacted Commander Anhur through his implants and

explained what he'd learned. "Normally, I'd ask Salvatore or Brian about this, but I can't reach them."

"Yes, we've lost contact with them, too. And they're long overdue," Anhur replied. "We'll be meeting to discuss a rescue operation shortly, and I'd like you to join us. But hang on a moment."

Jaden waited. Then someone else contacted him through his implants. "This is Lieutenant Malik." Jaden told her everything he'd explained to Anhur. "Hm... that's intriguing. And regular scans don't show anything?" Jaden could tell from her tone that she was taking the information much more seriously than Vincent had. "Jaden, try running a scan for transdimensional radiation signatures. I can only imagine what kind of technology such an advanced species might be using. Still, we have solid evidence that whoever is behind the disappearances is using that kind of system. It's possible they'd use that for their prison, too."

"All right, give me a minute," Jaden replied. He ran the scan but came up empty again. "The only signature I'm showing is the one from when Venus disappeared. There's no other transdimensional radiation anywhere near here."

"Weird. Let me put some thought into this, and I'll get back to you if I come up with any other possibilities."

"Great, thanks," said Jaden.

"This is Anhur again. Jaden, it sounds to me like the compound isn't in any immediate danger. Would you agree?"

"Yeah, I would."

"Very well. I'd like you to join us on the warship. I daresay your talents will help us make contact with our people and find out what's going on in there."

Jaden bade farewell to Sydney, pointedly ignoring Vincent, and boarded his saucer. Moments later, he was en route to the warship's location high above the Earth. Once he'd secured the ship in its berth inside the hangar bay, he hurried down to the docking platform and found Nadia waiting for him.

"Hey," she said with a grin, pulling him into a hug. "I'm glad you're here in an official capacity. I had about enough of that cloak-and-dagger nonsense."

"Yeah, sorry about that," Jaden replied. "So what the hell happened down there?"

Nadia filled him in with more detail as they made their way up to the bridge. The second in command, Captain Patel, told them that Anhur had already assembled the rest of his team in the conference room. Nadia and Jaden entered the room and took seats at the end of the table. Jaden recognized Lieutenant Malik, Ensign Shurani, and Lieutenant Bukhari.

"Thank you for coming," Anhur said to Jaden. "Let's get started. We've got five people inside the Malor base. We are unable to penetrate their shields with sensors, and Malia reported before going in that she could not get through them telepathically, either. So they've been out of contact since entering the base. That's to be expected.

"But this was supposed to be a recon mission. They should have been in and out by now, or at least have sent someone out to report. So we have to assume that they've been captured."

"But they may not be inside the base anymore," Bukhari added. "Shortly after they went in, we detected three Malor saucers leaving through the hangar bays at high speed. Our sensors couldn't penetrate their shields, but they might have been transporting our people somewhere else."

"Where?" Jaden asked.

"We don't know," Anhur said with a sigh. "The vessels went invisible almost immediately, and we couldn't track them. So we'll need to send a team inside the base first and see if our people are still there. If not, we'll have to try accessing their control system to find out where they took them."

"What about my mom and Venus?" asked Jaden. "Do we know if they found them in there?"

"We don't know," Anhur replied with a shake of his head.

Jaden took a deep breath. "How do we get inside?"

"We can't get through their shields with our weapons, and even if we could, we detected heavy armaments positioned around the entry," Bukhari told him. "They'd vaporize us if we tried it."

"Salvatore's last report indicated that they'd found an air vent on the top of the ridge. It's inside the shielding, but they detected the air current coming out of it," said Nadia. "Malia used her powers to create an opening in the shields directly above the vent, and they used that to get inside."

"We believe our best shot at mounting a rescue is to send an armed team inside the same way," said Anhur.

"And that's why you needed me here for this," Jaden said with a nod.

"Yes," Anhur confirmed. "Once inside the shielding, we can attempt to contact our people and find out what went wrong. Hopefully, that way, the rescue team can avoid capture and get our people out of there."

"I'm in," said Jaden. "Let's do it."

"Very well," Anhur replied. "Lieutenant Bashandi, assemble a team. You're leading this mission."

"Yes, sir," said Nadia.

"If you discover that our people are gone, you'll need to access the Malor control system and find out where they took them," Anhur told them. "But if that's the case, you are *not* to engage the Malor. You should be able to scan the base and access their computer once you've penetrated the shields. And if they're gone, there's no reason to go any farther inside."

"Yes, sir," Nadia repeated.

Anhur dismissed them. Jaden followed Nadia through the ship back to the hangar bay. She contacted six soldiers on their way there and ordered them to prepare for the mission. Once everyone had reached the docking port, they boarded one of the saucers and flew down to the surface. Nadia approached the Malor base from the south, taking them in low. They stopped a quarter of a mile out, and Nadia took detailed scans.

"Salvatore's saucer is still there, right on top of the air vent," she reported. "I'm sending it back up to the warship. All right, we're clear. Let's go."

Nadia moved them around the ridge and up to the top, flying only a dozen feet above the ground. Once they'd reached the air vent, Jaden and Nadia went down to the main level and moved into the airlock with the soldiers. Nadia opened the hatch, and Jaden got to work.

Jaden could see nothing but the rocky surface below. But he knew it had to be a hologram. Reaching out with his mind, he tried to focus on the projection but still sensed nothing but rock. *Come on*, he thought to himself. Malia had figured this out; he could, too. He concentrated harder, trying to imagine what must lie beneath the hologram. Finally, he started to sense the projection as energy flowing along the actual surface. Once he had that, he was able to divert the flow. It began as a flickering, but then an opening formed, exposing the air shaft beneath.

"Salvatore, this is Nadia. Do you read me?" she said through her implants. "Brian? Malia?"

There was no response.

"These shields could be interfering with the signal," Jaden suggested to her through his implants. "Let me try it telepathically." Nadia nodded. Reaching out with his mind, Jaden tried to sense his sister or any of the others inside. At first, he found only the Malor, careful not to touch their minds and alert them to his presence. But then he reached Malia and couldn't help but grin.

"You've got them?" Nadia asked.

Jaden nodded. "*Malia, it's me. Are you all right*?"

Chapter Twenty-four

Malia assessed her situation. She felt confident she could get out of the Malor shackles; she was familiar with the device from her last encounter with them and could visualize it. But what then?

Malia knew for sure that her telekinesis would no longer work against the Malor now that they had activated their shields. And their weapons didn't work against them, either. She hadn't attempted her telepathy yet. When she'd tried touching a Malor mind three years earlier, it was *too* alien for her to establish any meaningful communication. But her powers had evolved significantly since then, and she'd managed to surface *some* memories in the one they'd encountered over the Atlantic. So she decided it was worth a shot. But she'd have to be careful; if they realized what she was attempting, there was a good chance they'd knock her out.

Gazing around the hangar, she chose one of the Malor in the medical lab room. She had a clear view of him through the window. Malia reached out telepathically, trying only to sense the Malor's thoughts. But it was no good. It was as if he weren't even there. Tapping into the magnetic field to augment her powers, she tried again—still nothing. However the Malor had done it, they'd managed to develop a shield far more powerful than the ones Isis used.

Malia sighed. Now what?

Without her emitter, she couldn't go invisible anymore. She could remove her shackles and fly, but they'd see her. If she could use her telekinesis to grab one of *their* weapons, maybe that could get through their shields. But she wouldn't know until she tried. And there were still quite a few of them here in the bunker. Could she take out all of them before they recaptured her?

No, that wasn't likely.

Instead of trying to fight her way out, she could fly directly to the air vent and escape, except that they were sure to be guarding that exit now. And even if she did manage to make it out that way, she'd be leaving the others behind.

They'd been in here for a long time, though. There was a good chance Anhur and the others were planning a rescue by now. But there was no way to communicate with them to find out. So maybe the best thing to do was to wake the others. Four minds were better than one.

Malia tried rousing Brian through her implants, but this had no effect. She figured he must be too far under. Reaching out with her thoughts, Malia touched his mind. He started awake, opening his eyes with a groan. The Malor noticed; one of them pointed his weapon at Brian.

"*Be quiet*!" Malia told him with her mind. "*We don't need them knocking you out again*!"

"*Right, sorry,*" Brian replied, shaking his head as if to clear it.

Malia spent a few moments discussing her ideas with him. And she told him about the saucers departing.

Brian nodded. "*Anhur's sure to be mounting a rescue. The best thing we can do at this point is to prepare ourselves for that. Why don't you wake up the others and let them know what we're thinking? I'm going to take another shot at their computer.*"

"*Is that wise?*" Malia asked. "*That's what got us in this predicament in the first place.*"

"*Yeah, yeah, I know,*" he replied. "*Don't worry. I've got a couple of ideas. First, it would be best if we could figure out how to open the hangar bay doors by the time the rescue team gets here. And I'd still like to check their system to see if there's any record of them taking our people.*"

"*All right,*" Malia agreed. Next, she reached out to Griffin, penetrating his mind more deeply than she had Brian's. Bringing him up to consciousness, she took greater control of his reactions to try and avoid alerting the Malor this time. "*Hey, it's me, Malia. You all right?*"

"*Whoa... hey,*" he said, suddenly highly anxious. "*What's happening? I can't move! They paralyzed me!*"

"*No, that's me. Relax. I just wanted to make sure you didn't jump or anything. The Malor might have shot you again.*"

"*Oh... that makes sense.*" Malia could feel him relaxing. "*Well, I'm good. You can get out of my head now. Please.*"

"*Okay, I am, but listen.*" Malia told him the plan, then woke

Selena next. Thankfully, her reaction was less dramatic. Once she'd brought her up to speed, she checked in with Brian.

"*Nothing yet, but this looks promising. I've been able to initiate a subroutine without them detecting me. Just a couple more steps, and then we should be in.*"

Malia had no idea how he might be doing it, but she could sense his confidence. She took another look around the hangar, trying again to see if there was some way they might make it out of here on their own. But waiting for the rescue party still seemed like their best bet. Then, a few minutes later, Brian caught her eye.

"*Are you in*?" she asked him telepathically.

"*Yeah, I am,*" he replied, his expression grim. "*I'm afraid I've got bad news and terrible news. What do you want first*?"

"*Ugh. Give me the bad first. I'm not ready for terrible.*"

"*While I was able to access their primary control system, they've got security running through a separate machine. The doors, the exterior weapons, and the shields are all on that. Maybe Jaden could break into that thing, doing whatever it is that he does. But there's no way I'm getting into that.*"

"*So either Jaden can do it and open the front doors for us, or we'll fly out the same way we came in,*" Malia replied. "*That's not* so *bad. Give me the terrible.*"

"*I found out what they're trying to do here.*" Malia could sense his dread and steeled herself for the worst. "*Anhur was right. The transdimensional drives in their saucers were already there. They're trying to build a new one, but they've reached some sort of technological hurdle. Apparently, they need a tool that they can't build with anything we primitive humans possess."*

"That's not terrible at all—"

"I wasn't done. That tower was supposed to be a transdimensional antenna. But they ran into the same problem. And the terrible part is who they wanted to reach with it." He paused for a moment, fixing her with a stare. *"Malia, there's a second mother ship out there. They're trying to send a distress call."*

"A second *mother ship? But I thought their entire civilization was on that first one?"*

"So did I. But we were wrong. From what I can glean, it's on the other side of the Milky Way. When they left their world, they each claimed half of the galaxy. They figured that by splitting up, they doubled the chances of their species surviving."

"Well, as frightening as that is, you said they couldn't build the tool they need to complete the antenna. So they don't have any way to contact them."

"The three saucers that left here are going to the Othali power station on Puerto Rico. They're going to use the transmitter there to contact the other mother ship."

Malia stared at him in disbelief for a long moment. But then her heart jumped into her throat, and a wave of dread washed over her. *"We've got to stop them!"*

"My thought exactly," said Brian. *"But if that rescue team doesn't get here soon, it'll be too late."*

"*Hang on,*" said Malia, thinking it through. "*Why didn't they just start with that? Instead of trying to build their own first?*"

"*They didn't know about the Puerto Rico station. Only the other two. And they thought those were destroyed in the attack.*"

"*So, how did they find out about Puerto Rico?*"

"*During their battle with the chariot, they attacked Isis's computer, too. They downloaded an enormous amount of data, including Majestic's information about the power stations.*"

Malia sat quietly for a minute, contemplating the ramifications. They'd only managed to defeat the first mother ship because the Malor didn't know about Malia and Jaden then. Or that the Othali had come to investigate the beacon, too. They'd had the element of surprise on their side on two fronts. There was no such advantage this time. The Malor knew all about Malia and Jaden and the Othali, and if they had Isis's data, they'd be aware of the Collective's capabilities, too. As powerful as they'd become, there was no way Jaden and Malia could take out a fully operational mother ship.

"*Brian, if these Malor couldn't even build a transdimensional radio, then there's no way they could be the ones taking our people.*"

"*But who else could it be? They took Salvatore right before our eyes. And those Malor didn't look surprised to see him go. So I'm betting they've modified one of their existing drives for that purpose.*"

Malia shook her head. "*I don't buy that. Our people aren't here. I would sense them if they were. We looked everywhere. This is their base now; where else would they be taking them?*"

"*I don't know, but I can't believe there's* another *group of ancient aliens running around this planet. Wouldn't the Othali have detected them? They were here for millennia. Surely they would have crossed paths at some point."*

"The Anunnaki could have hidden from the Othali."

"I'm sorry. I don't think so. The simplest explanation is almost always the right one. We know *the Malor possess transdimensional technology. And we know this particular group of Malor has been working on it to adapt what they have for other purposes. So we just have to figure out* where *they're taking them."*

Malia was about to retort, but suddenly another voice touched her mind.

"Malia, it's me. Are you all right?"

"Jaden? Yeah, I'm fine. Are you here? In the Malor base?"

"We're up at the top of the ventilation shaft."

"Thank God. Now, listen carefully."

Chapter Twenty-five

Malia told Jaden everything they'd learned inside the bunker and warned him about their defensive capabilities. Jaden took a quick scan to confirm that she was right about there being two guards at the bottom of the shaft, then relayed Malia's information to Nadia.

"This could get messy," said Nadia. "Your telepathy doesn't work on the Malor, does it?"

"Only to a limited extent the last time we encountered them," Jaden replied. "But it doesn't matter. Malia says that their personal shielding blocks it. They must have found a way to let their own telepathic signals through, but not anyone else's."

"Which means we're going to have to get through the bottom of the shaft and take out the two guards before they warn the others about us," Nadia pointed out. "Otherwise, this is going to go to hell fast."

"Forget that," said Jaden. "Let me get into their control system. Brian got in and found that the doors, shields, and exterior weapons are on a separate machine, but he couldn't hack into it. So I'll go in and disable everything and open the doors. Then we can get our people out."

Nadia considered this for a moment. "Are you sure you can get into their secure system?"

"Pretty sure," Jaden said with a shrug. "But we won't know until I try it."

Nadia took a deep breath. "The other problem is that they could take our people hostage the moment they realize something's wrong. And if they *are* the ones delta shifting everyone, then we won't be able to get them back."

"It'll need to be a coordinated effort," said Jaden. "I'll alert Malia the moment I get the shields down, and then they can all fly before the Malor can grab them. They're shackled, but that won't stop them from moving. The real problem is that our weapons don't work against their personal shields."

"We can provide covering fire with the saucer's weapons," said Nadia. "There's a good chance their shields can't handle that kind of power."

Nadia contacted Anhur and let him know their plan. He approved.

"Commander, this is Jaden. What do you think about bringing the warship down here and bombarding this place once we've got our people out?"

"Yes, it would be best to put them out of commission," Anhur replied. "Hold on."

A moment later, another voice spoke through Jaden's implants. "Jaden, this is Malik. The only problem with destroying the base is that the Malor might be the ones delta shifting your people. So if they're keeping them in some sort of transdimensional bubble, the portal to that place might be here. And if that's the case, blowing it up might mean losing them forever."

"Would something like that show up on our scans?" asked Jaden.

"Sure. Theoretically. But our people have never managed to create a bubble like that, so it's impossible to say for sure."

"We'll make the final decision about this once our people are out," said Anhur. "But we'll move the warship into range just in case. So make your preparations, and we'll contact you again once we're in position."

Jaden knew that the warship would have to descend from orbit somewhere outside of the base's sensor range, then move in closer. Unlike the Martian vessels, the Othali warship would create a giant fireball as it passed through the atmosphere.

"Understood," Nadia replied.

Jaden contacted Malia again and let her know the plan. Then he left the airlock and squatted down by the ventilation shaft. He'd have to remain here; otherwise, he wouldn't be able to penetrate their shields telepathically.

Nadia moved the saucer down to the base of the ridge, fifty feet away from the hangar bay doors. They left the airlock and floated down to the surface. The warship contacted Nadia fifteen minutes later to let her know they were in position. Anhur gave them the go-ahead to proceed with the mission.

Taking a deep breath, Jaden reached out with his mind. He had no trouble locating the primary control system's neural processors.

It took him a few seconds to find the security node, but once he had, he wasted no time. The machine put up a good fight, trying to keep him out, but Jaden overwhelmed its defenses by sheer force of will. Luckily, the Malor had never imagined someone could penetrate their system the way he was doing and hadn't built in protections against it. Unlike the Anunnaki, it didn't seem like the Malor accessed their technology telepathically.

Jaden issued commands to drop the shields, take the weapon systems offline, and open the hangar bay doors. The moment he sensed the commands being processed, he reached out to Malia. "*This is it. Time to fly!*"

"*We're on our way,*" Malia told him.

Jaden flew down to Nadia's position on the ground before the doors were even open all the way. He could see the Malor scurrying around inside, trying to figure out what was going on. Their people were flying across the hangar bay toward the exit, but their Malor guards were firing their weapons at them. Malia flew out the entry, Brian close behind. Nadia's saucer fired several cannon shots, and sure enough, they packed enough power to burn through the Malor's personal shields, vaporizing their targets, including the two firing at their people.

But it was too late. One of the guards had hit Griffin mid-flight. He plummeted to the floor, still inside the base. Selena was behind him; seeing what had happened, she landed by his side. Several more Malor were running toward the pair. Nadia hit them with the saucer's plasma cannons. Jaden reached out telekinetically, lifting Griffin off the floor and bringing him outside to him, setting him gently on the ground. Selena followed him out as the saucer repeatedly fired, blasting the rest of the Malor and much of their equipment.

Jaden dropped to one knee to examine Griffin, gasping as he realized the extent of his injuries. The Malor weapon had torn several chunks out of his torso, leaving severe burns around the wounds. Griffin was unconscious.

Malia reached them then, tears streaking down her cheeks. The Malor had handcuffed her arms behind her back, but she used her powers to free herself. Falling to her knees, she grabbed Griffin's face with both hands, and Jaden knew she was penetrating his mind to heal him. He felt tears welling up in his eyes, too. The damage to Griffin's body was extreme; he didn't know if Malia would be able to help.

Suddenly, Griffin's eyes opened. He saw Jaden first, then spotted Malia. She took one of his hands in both of hers, and he said, "I'm sorry. Malia, I'm so sorry... please tell the others..."

Jaden didn't know what he was talking about. Malia held Griffin's gaze, and Jaden knew she was communicating with him telepathically. But then Griffin's eyes closed, and Malia sobbed, collapsing on top of him.

Griffin was gone.

Getting to his feet, Jaden took in his surroundings, realizing that Nadia was right next to them, looking on in horror. She told him that she'd managed to vaporize all the Malor and had sent the soldiers inside to search for stragglers.

"Jaden," Malia said between sobs. "It… it was Griffin."

"What?" he replied, meeting her gaze. "What are you talking about?"

Malia got to her feet, taking a steadying breath. "He was the one passing intel to Isis."

"*What*? No, no way. That can't be. Griffin wouldn't do that—"

"They had his sister!" Malia told him, her voice cracking. "Isis took Judith when her ship went down. They wiped her system to hide the evidence. And then Isis contacted Griffin and threatened to kill her unless he cooperated."

"That can't be," Jaden insisted. "They would have intercepted the transmission—"

"No. The signal was delta shifted. We were right: Isis managed to build a transdimensional radio. She reached him at the compound the first time, but he warned her that they were monitoring communications. So he erased the data and reprogrammed Vincent's saucer to alert *him* of any incoming transmissions. After that, Isis initiated communications through the saucer's system."

Jaden shook his head. This was too much to take in.

"There's more," Malia said shakily. "Griffin gave Isis the location of that planet the Othali were going to settle. That's where she wants to take her people."

Jaden felt his insides twist. Isis had compromised his best friend. Why hadn't he come to them for help? They could have found a way to save Judith. Jaden took a few steps away from the others, moving toward the Malor base as the soldiers emerged. They walked by him to confer with Nadia. He heard their leader telling her that none of the Malor had survived.

Jaden's eyes blurred with tears. Wiping them on his sleeve, he focused on the base, reaching out with his mind and tapping into the magnetic field.

"Jaden, no!" said Malia, coming up from behind him and putting her hand on his shoulder.

He shook her off, turning to face Nadia. "Did the warship detect any kind of transdimensional bubble inside?"

Nadia shook her head. "No. Nothing."

Turning back toward the ridge, Jaden focused with all his might, hitting it with everything he had and screaming at the top of his lungs, his rage pouring into the effort. Finally, the ground began to shake, and suddenly the mountain imploded, crushing everything inside.

Chapter Twenty-six

Jaden had collapsed after destroying the mountain, sobbing and crying. Malia felt devastated, too, but was keeping her composure. For now. Together, she and Nadia managed to coax Jaden back up to the saucer. Then, Malia used her powers to remove the others' handcuffs. Once they were all inside, Brian went up to the cockpit with Nadia. Malia sat down next to Jaden on the main level, each of them leaning against one of the pods.

"I can't believe he betrayed us like this," Jaden said after a minute. "Griffin, man..." He choked up for a moment and couldn't continue. "Why would he do it? He had to know we would have found a way to rescue Judith. So why didn't he come to us?"

"He was terrified of Isis," Malia told him. "I could sense it in him at the end."

"But why?" Jaden demanded. "We beat her ass, and he knew it."

"Put yourself in his shoes," she said, tears slipping down her cheeks. "He grew up in a Majestic compound. They knew Isis only as the mysterious Sphinx. All of them held her in fear and awe. Don't forget that their organization was like a cult."

"Yeah, I guess," he said with a sigh.

"But... now I understand why he was always so reluctant to let me inside his head," said Malia.

"He was worried you'd discover his secret," Jaden replied. "Damn. I still wish he'd let us know."

"I f-feel so guilty," Malia told him with a sob. "I gave him information from the council meetings. *I* was responsible for the leaks. He was relaying everything I told him to Isis."

"You can't take the blame for that," Jaden said, shaking his head. "I told him plenty of stuff, too. Hell, he was on the security force, so there was plenty he knew that didn't come from either of us."

Malia was heartbroken; she shook with silent sobs for a moment. Griffin had been her lover and best friend. And just like that... "I can't believe he's g-gone."

Jaden nodded. "Me too."

"His dying wish," Malia began, suddenly feeling her throat constricting. She took a deep breath. "He wanted us to rescue Judith."

"Yeah," said Jaden, closing his eyes tight for a moment. "We need to do that. And this time, we're not letting Isis get away."

Malia had to agree. As long as she survived, Isis would find a way to cause misery for their people. But they had more immediate issues at the moment.

As if she'd been reading Malia's mind, Nadia contacted her through her implants, asking her and Jaden to come up to the cockpit. Malia was momentarily surprised to see that they were streaking across the sky and that Commander Anhur's hologram was sitting in one of the seats, between Nadia and Brian. But remembering what they'd found on the Malor control system, she knew she shouldn't have been surprised at all.

Malia and Jaden each took one of the remaining seats. Checking the control system, Malia could see that they were en route to Puerto Rico, flying at top speed. Of course, Isis's people would be able to detect them this way, but Malia knew their need for haste trumped all other concerns.

"We don't have much time, so I'll make this brief," Anhur told them. "We incinerated the remains of the Malor base, just to be thorough. Right now, we are on course for Puerto Rico to provide support for your team, although we'll arrive a few minutes behind you. We've dispatched two other saucers to eliminate the Miami and Bermuda power stations. We don't want the Malor to have any backup plan available to them.

"I don't need to tell you how critical it is that we prevent them from sending any kind of transmission. Were this second mother ship to come here... well, you all know what we'd be facing.

"There's a good chance the Malor will have locked us out of our own systems by the time you get there. So don't waste any time trying to gain access. Just hit that station with everything you've got."

"Yes, sir," said Nadia.

Anhur nodded to them. "Good hunting." His hologram faded away.

Minutes later, they reached Puerto Rico and moved into position near the island's northwest corner.

"I'm not detecting any Malor vessels, but I'm reading nine

Malor life signs inside the power station..." Nadia said with a look of confusion. "Shit. They've raised the station's shields."

"Can't we get through them with the plasma cannons?" asked Malia.

"Maybe. But it's going to take a prolonged bombardment."

"We've still got to try," said Brian.

"Of course," Nadia agreed. "But the moment we open fire, the Malor vessels will strike. We can't see their saucers, but they're out there somewhere. It would have been an easy hit-and-run were it not for those shields."

"They haven't initiated the transdimensional beacon yet," said Jaden. "I can access the system and shut everything down."

"Do it," said Nadia.

Jaden stared out the windows, his brow furrowed in concentration. Malia knew he was taking control of the station's neural processors. But at that moment, a red beam shot out of the ocean, piercing the night sky. Malia accessed the saucer's control system through her implants to monitor the situation.

"Jaden! Now!" Nadia screamed.

The saucer's sensors detected the station's shields dropping, but the transmission continued.

"JADEN!" Nadia repeated. But at that moment, she fired the plasma cannons.

Finally, the transmitter went down, and the beam of light disappeared. At the same moment, the plasma shots hit the station, incinerating it in an enormous fireball. Nadia engaged the engines, but the Malor saucers fired on them. Through the cockpit windows, Malia could see that they'd vaporized a giant section of the hull.

"We've lost engines," Nadia announced. "We're going down!"

The saucer was plunging toward the ocean. Malia reached out with her mind, arresting their motion just before impact. But as she moved them toward land, there was a burst of laser fire above them and three giant explosions. The warship had arrived, taking out the Malor saucers.

Once they'd reached the shore, Malia set them down on the beach. She moved down to the main level with Jaden, Nadia, and Brian. They found Selena there with two of the soldiers, clinging to pods along the remaining section of the wall. But the other soldiers and Griffin's body were gone. Malia fought back a sob.

"So… are we screwed?" Jaden asked.

"It's hard to tell," Nadia said with a sigh. "As you saw, they did manage to activate the beacon."

"But it was only for seconds," said Brian. "And if it was like the transmission that brought the first mother ship, then it was only a general distress call. So those other Malor might not detect it. And even if they do, they could ignore it."

Nadia shook her head. "They focused the beam on a location on the other side of the galaxy, where we know the other mother ship to be. And they piggybacked their own signal on the distress call. That's probably why it took them so long to initiate the transmission."

"I think we're in trouble," said Jaden.

Malia felt panic threatening to overtake her. She forced herself to take a deep breath and remain calm.

"Shit," Brian muttered.

Anhur sent a saucer to take them up to the warship. The wrecked saucer was damaged beyond repair, so they vaporized its remains to make sure nothing important fell into the wrong hands. Once onboard, Malia and Jaden headed up to Anhur's conference room with Nadia and Brian. Anhur and his staff were already there. The newcomers took seats around the end of the table. Nadia gave Anhur the same report she'd shared with the others down on the surface.

Anhur took a deep breath. "What information was in the Malor signal?"

"Not much. Only that there were three dozen survivors here from the first mother ship. And that the Othali are still here, and that the Collective is sharing technology with the humans," she added with a shrug. "I'm not sure why they'd bother reporting that part."

Brian sighed, covering his face in his hands.

"I'm going to guess that the first mother ship probably communicated with this other one once its fate became clear during the invasion," said Anhur. "These other Malor must have known that there *could* be survivors. Yet, in all this time, they haven't attempted a rescue. Or an invasion of their own. Do we have any reason to believe this new transmission changes anything?"

"Yeah, right?" said Jaden with a hopeful tone. "And now there *aren't* any Malor survivors here because we just killed them. No need for the other ones to bother making the trip!"

"They have no way of knowing that," Brian pointed out, his expression grim. "But I doubt they'd come here for the survivors anyway. The commander's right. They surely would have known that the other mother ship perished and that there *could* be survivors. Yet they didn't come."

"But?" asked Nadia, looking worried.

"But they *will* come now. The Malor are a predator species. They wait until a world reaches a certain level of technological sophistication before invading. In part, this is because it makes it easier for them to harvest the world's resources. As we know, they use existing infrastructure. But there's more to it than that. To stay dominant in the galaxy, they've got to eliminate other species before they become sufficiently advanced to pose a threat to them."

Malia suddenly realized where he was going with this. "And now that the Collective is sharing technology with the humans, they'll see Earth as a potential threat."

"Yes, exactly," Brian agreed. "More, they know that the Othali possess the ability to delta shift. And if they were to share that technology along with their weapons, then it would only be a matter of time before humans could challenge them."

"But that's insane," said Jaden. "The Othali *aren't* sharing transdimensional tech with the humans."

"And our people possessed that technology for almost two hundred years before the Malor attacked," Anhur told them. "They must have had scout ships on our world just like they did on Earth. So if what you're saying is correct, then why did they wait so long before targeting Othal?"

"They've been roving the galaxy for hundreds of thousands of years," Brian said with a shrug. "On their time scale, two hundred years is the blink of an eye. Look, maybe this second mother ship won't show up *tomorrow*. But they would have targeted us eventually, even without that transmission. And that signal will almost certainly accelerate the timetable. So one way or another, we need to prepare."

"How?" asked Malia. "It's a Malor mother ship. We only defeated the first one because they didn't know about Jaden and me—or the Othali warship. We won't have that luxury next time."

"The Anunnaki," said Jaden.

"*What*?" said Brian, as all eyes turned to Jaden.

Jaden took a few minutes to tell them everything he'd discovered with Ezra, including the Anunnaki outpost on Earth and their Moonbase, as well as the information about their prison.

"Wait a minute," said Brian when he was done. "You're telling me that as advanced as they were, there was another species even more powerful than them?"

Jaden nodded. "That's what the alien in the recording said. And then he vanished in a flash of light. So the aliens who imprisoned them must be the same ones taking our people. We've proven beyond the shadow of a doubt that it wasn't the Malor. So if we can find them, whoever they are, then maybe we can get our people back *and* get them to help us with our Malor problem."

"If they are the ones abducting your people, what makes you think they'd be willing to help against the Malor?" Anhur asked.

"You're right," Jaden admitted. "I guess we have no way of knowing that. But maybe the Anunnaki, then. That one I saw in the Malor data wiped out their ship with a wave of his hand. If we can find that prison, and find a way to free them, then maybe they'd be willing to help us in return. Against the Malor, and with getting our people back."

"Wait a minute," Nadia said, her eyebrows raised. "You told us that entire civilizations disappeared everywhere these Anunnaki went. And these are the people you want to free from prison?"

"We don't know that they were harming them," Jaden said with a shrug. "Ezra believed they were taking the people to their homeworld to live. But we don't have any proof they were the ones responsible for the disappearances in the first place."

"Correlation doesn't necessarily imply causation," said Malia.

"Right, thank you," Jaden agreed. "And one of those Anunnaki was living among the Mayans. They buried him in this fancy tomb. That sure doesn't make it seem like he posed any danger to them."

The others considered this in silence for a moment.

"You said the Anunnaki recording showed the Collective's compound as the location of this prison?" Anhur asked. "But your scans showed nothing in the area that could have been it?"

"Right," Jaden confirmed. "I mean, whoever imprisoned the Anunnaki must have been ridiculously advanced. So, maybe they put them in some kind of transdimensional bubble like Malik was talking about. But our sensors didn't show any sign of that anywhere near the compound."

"You said the hybrids got to the Moonbase before you?" asked

Brian. Jaden nodded. "Then that's it. Isis must have altered the recording to hide the prison's true location."

"Which means that Isis must have already found it," said Malia. "She altered that hologram to make sure we were chasing our tails while she made contact with the Anunnaki."

"We need to go to the Moon," Brian told them. "Now that we know what she did, there's a good chance we can recover the original data."

"How could Isis have altered that hologram if the base's AI is so advanced?" asked Nadia.

"I tried getting into the protected area of their data storage units, and I couldn't do it," said Jaden. "So I doubt Isis could, even if she's developed the same ability with neural processors that I have, and we don't know if she has or not. But this message wasn't in the protected area. I'm pretty sure I could have modified it if I'd wanted."

"Without the AI knowing about it?" Nadia asked skeptically.

"Yeah, that would've been tough," Jaden admitted. "But this is Isis we're talking about. She's a master of deception. I bet she could've pulled it off."

"But why go to the trouble?" asked Nadia. "Why not erase the entire message?"

"I'm sure the AI would have noticed *that,*" said Brian. "The only hope it has of reuniting with its people is for someone to find that message."

"Well, we know for sure this prison isn't at the compound," said Anhur.

"How do we know that?" asked Nadia. "Their technology is way beyond ours—"

"Because Isis hasn't turned up there," Anhur replied, talking over her. "That alone makes me believe she must have altered that hologram. I agree with Brian. It's time to go to the Moon."

Chapter Twenty-seven

Jaden got to his feet. "Hell, yeah. Let's get this done!"

"We should take a saucer there," Brian suggested. "It's faster, for one thing. And if Isis realizes that the warship has left, she might use the opportunity to attack the compound."

"I agree," said Anhur. "But take two saucers. Jaden on one and Malia on the other. If the hybrids are still there, we want to be ready for them."

Jaden and Malia hurried down to the docking port with Brian and Nadia. Anhur had ordered two dozen soldiers to meet them there. Jaden boarded one of the saucers with Nadia and half of the Othali, while Malia and Brian moved into the other with the rest of the soldiers.

Nadia took them out of the docking port and set a course for the Moon. Malia piloted the second vessel. Once they were on their way, Jaden and Malia used their powers to accelerate them.

"Well, Jaden," Brian said over his implants, "it appears I owe you an apology. I'm sorry for not believing you about these Anunnaki. It turns out Ezra was right all along."

"No worries," Jaden replied with a grin. "We got there in the end."

"It is astounding, though... Not one, but two more alien species that have interacted with Earth over the eons. Makes you wonder how many more are out there."

"It's like Carl explained," said Jaden. "A lot of civilizations could have developed in the twelve billion years since the galaxy formed."

They reached the Moon and inserted the ships into lunar orbits. Jaden reached out with his mind as they moved around the far side, searching for the presence of any hybrids in the area. Sure enough, he found them.

"We've got three enemy saucers out here," he told the others through his implants.

"I'm sensing them, too," Malia agreed.

"They don't seem to have noticed us," Brian observed. "Jaden, I'm not detecting any kind of access point to the base's control system. Can we access this AI from out here?"

"Yeah, hang on," Jaden replied. Then, reaching out telepathically, he contacted the Moonbase's AI and explained the reason for their visit.

"*That's impossible*," the AI replied. "*Nobody could alter the message without my knowledge.*"

"*Yeah, yeah, well, we'd just like to check it to make sure. Can you let us access the system electronically from out here?*"

"*Not through the shields.*"

"*All right, then can you drop the shields?*"

"*One of my people would have to authorize that. You will have access if you enter the base, but I assure you, nobody has tampered with the message.*"

"We're going to have to do it from inside the base," Jaden notified the others. "Let's take out those hybrid saucers, first, though. We don't want any nasty surprises waiting for us on our way back out."

"Do you think you two could crash them into the Moon?" asked Nadia. "We've got the element of surprise, but if it comes to a firefight, their capabilities are identical to ours, and they outnumber us three to two."

"That's going to be tough out here," said Malia. "I don't know if we can overpower their shields without the Earth's magnetic field."

"Let's do it telepathically instead," Jaden suggested. "I'll take over their control system."

"Wait, I didn't think Malia could do that?" asked Brian.

"I can't," Malia replied. "Jaden likes rubbing it in. But don't worry. I can force the pilot to crash."

"Let's coordinate the attack," Nadia said. "We'll hit the third ship with a full weapons barrage from both of our saucers."

Jaden calculated the enemy ships' spatial coordinates and entered the data into their control system. They selected their targets, and then Nadia initiated a countdown. Jaden reached out telepathically when the time came, accessing one saucer's neural processors. He set a course for the lunar surface and engaged their engines at full power. At the same time, Nadia and Brian both opened fire on one of the others. Moments later, Jaden's target slammed into the Moon in a fiery explosion, followed quickly by Malia's. But then Nadia said, "Shit."

"What's wrong?" asked Jaden.

"Our target got away," Nadia replied.

"How can that be?" said Jaden. "With that much firepower, you shouldn't have had any trouble."

"There was nothing at the coordinates you gave us," she said. "It must have altered course before we could fire."

Reaching out with his mind, Jaden tried to locate the missing ship. But he couldn't sense them anywhere. Malia reported that she couldn't find them, either.

"They're probably calling for reinforcements," said Jaden. "Let's go inside and get this done before anyone else shows up." They moved in closer to the crater masking the entry to the base, and Jaden contacted the AI again. It opened the portal for them. Nadia moved their saucer through the force field and into the access tunnel, Malia's ship right behind them.

Once they'd reached the hangar bay, Jaden reached out telepathically to make sure there were no hybrids inside. But he found a dozen of them waiting to ambush them in the passage to the central hub.

"*You didn't tell me the others were here*!" he complained to the AI.

"*You didn't ask.*"

Jaden rolled his eyes. "*What are they doing here*?"

"*They've been trying to access the data on the primary storage system.*"

"*Have they succeeded*?"

"*Of course not.*"

Jaden let the others know that they had company. Then he targeted the hybrids with the saucer's weapons and vaporized them.

He checked the rest of the complex once more to make sure nobody else was waiting for them, but it was empty.

Nadia stayed behind on the saucer while Jaden left through the airlock and met Malia and Brian down on the flight deck. He led them through the tunnel and into the central hub.

"This is incredible," Brian said, scanning the area when they reached the command center. "Their technology is radically superior to ours. Looks like… organic quantum processors with DNA storage devices. Wow."

"Yeah, pretty crazy, right?" Jaden agreed. "Can you access the message through your implants?"

Brian focused for a moment. "Yes, here it is." The holographic recording appeared next to him and began playing. "Give me a moment." The hologram disappeared again, and Brian's eyes went unfocused for a minute. "Well, this system is unlike anything I've seen before. But it does appear the section of the hologram showing the prison's location is much newer than the rest of it."

"So Isis definitely altered it," Jaden said.

"Someone did. I cannot determine who or when, and I can't seem to access the overwritten data. But yes. Someone changed the map for sure."

Jaden reached out to the AI telepathically and told it what Brian had found.

"*That cannot be.*" But then a moment later, it added, "*This is shocking, but you are correct. That woman who came here with the others must have changed the data.*"

"*You mean Isis*?" Jaden asked.

"*Yes. It seems she distracted me with her efforts to access the primary storage system long enough to alter the welcome message. I must apologize.*"

"*Yeah, no worries,*" Jaden said impatiently. "*Can you recover the original message*?"

"*Yes. If you access it now, you will see the restored data.*"

"Play it again," Jaden said to Brian.

He did and moved to the segment showing the Earth. The view zoomed in on an area in Siberia, only about five hundred miles south of the Malor base. Then it froze, and a red circle appeared over a massive clearing in a forest. Brian gasped.

"What is it?" Jaden asked.

"I know where this is," said Brian. "It's a place called Tunguska. There was some sort of impact event there in 1908. It destroyed over 800 square miles of forest with the force of a twelve-megaton bomb."

"Seriously? What could have caused that?"

"Nobody knows for sure. Scientists believe it was a meteoroid, but nobody has ever found an impact crater. For years, the leading theory was that the object exploded in the atmosphere, and the shockwave caused the destruction on the surface. But more recently, some have postulated that it could have been an iron-heavy asteroid that bounced off our atmosphere and back into space. It must have come in at a shallow angle. If it had been a direct impact, it could have destroyed all life on Earth.

"But after seeing this, I'd say both theories are wrong. It must have been the enemy aliens creating the prison for the Anunnaki."

"That's where we need to go," said Jaden. "Come on!"

He hurried toward the tunnel, Brian and Malia right behind him, but just then, Nadia contacted them over their implants.

"We've got a problem over here," she said.

"We're on our way," Jaden told her.

They reached the hangar bay and boarded the saucers. Jaden flew up to the cockpit. "What's going on?"

"Someone buried us down here. They blew out the crater walls and filled the basin with debris."

"Great," Jaden replied sardonically, scanning the area with the ship's sensors to get a look himself. "*The hybrids filled the crater with rubble,*" he told the AI. "*Can you lower the shields up there so we can blast our way out?*"

"*Not without authorization from my people.*"

"Yeah, yeah," Jaden said out loud. "Malia, we're going to have to clear a path with our telekinesis."

"Understood."

They took the saucers up to the top of the access tunnel. Gazing up through the cockpit windows, Jaden reached out with his mind and began clearing a path through the debris. He could feel Malia's doing the same thing. But every time they moved some of the rubble out of the crater, more slid down to replace it. Jaden felt sure they could have blown it all out at once if they had access to the Earth's magnetic field, but it took much longer without that.

But finally, they managed to create a clear path. Nadia was about to take them through the force field, but Jaden said, "Wait."

Reaching out with his mind, he checked to see if the hybrid saucer was still out there. He found much more than that. "I'm sensing at least a dozen ships out there," he reported to the others. "They only buried us in here to buy time for their reinforcements to arrive."

"Now what?" Brian asked through his implants.

"They shouldn't be able to detect us as long as we keep our shields up, right?" said Jaden.

"No, but they will detect the disturbance we create on our way through the force field," said Nadia.

"And then they'll hit us with everything they've got," Brian added.

"Malia, we'll have to crash them all into the surface before we go," Jaden told her.

"I've got a better idea," she replied. "If we exit the tunnel at full power, we'll be clear by the time their weapons make impact. And if we change course the moment we're out and drop engines below the detection threshold, they won't be able to track us, either."

"Good thinking," said Nadia. "Let's do it. But they're sure to figure out we're heading straight to Earth, so I want you two monitoring our back trail. If you sense any pursuit, take them out before they can fire on us."

"Sure thing," Malia replied.

Nadia set a course and engaged the engines at full power. They blew through the force field, and Jaden detected explosions at the tunnel entry moments later on the ship's sensors. But they were clear and on a course around the Moon.

Neither Jaden nor Malia detected anyone behind them at first, but once they'd left lunar orbit, Jaden sensed several saucers approaching at high velocity.

"Incoming," he said to Malia.

"I see them."

Reaching out with his mind, Jaden accessed the nearest ship's control system and triggered an overload in its engines. Seconds later, the saucer went up in a giant fireball. Malia forced one of the pilots to crash his ship into another, taking them both out. After that, the others moved out of range.

"Good work, you two," Nadia said. "I've alerted the warship to the situation. They're going to meet us near Tunguska."

Chapter Twenty-eight

They reached Earth, and Malia followed Nadia's saucer through the atmosphere, approaching Tunguska from the west. It was a little after sunrise here. As they drew closer, Malia scanned the area, bringing up a holographic image in the center console.

"I'll be damned," Brian muttered.

There was an enormous clearing in the trees and a massive excavation project in the center of that. Isis and her people had dug a giant shaft into the Earth, and scans showed a tunnel complex far below the ground. But there was a vast spherical area in the center of the complex that the sensors couldn't penetrate.

"Whoever imprisoned the Anunnaki must have planted... whatever that is down there," said Brian. "The Tunguska event wasn't a meteorite or an asteroid, after all. It was *this*."

"I'm getting some strange readings down there," Malia told the others. "Sensors can't penetrate the central structure, but the transdimensional radiation it's emitting is off the charts."

"We're detecting the same thing," Nadia agreed.

"The entire complex is crawling with hybrids," said Malia. "Sensors show a few hundred of them on the surface and underground."

"They're not bothering to make themselves invisible," Nadia noted.

"Yeah, that's because they've got about a hundred saucers in the air up here," Jaden reported. "Maybe more. The airspace is thick with them. I'm sensing hybrid minds everywhere I look."

"Sensors aren't showing any kind of computer or control system for that... thing," said Nadia.

Malia reached out with her mind, trying to understand what was going on in the central core. But she couldn't get through its outer barrier. "I can't get in there telepathically," she told the others. "It's weird... it almost felt like there was some kind of psychic wind pushing against me."

"Psychic wind?" Jaden asked with a note of derision in his tone.

"You try it," Malia told him.

A few seconds later, Jaden said, "Wow, you're right. I've never experienced anything like that before. I don't sense any kind of control system, either."

"Anhur here. I've asked Lieutenant Malik to take a look at these readings. Stand by."

Moments later, Malik said, "Hey, everyone. I'm not sure about this, but I believe what we're seeing down there is a transdimensional bubble. Most of that thing isn't in our universe, and that's why we're having so much trouble detecting anything."

"Not in our universe?" said Jaden. "What does that even mean?"

"It's a structure that someone constructed in extradimensional space," said Malik. "Or I guess, based on what we know about the

Tunguska event, it's more accurate to say someone placed it here. But it doesn't exist entirely within our everyday spacetime continuum. Now, I risked an active scan to see if I could penetrate it that way. Only for a fraction of a second, so I don't think our friends down there detected it. And there is one little section of that thing that is solidly here in our universe. I believe it must be the portal to the rest of the bubble. But the scan wasn't able to penetrate that portal, so I have no idea what might be inside."

Malik sent the active scan data. Malia added it to her scans to plot the portal's position relative to the rest of the complex, then sent the combined data to the others.

"We're going to have to go down there," said Jaden. "Malia and I might be able to communicate with whoever's inside that thing if we can get closer to that portal."

"Out of the question," said Anhur. "One misstep, and the hybrids will realize you're there. Isis must have her entire force here, which means the chariot is probably nearby, too. If they capture you, a rescue may not be possible."

"We've got to try," said Malia. "Salvatore, Venus, and Mom might be inside that thing. And if we can make contact, they might be able to tell us how to free them. Or, at the very least, the Anunnaki in there might be able to help us find their jailers. One way or another, those beings have the answers we need."

"What about this," said Brian. "Let's capture one of the hybrids. See what they know about this place. It's clear they've been working on this for quite some time. We're starting from scratch here, so this might be a good way to give ourselves a crash course."

"We'll have to find someone who knows something," said Nadia.

"Of course," Brian agreed. "But our scans are working right up to the perimeter of that bubble. They've got a team at the portal. One of them is bound to be in the know."

"How do we get to them?" asked Jaden. "Going down there to abduct one of them runs the same risk of detection as trying to get to that portal."

"Not if we bring them to us," Malia replied. "Every hybrid I've scanned is wearing an emitter; they're just not using it. So once someone from their portal team comes up to the surface, you and I can grab them. One of us can penetrate their mind and force them to go invisible while the other moves them into the airlock."

"That would work," said Anhur.

But at that moment, Malia spotted someone else making their way down the main shaft. "Well, look who's here," she said to the others.

"Is that Isis?" Jaden asked.

"Sure is," said Malia. She tracked their nemesis as she moved through the complex toward the portal. Then she reached out with her mind to get a closer look. Careful not to alert Isis to her presence, she tried to sense what she was doing. And as she'd suspected, Isis was attempting to communicate telepathically with the beings inside the bubble. Malia could feel her using her powers but couldn't tell if she was getting through to them or not. But she kept it up for several minutes. Malia told the others what she was witnessing. But then

Isis abruptly stormed away, flying back to the main shaft and up to the surface. "I couldn't tell what was going on in there, but her body language certainly isn't conveying happiness."

"All right, the rest of the portal team seems to be breaking up," said Brian. "If you two are going to grab one of them, this is probably the time to do it."

Malia checked the sensors. Sure enough, the other hybrids around the portal were moving out of the complex. She monitored their progress and got a visual scan of each of them as they reached the surface. One of them stood out. She was leading a group of four other hybrids, and based on how she carried herself, Malia suspected she was the one in authority.

"Jaden, let's take the older Black woman at the head of that group that just came out," she said to her brother.

"Not now; the others will see it."

"Obviously," Malia replied. "Hang on—she's moving away from the group." But there were so many hybrids down there that this would be difficult to pull off without anyone noticing. Malia was about to give up and look for someone else when the woman rose off the ground. She realized she must be flying up to one of the saucers. "Jaden, now! I'll make her invisible, and you grab her."

"I'm on it."

Reaching out with her mind, Malia penetrated the woman's thoughts. She took over completely, accessing her implants to activate her emitter, making her invisible, and to sever her communications. Then she knocked her out.

"I've got her," said Jaden. "Bringing her into the airlock now."

"Put her in one of your pods," she told Jaden. "I'll be right there."

Malia went invisible as she moved down to the airlock, then left her saucer and flew to Jaden's ship. She deactivated her emitter once she was inside. Jaden had their prisoner in one of the pods already.

"She's all yours," Jaden told her.

Malia nodded. She accessed the pod's control system and administered an injection to inhibit the woman's motor control, ensuring she couldn't use her fake tooth. Then she penetrated her mind telepathically, returning her to consciousness.

"*You two*," the woman said in her mind. "*What do you want with me?*"

"*Has Isis made contact with the Anunnaki inside the transdimensional bubble?*" Malia demanded.

The woman made no direct reply. But Malia could tell from her sense of disappointment that she had not.

"*So, Isis hasn't made contact, then*," Malia said.

The woman gave the mental equivalent of a sigh. "*You're going to pull the answers you want directly from my mind even if I refuse to cooperate.*"

It wasn't a question, but Malia replied, "*Yes.*"

"*Isis can sense them in there. Telepathically. But only when she goes down to the portal. There are hundreds of them. She can feel their desire to escape, but no, she has not been able to make contact.*"

"*Have your people found any kind of control system?*"

"*We think so. But it's woven into the structure of the bubble. We can't access it. The technology is radically advanced—so much so that 'technology' may not be the right word."*

"*What do you mean?*"

"*It almost seems like the entire thing is biological in nature. We haven't been able to penetrate the barrier with our scans, but the barrier itself has a cell structure. It doesn't register as living tissue, but we've detected biological processes. Respiration chief among them.*"

"*That thing is* breathing?"

"*Yes. We also believe it's metabolizing thermal energy from the Earth. It's also demonstrated an ability to heal itself.*"

"*How would you know that?*"

The woman was reluctant to respond. But a memory floated to the surface—a group of hybrids firing laser rifles at the area around the portal.

"*You tried cutting through the barrier with weapons?*"

Another mental sigh. "*It didn't work. The outer membrane heals itself almost instantaneously. So at first, we didn't think we were damaging it at all. But scans revealed that we were creating small incisions in the cell walls, but they were healing faster than we could overcome.*"

Malia could sense that the woman was holding something back. Once she focused on it, the idea revealed itself to her. "*Isis is planning on hitting it with a massive barrage? Firing weapons from all your saucers at once?*"

"*Only as a last resort. We've calculated that it could be enough energy to overwhelm that thing's healing abilities.*"

"What is Isis waiting for?"

"As you already know, we've got teams at the Anunnaki Moonbase and their Earth outpost. We're trying to crack their systems and see if we can learn anything about this structure. But if she gets what she wants, then we may no longer need to get inside this thing."

"Why?"

"Haven't you figured it out yet? We only want their transdimensional technology. If we can acquire it from the Anunnaki systems, then we're done here."

"She's going to an awful lot of trouble. Why haven't you tried taking what you want from the Othali warship?"

"Too risky. You people left us with only one chariot and eliminated our ability to build another. Our weapons are no match for the warship. Meanwhile, this radically advanced technology is just sitting here for the taking."

Again, Malia could tell she was holding something back. The woman tried to stop her from surfacing it, but Malia quickly overpowered her. Isis was waiting for her twins to grow into their powers. She hoped that Jaden's clone would develop the same ability he possessed to access neural processors telepathically, in which case they could take whatever they wanted from the Othali data banks. Isis had tried replicating Jaden's new power numerous times but was unsuccessful.

"Isis warned us that your powers would be stronger now," the woman said. Malia could sense her irritation at having her thoughts taken from her so easily.

"*Isis was able to communicate with the Anunnaki AI*," Malia pointed out, ignoring her comment.

"*Only because that system was built to interact telepathically. The neural processors our people and the Othali use were not.*"

Malia nodded; that made sense. "*You've been very helpful. Thank you.*" Malia put her under again.

Chapter Twenty-nine

Jaden listened as Malia told everyone what she'd learned through their implants. "We need to go down there," he said when she was done. "Malia and I might be able to communicate with the Anunnaki if we can get closer to that portal."

"Isis couldn't," Brian pointed out. "What makes you think you could?"

"Our powers have developed more than hers," said Jaden. "I can control neural processors telepathically, and she can't, for example. Just because she couldn't make contact doesn't mean we can't."

"It's dangerous," said Anhur. "There are hundreds of hybrids down there. If Isis is going to try breaking that structure open by force, we should wait and see what happens with that effort first."

"We can't wait that long!" said Jaden. "Our *mom* is probably in there, along with Salvatore and Venus."

"We don't know that," Nadia reminded him.

"I agree with Jaden," said Malia. "We don't know for sure that our people are in there, but if we can make contact, we could confirm it. And there's no telling if Isis's plan will work. For all we know, she could end up destroying the portal, trapping the people inside forever."

"Let us make the attempt," Jaden pleaded.

There was no reply from anyone for a moment until Anhur said, "This is not our decision. It's a Collective matter."

"And that puts it squarely on my shoulders," Brian said. "If I authorize this, and you two get hurt—or worse—your mother will have my head."

"And if you don't, we'll probably never see her again," Jaden replied.

"All right," he agreed finally. "Go. Do it. But no unnecessary risks. If at any point you feel that proceeding would compromise your safety, then abort and get your asses back up here. Agreed?"

"Yes," said Jaden.

"You have our word," Malia agreed. Then she caught Jaden's eye and said out loud, "I'm going to hold you to it."

Jaden nodded. He made to grab a plasma cannon from the weapons compartment, but Malia pointed out that those would be too bulky with all the hybrids in the area. If they bumped one of them against someone, it was all over. Instead, they each grabbed a laser pistol, made themselves invisible, and disembarked through the airlock. Malia led the way, and they flew down the central shaft. They flew around numerous hybrids coming and going to different areas of the complex. Finally, they found the passage leading to the portal near the bottom. This area was still empty, and they had no trouble making it to their destination.

"*This is the weirdest thing I've ever seen,*" Jaden told Malia telepathically. The portal itself looked like a pool of water embedded in the rock, except it was suspended vertically. He touched it with one finger, and the surface rippled with waves, but he couldn't push through it.

"*Isis was right*," Malia said. "*I can sense them in there.*"

Jaden reached out with his mind, trying to penetrate the barrier. He still couldn't get through it—it felt like the portal was pushing back. But he could also feel the minds of the beings trapped in there, too many to count. Jaden focused on individual thought patterns, trying to identify them and see if he could find their missing people, but it was no use. Other than a general impression of individual minds, he couldn't sense anything more specific. So instead, he chose one and attempted to make contact. But again, he felt the portal resisting his effort.

Expanding his focus to include the entire structure, Jaden tried to find its control system. Again, the hybrid was right: Jaden *could* sense a consciousness there. But try as he might, he couldn't make contact with that, either. And without being able to find a centralized processor, it was impossible to force his way in, as he did with the other neural systems he'd encountered.

"*Jaden, this portal is functioning as a force field*," Malia told him. "*It's similar to the Malor holographic shields, but it's using transdimensional energy.*"

"*You think we can create an opening through it like we did at the Malor base?*"

"*That's exactly what I think.*"

Jaden could sense her reaching out with her mind, trying to

create a rift in the portal's surface. He added his power to hers, and slowly, they disrupted the flow of energy. Suddenly, Jaden felt someone's thoughts touch his mind. It was weak, but it grew stronger as they increased the disruption.

"*Jaden*?" a voice said in his head. He could sense the being's mind now, but it was nobody he recognized.

"*Yes. Who are you*?"

"*You may call me Enki.*"

"*Are you one of the Anunnaki*?"

"*Yes, Jaden. That is correct.*"

"*Some of our people have disappeared—are they in there with you*?"

"*Melissa, Venus, and Salvatore are here. The beings who imprisoned us brought them very recently.*"

Jaden felt his heartbeat accelerating. "*Why? What do they want with them*?"

"*I do not know.*"

"*Who are these people who imprisoned you? Where can we find them*?"

"*We call them the Founders. Their species was the first in the galaxy to achieve technological intelligence billions of years ago. They rule with an iron fist, and any species that violates their edicts faces the consequences. But you cannot find them. They do not exist on your plane of existence.*"

"*Then how do we get our people out of there*?"

"*Melissa has told me about the way your abilities have developed. I believe that you, Jaden, possess the power to free your people—and mine.*"

Jaden started as if an electric shock had passed through his body, so surprised was he by this statement. "*What? How? I don't—*"

But at that moment, Brian intruded on his thoughts through his implants. "Malia and Jaden, you've got incoming!"

"Hang on," Jaden replied. "We're almost done!"

"*Jaden—they're coming*!" Malia said telepathically. "*We've got to get out of here*!"

"*Malia, no! I made contact with one of the Anunnaki. Our people are in there! He says I have the power to free them*!"

"*You* promised! *We've got to get out of here before they catch us*!"

Jaden reluctantly agreed. At least a dozen hybrids were approaching the same way they'd come, so Malia led them farther up the tunnel. But as they neared an intersection, they detected a dozen more hybrids closing in quickly from this direction, too.

"*We're trapped*!" Malia told him.

Jaden reached out telepathically, penetrating the mind of the nearest hybrid. But before he could knock him out, the hybrid kicked him out of his mind. Jaden tried another one with the same result.

"*Shit, they're all Omega Group*," he told Malia.

"*Who?*"

"*The ones Isis trained specially to fight* us. *She must have brought them here because she knew we'd show up eventually*."

"*What do we do now?*"

"*Let's go back the other way*," Jaden suggested. "*That's the quickest route to the main shaft. We'll have to fight our way through, but at least we'll have a direct path out of here after that*." Malia nodded. Taking a deep breath, she followed Jaden back the other way. *"Let's use our powers first—no weapons. They could use the laser fire to track—"*

Jaden stopped short. Heading the group marching toward them was Isis. "I know you two are in here. I sensed you reaching out to the prisoners telepathically." Holding out one hand, she hit them with active scanning beams. "There you are. Now, drop your weapons and emitters, or I'll order my people to fire." The second group of hybrids came up behind them, cutting off any chance of escape.

"Shit," Jaden muttered out loud. He tossed his pistol and emitter toward Isis's feet. Malia did the same.

"Did you make contact with them?" Isis asked as one of her hybrids picked up Malia and Jaden's equipment.

Jaden glared at her for a moment. But then it occurred to him. Isis wanted to communicate with the Anunnaki as much as he did. Telling her the truth might actually help. "I did. I reached one called Enki. He was about to tell me how to release them when you interrupted."

Isis's eyes grew wider, and Jaden could see the desire in them. "Do it."

They moved back to the portal. Malia and Jaden disrupted its energy flow again, then Jaden reached out to Enki.

"It's me again. Sorry about that. So how is it that I'm going to get you out of there?"

"The Founders bridged the gap between the biological and technological eons ago. And in learning to control neural processors telepathically, you have taken the first steps along that path. You must

continue developing that ability, and in time, your power will become sufficient to open this portal and set us free."

"*In* time? *I thought you were going to tell me how to do it* now?"

"*I am sorry, Jaden—*"

"What the hell is going on?" Isis demanded. Jaden told her. "You expect me to believe that? If you don't—"

"Read my mind then!" Jaden said. "You'll see that I'm telling you the truth!"

Isis penetrated his thoughts, surfacing his memory of the engagement he'd just had with Enki. Jaden didn't fight it. "*Dammit*!" she shouted as she left his mind, turning and striding away. "Take them with us," she ordered her people.

But as they started moving, Anhur contacted them through their implants. "Our long-range sensors have detected the Malor mother ship in orbit around Jupiter, building up velocity for a slingshot toward Earth."

"Oh, no," Brian replied. "Malia and Jaden, what's your situation down there?"

"Hold on," said Jaden. Then he called out to Isis.

She rounded on him. "What is it now?"

"The Malor mother ship just entered orbit around Jupiter. They're headed here—"

"What nonsense is this?" she demanded, cutting him off. "You two already destroyed the mother ship."

"There's another one!" Malia told her. "Those rogue Malor sent a signal from one of the power stations!"

Isis's eyes unfocused for a moment, and Jaden knew she was probably communicating with her ship. "Shit," she muttered, fixing Jaden with a stare. "My people have detected it, too."

"The Anunnaki have the power to destroy them!" he told her. "I watched one of them take out a Malor vessel with a wave of his hand. It wasn't a mother ship, but he did it with *ease*."

"What the hell are you talking about? The Anunnaki are all in that prison back there!" she said, pointing toward the portal.

Jaden explained what he'd found on the crashed Malor ship in Greenland. "Penetrate my mind again. I'll show you." So she did, and Jaden recalled the hologram in which he'd watched the Anunnaki singlehandedly defeat the Malor vessel.

"We've got to free them!" Jaden told her. "They can destroy the Malor, you can get them to give you their transdimensional technology, and we'll get our people back. Execute your plan *now*. Hit that structure with all your ships' weapons before it's too late!"

Isis's eyes narrowed. "How do you know about that?" she demanded. But then added, "Never mind," before striding away again.

Her people brought Malia and Jaden along behind her. They flew up to the surface, and Jaden thought about flying back to his saucer. But a couple dozen more hybrids were waiting for them, and he was pretty sure that without his emitter, he'd never make it that far without being shot.

"Move everyone to the edge of the clearing," Isis ordered her people before launching into the air. Jaden kept an eye on her progress as the hybrids prodded them forward. But Isis vanished high above the clearing. Jaden suspected she must have boarded one of her vessels. Probably the chariot.

Jaden contacted their people through his implants and let them know what was happening. He was surprised Isis wasn't jamming their communication, but at this point, it probably didn't matter.

Moments later, Jaden heard another voice through his implants. "Chariot, this is Command Anhur from the Othali warship. Do you read me?"

There was a short delay, then a voice said, "Go ahead, Commander."

"It is our understanding that you plan on firing on that alien structure down there. We would like to assist. Please send targeting and timing information so we can coordinate our efforts with yours."

"Stand by," the other voice said. Jaden couldn't believe what he was hearing. Never did he think he'd see the day when the Othali and the Collective would work together with Isis. But a moment later, the voice said, "Confirmed, Othali warship. Sending the data now."

Less than a minute later, Jaden watched as first one, then a dozen, and then well over a hundred lasers fired on a point near the center of the clearing. Their power steadily increased, but a shockwave suddenly emanated from the underground structure. It hit Jaden and Malia, knocking them to the ground. Jaden wondered why the hybrids hadn't fallen for a moment, but then everything went black.

Chapter Thirty

Brian Kwan had monitored their progress as Malia and Jaden descended into the shaft and traversed the distance to the portal. Yet, despite authorizing this endeavor, he still harbored deep misgivings. Yes, he'd sent them into the heart of a hybrid stronghold. But more than that, this wasn't the first time he'd been responsible for the twins having a close encounter with alien technology. And the results had been disastrous when he took them to the Othali power station.

This time could be worse. They knew almost nothing about these Anunnaki. And the little they did know was concerning. Every civilization they'd interacted with ended up vanishing. Now, Brian knew that hardly proved they were responsible for those disappearances. Maybe the ones who imprisoned the Anunnaki were behind it. But this transdimensional bubble still represented a technology vastly more advanced than anything their people understood. Who knew what might happen when Malia and Jaden tried to interact with it?

Sensors indicated a large group of hybrids moving into the primary shaft, snapping Brian out of his thoughts. He warned Malia and Jaden. But then he spotted the second group of hybrids moving in from the other direction. They were trapped in there. Brian alerted the warship.

"Stand by," Anhur replied. "We've got another situation developing up here."

Now what? Brian thought. But only a couple of minutes later, Anhur told them that they'd detected the Malor mother ship orbiting Jupiter. The entire situation had gone to hell. Brian tried getting an update from Jaden, but he told him to wait. He was about to contact Anhur about mounting a rescue mission but saw that the twins were moving. They flew back up to the surface with their captors. Isis flew up to one of her ships while the hybrids moved Malia and Jaden to a position at the edge of the clearing. Finally, Jaden contacted them and told them what was going on.

"I'd like to reach out to Isis and offer to help," Anhur said through his implants, and Brian could see that this communication was private. "Adding our firepower to hers will increase our chances. What do you think?"

"I think this whole plan is insane," Brian replied. "We have no idea what this might do. That much energy hitting an alien structure that we hardly understand..."

"Isis is going to hit it with or without us," Anhur pointed out.

"Sure, yes, that's true. But I worry about these Anunnaki. There's an old Earth expression: Better the devil you know than the devil you don't."

"I understand your concern," Anhur replied. "But we know what that mother ship will do to this planet, and we don't stand a chance against it. These Anunnaki lived among humans for millennia without wiping out all life on Earth. So I like our odds."

Brian let out a long sigh. "All right. Let's do it."

Anhur contacted Isis's ship, and they agreed. Anhur sent him and Nadia the coordinates and timing for the attack moments later. When the time came, Brian fired his saucer's weapons, along with well over a hundred hybrid vessels and the warship. Nothing happened at first, so they increased power. And then, suddenly, something overloaded his control system. Brian had lost weapons along with shields, communications, and sensors. But he wasn't the only one—all the ships had stopped firing at the same time. Communications returned a moment later, and he reached out to Anhur.

"What happened?"

"We're not sure yet. Some sort of feedback through the weapons system. Stand by."

Brian's sensors came back online, and he checked on the twins. But they were gone.

"Malia? Jaden?" he called out through his implants. "Please respond. Where are you?"

There was no reply. Brian did a wide-area scan but couldn't find their life signs or any trace of their DNA in a 100-mile radius.

"This is Anhur. Our systems are back up now. Sensors show no change in the alien structure. So it would seem Isis's calculations were wrong."

"Commander, we have another problem. Malia and Jaden are gone."

There was a brief pause. "Confirmed. We can't locate them on sensors. Hold on..." Brian's heart had jumped into his throat. Was it possible Isis had taken them in the confusion? If they were on one of her ships, then they *wouldn't* show up on sensors. But, no, that wasn't correct—all the hybrids' ships had lost shields, too. Including the chariot, which was holding position in the exact spot Isis had vanished earlier.

Unless they had them inside the chariot's command module. They'd learned from their battle with the first chariot that they had physical shielding over that area—

"This is Anhur. The alien structure emitted some sort of transdimensional shockwave. That's what overloaded our systems. Sensors show Malia and Jaden disappearing a tenth of a second before we went offline. And we are now detecting a transdimensional radiation signature at their last known location."

"A radiation signature?" Brian repeated, hardly able to process this information. "You're telling me they vanished like the others?"

"That's precisely what I'm telling you," Anhur confirmed.

"They must be inside that thing," Brian said. "We've got to find a way to get them out!"

"Unfortunately, we've exhausted our options for the time being. And right now, we need to turn our attention to that Malor vessel."

Brian knew he was right. It tore his heart out to admit it, but Malia and Jaden would have to wait.

To be continued...

Made in the USA
Middletown, DE
25 October 2022

13499478R00191